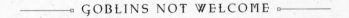

GOBLINS NOT WELCOME

Finn had a knife in his hand, and Teagan didn't know where it had come from. He didn't look a little scary anymore. He looked a lot scary.

"Finn!" Mr. Wylltson said sharply. "That's not necessary—"

"It is." Finn moved between Teagan and the goblin. "This thing isn't human. It doesn't follow your rules. You heard what the man said, goblin. Get out of this house. You're not welcome here."

"Finn?" the goblin spat. "The *Mac Cumhaill?* Keep the girl while you can. I'll take the little one first. He'll cry the longest." It spun toward Aiden.

"No!" Teagan shouted. Finn threw his knife as the goblin lunged.

TYGER TYGER

A Goblin Wars Book

KERSTEN HAMILTON

Houghton Mifflin Harcourt
New York • Boston

The text of this book is set in 11.5-point Celestia Antiqua Std.
Book design by Sharismar Rodriguez

The Library of Congress has cataloged the hardcover edition as follows:
Hamilton, K. R. (Kersten R.)
Tyger tyger: a goblin wars book / by Kersten Hamilton
p. cm.
Summary: Soon after the mysterious and alluring Finn arrives at her family's home,
sixteen-year-old Teagan Wylltson and her disabled brother are drawn into the battle Finn's family
has fought since the thirteenth century, when Fionn MacCumhaill angered the goblin king.
[1. Goblins—Fiction. 2. Magic—Fiction. 3. Imaginary creatures—Fiction. 4. People with mental
disabilities—Fiction. 5. Irish Americans—Fiction. 6. Zoos—Fiction. 7. Finn MacCool—Fiction.]
I. Title
PZ7.H1824Tyg 2010
[Fic]—dc22
201001337

ISBN 978-0-547-33008-2 hardcover
ISBN 978-0-547-57732-6 paperback

Manufactured in the United State of America
DOC 10 9 8 7 6 5 4 3 2 1
4500304582

For Mark, of course!

 ACKNOWLEDGMENTS

I would like to thank Mark Hamilton, Rion Reece, Mona Holten, Meghan Wilson, Tam Owyoung, Linda Jewell, and Melinda Beavers for all they have contributed and endured during the writing of this book. Without their collective knowledge, wisdom, and patience, *Tyger Tyger* would not have been possible.

I am especially grateful to Lynne Polvino and the entire crew at Clarion and HMH, who have done a stellar job of editing, designing, and marketing. They've been incredibly helpful and creative every step of the way.

PART I: FINN

ONE

PLEASE. Teagan Wylltson's fingers curled in American Sign Language as she spoke. *Trade sweater for banana?* She leaned over the fence around the chimp enclosure. *Come on, Cindy,* she coaxed. *Be a good girl. Trade.*

Cindy bared her fangs in a grimace, ignoring the ripe banana Teagan offered. She draped the pink cashmere over her shoulders and did the ape equivalent of a runway strut all the way to the bamboo along the back wall, turning to glare at Teagan before she disappeared into the greenery.

"Ms. Wylltson doesn't appear to be getting anywhere, Dr. Max," Ms. Hahn, the head of the youth docents, said.

"Tea can handle it." Dr. Max wiped his balding dome with a handkerchief.

"You should ask Cindy to give it back, Max," Ms. Hahn said. "The chimp listens to you."

"She used to." Dr. Max shook his head. "Lately she just throws things every time I come in sight."

"How did she get your sweater, young lady?" Ms. Hahn's eyes narrowed. "That could be dangerous for the animal!"

3

"I left it on the railing," Teagan said. "Cindy used a stick to fish it into her enclosure."

"And you didn't notice that this was happening, Max?"

"Dr. Max wasn't here."

Ms. Hahn's pencil-thin eyebrows rose. "The girl was here *unsupervised*?" She sniffed. "That is against regulations. Youth never work with the animals unsupervised!"

"Teagan's not a youth-docent volunteer," Dr. Max said. "She is an employee."

"A sixteen-year-old employee." Ms. Hahn's voice was growing louder. "Youth-worker rules still apply."

"Teagan is very responsible, and she was never in the cage with Cindy," Dr. Max said calmly. "Really, Darleen, you're not helping here. Cindy is just like a child. She'll pick up the tension in our voices if we argue."

Teagan sneezed. She wished Ms. Hahn would find somewhere else to be. She wished she'd taken her Benadryl during her break. And she wished Cindy would just give the sweater back so she could head to the animal clinic.

The bamboo shook where Cindy had disappeared. Teagan held the banana to her nose and pretended to sniff.

"Smells good." The words came out sounding like *thmells dwood*. Her nose was so plugged up she couldn't smell the Primate Research House, much less the ripe banana she was peeling.

The bushes at the back of the enclosure shook harder.

"Cindy," Dr. Max coaxed, "come out and talk to Teagan."

Cindy came out of the bushes, the sweater wadded into a ball. She held it over her head like a trophy, then put it down and started signing madly.

"*Bad girl, bad girl*," Teagan translated.

"*Cindy's a good girl*," Dr. Max said as he signed. "*Give Tea's sweater back. Say sorry.*"

Teagan met Cindy's icy glare. The chimp didn't look one bit sorry. In fact, she looked just like . . . Teagan glanced at Ms. Hahn. It couldn't be. Could it?

Bad boy, Teagan signed.

Cindy bared her fangs.

Ugly boy, Teagan signed, then gave Dr. Max a push.

"Hey," Ms. Hahn said. "What do you think you are doing?"

Cindy screamed and threw the wadded-up sweater at Teagan, who caught it with one hand.

"What . . . how did you do that?" Ms. Hahn demanded.

"Cindy wasn't saying that *she* was a bad girl." Teagan shoved the sweater into her backpack. "She was telling Dr. Max that *I* was a bad girl."

"What?"

"Cindy's got a crush on Dr. Max. She wants him to stay away from me." Teagan didn't mean to look directly at Ms. Hahn when she said it. It was just so obvious. "Common primate behavior."

"Perceptive!" Dr. Max said. "Didn't I tell you she was perceptive, Darleen? This girl has a future ahead of her as a vet, or an animal behaviorist. She's going to get lots of scholarship offers out of her work here. 'Common primate behavior.' Of course, of course." He chuckled and turned mildly pink. "I should have known that. I just didn't consider myself—"

"It's the lab coat," Teagan said. "Very hot."

Ms. Hahn's glare made Cindy's seem warm and friendly.

"I have to clean the cages in the lab and feed the tiddlywinks,"

5

Teagan said before Ms. Hahn could open her mouth. "Gotta run! See you on Saturday."

Teagan took a deep breath—through her mouth, since her nose was too stuffy—as soon as she was outside. She couldn't help feeling sad at the zoo. The animals here would never live the way they were meant to live. The primate house was the worst, because the apes were so much like people. Especially Cindy, with her acquired language.

Teagan had learned ASL in middle school so she could teach a preschool signing class at the community center. Community service had seemed like a good idea for her college applications, but Dr. Max had offered her something even better.

He'd been one of the judges of the sophomore science fair. He'd seen her signing to her little brother and offered her a part-time job with his primate research team, socializing with Cindy. Because her science fair project had been on urban wildlife rescue, Dr. Max had agreed to work some clinic time into her schedule as well. If the chimp language program helped convince people that apes should have some basic rights, Teagan was happy to help. But her real love was the clinic. She worked for Dr. Max every Thursday after school, all day Saturday, and half a day on Sunday. As soon as summer vacation started, her position would be full-time, and she'd get to spend four hours a day in the clinic.

She dashed across the zoo grounds, punched the security code into the keypad at the clinic door, and waited for it to hiss open.

"Hey." Agnes, the vet tech, was sitting at the office desk when Teagan came in. "Look at this."

Teagan leaned over to look at the computer screen. It was a cryptozoology site, of course. Agnes's hobby was debunking pseudo-scientists who thought they had pictures of everything from Big-foot to the Loch Ness Monster. The screen showed a flat, mummified creature with what appeared to be a grimacing face. The caption read, "Alien body found in New Mexico?!"

"What is it?" Teagan asked.

"It's a dead sea skate. What it's doing in the middle of the desert I don't know. Somebody must have brought it home from vacation and thrown it out with the trash."

"So you told them?"

"Of course I did. More science, less ignorance."

Teagan left Agnes to her debunking and went to feed her pa-tients in the next room. She put a fresh lettuce leaf into Methuselah's cage, and the tortoise winked a red eye at her. He'd been someone's pet until he wandered into the street. She ran her finger along the mended crack in his shell. Shells didn't heal, of course, but the su-perglue she'd used to put him back together would probably last his lifetime. Now all he needed was a new home—one that could keep him out of traffic.

Teagan heated some goat's milk in the microwave, mixed it in a bowl with canned puppy food, then tapped on the nest box behind Dr. Max's desk.

"Tiddlywinks, wake up," she whispered. The mass of prickles and paws in the middle of the nest started moving, sorting itself into five baby hedgehogs. Dr. Max had not been hopeful when they were orphaned at two days old, still so young that their prickles were white. He'd said that African hedgehogs were next to impossible to hand raise, but Teagan hadn't lost even one of the babies. For the first two weeks, she'd carried them with her in a basket night and day, feeding them every two hours. It would have been easier if they hadn't been nocturnal and done their best feeding at night.

Now that they were almost weaned, they didn't have to eat as frequently, so they stayed at the clinic. Dr. Max and his lab techs did most feedings these days, but Teagan still loved taking care of them when she could. Fats waddled toward the food she'd prepared for them, but Arwin the Adventuresome beat him there. Tiny Tiddly, the smallest, sat blinking in the corner while Sonic and Speed Racer pushed in beside Fats.

Teagan filled an eyedropper with goat's milk and picked Tiny Tiddly up carefully. He was her favorite, and not quite as ready as his brothers and sister for solid food. He patted her finger with his plump pink hands while he sucked milk from the eyedropper. When they had all eaten, Teagan cleaned them and took the bowl out of their nest box.

"Don't give Agnes any trouble." She checked the clock. She was going to have to run to catch her bus.

"See you Saturday," Agnes called as Teagan went out the door.

"Saturday," Teagan said.

The early May wind off Lake Michigan was cool enough to make her shiver, even after her mad dash to the bus stop. Teagan took her sweater out of her backpack and held it up. Cindy had been very careful with it, really. She hadn't even snagged the loose knitting.

The bus hissed to a stop, and Teagan pulled the sweater over her head before she jumped up the steps. The driver gave her a sour look as she flashed her student pass, and nodded toward the back.

Two grandmotherly ladies frowned at her. One of them said something to the other in German, and they both shook their heads.

Teagan sneezed as she took the empty seat behind them. The old man sitting by the window blinked at her through thick glasses and tried to press himself into the corner.

Teagan smiled apologetically. "It's just allergies," she said, digging her Benadryl out of the front pouch of her backpack. "Nothing contagious." She swallowed the pills with a swig from her water bottle.

"Tea!" Abby Gagliano got on the bus at Clark and Addison. Abby liked to say she had a modeling job at her cousin's boutique and beauty salon, Smash Pad. Her purple military-style cap pulled sideways, tight black T-shirt, miniskirt, and cargo boots were a walking advertisement for Smash Fashions, and she did spend an hour or two a day posing in the store window. But most of the time she was the assistant pedicurist, specializing in art for the toenails of the rich and eccentric.

Abby rode the bus home with Teagan at least three times a week to spend the night. Her sister Clair had moved back in while her husband was deployed. The only place the Gaglianos had to put her was Abby's room, and it was small, so Abby and Clair worked out a time-share. They were never home on the same day of the week, and Abby kept half of her clothes in Teagan's closet.

Teagan looked around for an empty seat as Abby made her way down the aisle. There wasn't one.

"Thank god you're here!" Abby grabbed the post to steady herself as the bus started forward. "I've been trying to call you. Your life is totally in danger." Her face twisted. "What's that smell?"

"What?" Teagan said. "I can't smell anything."

The German grandmother turned around.

"You smell like shite," she said helpfully.

"Oh, my god. Abby, is there something on my sweater?" Teagan twisted so Abby could see her back.

"Yes," Abby said.

"Help me clean it off."

"I'm not touching it."

"Hold my blouse down while I take my sweater off, then," Teagan said.

Abby grabbed her shirttail, and Teagan wiggled the sweater up over her shoulders, careful not to turn it inside out. Whatever was on it, she didn't want to smear it on her blouse or in her hair.

"Eew," Abby said, and let go. Teagan felt cool air on her midriff as the sweater went over her head. She pulled it off her arms, then jerked her blouse down with one hand. Two high school boys across the aisle had goofy smiles on their faces.

"Nice shimmy," one said.

"Hey." Abby smiled at him. "You go to our school, don't you? Geoff Spikes, football team. Quarterback."

"Does your friend know who I am, too?" Geoff leaned around Abby to leer at Teagan.

Teagan ignored him and turned her sweater over. She should have checked the back before she put it on. Cindy had left a present for her—a thick brown-green gob stuck right between the shoulders. It had squished flat when she'd leaned back, leaving a lovely smear on the bus seat.

"Tell your friend to call me if she wants to hook up," Geoff said. "I could spend some time with that bod."

"She's into brains, not brawn," Abby said. "You might have a chance. Just one. What's your IQ?"

"Huh?"

"Wrong answer. You're out." Abby turned her back on him.

"Abby," Teagan whispered, "I'm going to kill you."

"I had to let go of the shirt," Abby whispered back. "That . . . stuff almost touched me."

"Did anything show?"

"Anything like wha—" Abby stopped. "You're wearing a bra, right?"

"Of course I am."

"Good," Abby said. "'Cause he had a cell phone."

"What?"

"You can kill me later. We have to get off at the next stop. Your life is in danger."

"What?"

"I said we have to get off here."

"I meant the other part. About my life being in danger?"

"I had a dream," Abby said.

"A dream."

Abby nodded. "I'm totally psychotic. You know I am."

The old man huddled in the corner threw a worried look at her.

"Psychic. She means psychic," Teagan assured him, using her sweater to wipe the brown goo from the seat.

"That's what I said," Abby agreed. "I should be working for the psychotic hotline, I swear." She grabbed Teagan's arm and pulled her down the aisle.

Several passengers cheered as they went down the steps.

"Does the ape poop really smell that bad?"

"My eyes are watering," Abby said.

"Where are we going?" Teagan asked as the bus pulled away.

"We're not going." Abby waved toward the building above them. "We're here. St. Drogo's."

"No, no, no." Teagan stopped. "I'm not going to church. Not with this sweater."

"Then throw it away."

"Never," Teagan said. "It's my favorite sweater."

"How long have I been your best friend?"

"Forever," Teagan said.

"Damn right." Abby started up the church steps. "I flunked first grade so you could catch up to me, didn't I? I gave up a year of my life for you—a whole year! And have I ever asked you to do anything for *me*?"

"Yes," Teagan said. "All the time."

"That's true. But this is life and death, Tea, I swear. You're always taking care of other people. Now I am going to take care of you. I'm going to light a candle so Drogo will intercede for you."

Abby *wanted* to go to church? She'd only been twice since they'd transferred from St. Joseph's Academy to public school, and that had been in the ninth grade.

"This is crazy," Teagan said, but she followed Abby up the steps and past the smiling statue of Saint Drogo leaning on the handle of a hoe. "How is my life in danger?"

"I'll tell you after we pray." Abby looked around nervously. "I want to get out of here before Father Gordon sees me."

They dipped their fingers in the laver and crossed themselves before they stepped into the familiar nave. A second statue of Saint

Drogo, his face grim and his hands lifted in petitioning prayer, stood to the side of the altar.

Teagan had asked her parents who Drogo was one Sunday morning when she was six.

"Frodo the hobbit's father, from Tolkien's *Lord of the Rings*," Mr. Wylltson had said. "Isn't it marvelous that they built a church for him?"

"Hist! John!" Her mother's Irish accent showed even in a whisper. "Mind you're in church, and don't mislead the girl. *Saint* Drogo was a holy man, and a bilocate. He could be in two places at once. The blessed man spent every Sunday face-down on the floor in front of the altar while simultaneously working in his garden to the glory of God."

"I think he was sleeping in church," Mr. Wylltson had said.

"John," Mrs. Wylltson warned. "I'm instructing our daughter in the things of the faith." She turned back to Teagan. "That's why we have two statues—the petitioner and the gardener. If I could do that, think how much painting I could get done."

"Come on." Abby tried to pull Teagan toward the altar, but she shook her head. The statues of saints along each wall looked unusually disapproving.

"I'll wait here." Teagan slid onto the pew at Saint Francis's feet. If anyone would understand bringing ape poop to church, it would be Francis.

Abby went to the front, lit a votive candle, and knelt with her head bowed. Teagan shifted on the hard pew.

"Abigail Gagliano." Father Gordon had entered the nave. "I haven't seen you for—"

"Laters, Father." Abby jumped up. "Gotta run." Teagan followed her out.

"So what was this psychic dream?" Teagan asked. "Did it have perverts with cell phones and a bus in it?"

"No." Abby shuddered. "Saint Drogo was in it. He was trying to tell me something, but his Italian was all mixed up. Like, not Italian at all. And some of your mother's paintings—the ones in your basement—came alive. I remember the goblins for sure. The goblins came upstairs, and they were after you, Tea."

"You're making me walk *six blocks home* because you had a crazy dream about my mom's paintings? You were right, back on the bus. You *are* psychotic."

"Whatever," Abby said. "The people on that bus thought I was a hero for getting you and your monkey poo out of there."

"Very funny." Teagan found a plastic grocery bag in the gutter, shook off the twigs and dirt, and wrapped her sweater in it. "And it's ape poop. Cindy is an ape."

Aiden was playing Super Mario Galaxy in an alcove off of the living room when they came in the front door. Lennie Santini loomed over him, waving the Wii wand to gather up the stars that appeared on the screen. The alcove was Aiden's den of boyhood, complete with video games, a Lego castle, and an army of Lego men set up around the room, ready to wage war.

"*Ai-den-is-the-hero,*" Aiden sang in sync to the synthesized music.

Teagan winced. If she had known her dad was going to get him a Wii for his fifth birthday, she'd have destroyed every compatible sound system in the house. Aiden was one chip short of being a high-end cell phone. His brain came bundled with an MP3 player and GPS. Every tune he had ever heard was stored in his gray matter. When the music had no lyrics, he made up his own.

"Hey, Tee-gan," Lennie's voice boomed. "Hey, hey, cousin Ab-by."

"Hey, Lennie," Teagan said. Lennie was a sweet six-year-old trapped in a plump, pimply eighteen-year-old body, and he was Aiden's best friend in the whole world. "Does Mom know you guys are playing Mario?"

"Dad said I could if I didn't sing too loud."

"Dad's home already?"

"Hey, choirboy," Abby said. "You still have that goochi-goochi I gave you?"

"*Tamagotchi.*" Aiden paused Mario and pulled the electronic pet out of his pocket. "I'm taking good care of it, see?"

"Hey!" Lennie squinted at the pixels on the tiny screen. "He's growing! Let me feed him, okay?"

"Okay." Aiden handed it to Lennie. "But you have to whisper. Dad said to be quiet because we have company. They're in the kitchen."

"Company?" Teagan asked.

Abby followed her through the door into the kitchen. It stretched across the whole back of the old house. They used half of it for food preparation and eating. The other half was an art studio. Teagan's mother was standing in the art-studio half with a woman in a purple pantsuit. A female water goblin leered out of the still-wet paint on the canvas before them, the strands of her thin hair plastered to her round face.

"You illustrate *children's* books?" The woman's head wagged disapprovingly.

"Write and illustrate." Aileen Wylltson turned to gaze at the woman.

The woman took a step back. "She's . . . frightening."

Teagan wasn't quite sure whether the woman meant the painting or her mother. She would have given anything to have inherited her mother's intense amber eyes, ringed by subtle green, but the gene lottery had given her her father's dark brown eyes instead.

"Of course she's frightening," Mrs. Wylltson said. "She's Ginny Greenteeth. She drowns travelers in bogs."

Teagan's father was filling the teakettle at the sink. He smiled at the girls. "How was work, Rosebud?"

"Fine." Teagan tossed the bagged sweater at the laundry chute. Her father had taken both the doors off, upstairs and down, six months ago to refinish and seal the ancient wood. Now the openings gaped like a monster's maw, offering up basement breath and the occasional death rattle from their old washing machine. The sweater dropped from sight as her mother and the woman turned toward Teagan.

"Tea, you're home!" Mrs. Wylltson said. "Ms. Skinner, this is our daughter, Teagan, and her friend Abigail. Tea, this is Ms. Skinner from Social Services."

Ms. Skinner's glance flicked from Teagan to Abby, and her thin lips pressed together. She clearly did not approve of Smash Pad's fashion statement.

"Pleased to meet you," Teagan said.

"A teenage daughter!" Ms. Skinner's ginger eyebrows drew together. "You should consider her safety when deciding who you take into your home."

"We always take our children's safety into consideration," Mr. Wylltson assured her.

Ms. Skinner ignored him and studied Teagan. "How do *you* feel about your cousin Finn coming to live with you?" she asked.

Teagan blinked. "Who?"

TWO

TEA won't remember Finn," Mrs. Wylltson said quickly. "His family hasn't visited since she was a baby."

"Would you like a cup of coffee, Ms. Skinner?" Mr. Wylltson asked.

"I drink only herbal tea." Ms. Skinner held up her clipboard. "We are not finished with this interview, but I hesitate to continue in front of the children."

"What children?" Abby looked around.

Mr. Wylltson frowned at Abby and nodded toward the door. Teagan grabbed Abby's arm and dragged her out of the kitchen. She shut the door behind them, then motioned for Abby to follow her up the stairs.

"'A *teenage daughter!*'" Abby's imitation of Ms. Skinner's tone was perfect. "What's that supposed to mean?"

"That harboring hormones is a crime," Teagan said. "Now, shh."

"What are we doing?" Abby whispered as Teagan sat down by the open mouth of the laundry chute in the second-floor hallway.

"Shh," Teagan said again.

"You had no idea he was in town?" That was Ms. Skinner's voice.

Abby's mouth made a little O and she sat down to listen as well.

"My brother's family moved frequently. They followed the work wherever it took them."

"What kind of work would that be?"

"Odd jobs," Mrs. Wylltson said. "They did what they could do to get by."

"Irish Travelers." Ms. Skinner's voice twisted around the words as if they were rotten.

"The Mac Cumhaills are fine people," Teagan's mother said.

There was a snorting sound. Teagan couldn't tell for sure who had made it, but she could guess.

"He walked into a hospital with a broken arm?" That was Mr. Wylltson, trying to change the subject. "Is that how you . . . got involved with him?"

"He was in our records," Ms. Skinner said. "A Finn Mac Cumhaill ran away from a foster home when he was twelve. When he showed up, the hospital contacted us. It's the same boy. If he'd waited a few more months, he'd have aged out of the system, and I wouldn't have to—"

"I'm sure your convenience was foremost in his mind when he went looking for help with a broken arm," Mrs. Wylltson said. "He gave them my name, didn't he? As a close relation."

"He didn't know your phone number or address. I'm the one who tracked you down. And you've had no contact with the family in years. I see from the guardianship petition that you've been institutionalized, Mrs. Wylltson. May I ask what for?"

"I had a mental breakdown," Teagan's mother said. "Four years ago."

"What a hag," Abby whispered. "That's none of her business, and—"

Teagan put her hand over Abby's mouth and scowled at her until her lips stopped moving.

Her mom had been coming home on the EL when she'd had her incident. She'd started screaming; shouting in a garbled, made-up language; punching and kicking at things that weren't there. Someone had called the cops.

Abby's mom had been watching baby Aiden while Teagan and Abby studied together. They'd both ended up staying with the Gaglianos for three months while their mom was in Lakeshore Hospital and their father worked all day and then spent every evening with his wife. *Psychotic episode*. Teagan had heard her father use the term one night when he was talking to Mrs. Gagliano. She never told anyone she'd looked it up. Not even Abby. *Hallucinations, delusional beliefs. Total break with reality.*

"Why is that relevant?" Teagan could imagine the look on her father's face as he asked.

"I'm just doing my job." Ms. Skinner's tone was defensive. "Finn's been sleeping in a derelict warehouse, climbing drainpipes, dropping in windows, eating from trash cans. Living with no running water or electricity." She sounded like she'd practiced the litany on the way over. "He's practically *feral*. I'm not sure that someone who is emotionally fragile would have the resources needed to deal with him."

"I'm not fragile," Mrs. Wylltson said. "I will be happy to let you speak to my psychiatrist. I have emotional resources out the wazoo, I assure you."

"I'm just doing my job," Ms. Skinner repeated. "What on earth is that smell?"

Teagan winced. The Benadryl was kicking in, and even she could smell the stench. Either the old plastic bag had broken open on its way down, or the ape poop had eaten through it.

"Something in the basement," Mrs. Wylltson said. "The drains must have backed up."

"I'd best be going," Ms. Skinner said.

"So we will be picking him up tomorrow?" Mr. Wylltson asked.

"Sending Finn here is against my best judgment, but I have limited options. He hasn't committed any crimes we can prove."

"So we will be picking him up," Mrs. Wylltson said triumphantly.

"I'm afraid so."

"Let me walk you to your car," Mr. Wylltson offered.

"I'll leave my number tomorrow. If he gets into any trouble . . ." Their voices faded as Mr. Wylltson led her toward the front door.

Teagan pulled open the door to the maid's stairs. The dark stairway went from the tiny guest room in the attic that had once been the maid's quarters all the way down to the basement. The house had been built with the notion that a servant should not be seen. The stairway had doors cut into the wood paneling where they would be most useful: in the hall between the bedrooms, in the kitchen, and in the basement.

"Where are you going?" Abby asked.

"To save my sweater," Teagan said. "If possible."

"I'm not going down there." Abby followed her as far as the kitchen door. "I'll wait with your mom."

"They're just paintings," Teagan said.

"You didn't have the dream I had."

"You lit a candle at church."

"For you, not for me. I'll just wait here."

Teagan went down one more flight. The basement was the largest room in the house, and it didn't smell like a Chicago basement at all. It smelled like an art gallery. A dehumidifier hissed in the corner, sucking any hint of dampness out of the air.

Teagan had always loved this place. It was almost like having her own private Narnia to escape to. The sprites, spriggans, phookas, goblins, and young girls in medieval dresses from her mother's books looked down from the canvases that covered every wall. Wonderful trees—oak, ash, and thorn, gnarled and ancient—appeared in almost every scene.

Teagan stopped in front of her mother's favorite painting. A beautiful little girl danced in front of a house made of trees, their upper trunks curved like the fingers of protective hands above her, while the Green Man, frightening and fascinating all at once, laughed at her.

"You guys planning on coming upstairs for supper?" Teagan asked the hideous band of goblins squatting around a fire in the next painting. "No? I didn't think so."

The laundry room was separate from the rest of the basement, a tiny space just large enough for a washer, dryer, sink, and the basket under the chute. Teagan retrieved her sweater, scraped the green mass into the basin and washed it down the drain, then left the cashmere soaking in Woolite before she headed upstairs.

Her dad hadn't come back from walking Ms. Skinner to her car, but Abby was perched on a kitchen stool, watching Mrs. Wylltson prepare her palette.

"This fat woman wanted Our Lady on her toe today," Abby said.

Mrs. Wylltson paused, paintbrush in the air. "On her toenail?"

"Left big toe. Putting Mother Mary down there where she'd be looking up some lady's skirt all day didn't seem right, you know?" Abby shrugged. "But she was a paying customer."

"What did you do?"

"Painted Bette Midler with a halo. I didn't think she'd mind filling in for the Virgin, right? And the fat lady couldn't tell the difference. I don't think she's seen her toes in years."

"You should go to art school." Mrs. Wylltson squeezed a drop of orange into a glob of yellow paint and mixed it with two quick strokes. "You have too much talent to be painting toenails."

"Gotta pay for art school somehow," Abby said. "Mama can't afford the Institute, not after all my sisters' weddings."

Mrs. Wylltson glanced up. "What on earth was that smell, Tea?"

"Ape poop," Teagan said. "Cindy got hold of my sweater."

"So, Tea's back. Now can we talk about Finn?" Abby had clearly tried to pry some information out of Mrs. Wylltson already and had gotten nowhere.

"Let the grilling begin," Mrs. Wylltson said.

"What happened to his parents?" Teagan asked.

"Car accident." Mrs. Wylltson added a yellow gleam to Ginny Greenteeth's eye. "Seven years ago. I don't understand why Mamieo didn't take him in. It isn't like the Travelers to leave a boy alone."

"Mamieo is Teagan's grandma?" Abby asked. "How come I haven't met her?"

"Because she hasn't been this way in fifteen years," Mrs. Wylltson said. "My brother's family, including Finn, was with her the last time I saw them. No one contacted me after the accident. I didn't know my brother was dead until Social Services called asking if we'd take Finn."

"Your family doesn't write or call on the phone?"

"They show up when they show up," Mrs. Wylltson said. "That's just the way they are."

"So how old is Finn?" Teagan asked.

"Seventeen." Mrs. Wylltson wiped a paint-smudged finger on her shirttail, then brushed a curl off her forehead with the back of her hand. "Almost eighteen."

Mr. Wylltson came back into the kitchen, looking slightly disgruntled. "I sent Lennie home. We could use a little peace around here after that woman. Now, how was *your* day, Rosebud?"

"Fine," Teagan said. It probably was not the right time to bring up cell-phone perverts on the bus.

"That's good. Now, your mom and I need a little time to talk. Aiden found a tribute to the King on Lifetime. That should keep him quiet. You girls want to watch it with him?"

"Dad!" Teagan said. "Not the one with the—"

Aiden screamed in the other room.

"Elvis impersonators." Mr. Wylltson winced. "I'd forgotten that bit. How does he hit that note? I'm surprised we have any glass left in the house."

When they reached the living room, Aiden was standing in front of the television set, his hands over his ears as a line of fake Elvises bumped and gyrated in their tight white pants. One of them held a microphone to his mouth and started to sing. Aiden screamed again. Mr. Wylltson put his fingers in his ears.

Teagan grabbed the remote and turned the TV off.

"That's . . . not . . . Elvis!" Aiden said. "He sounds all wrong!"

"Of course he does." Mr. Wylltson had taken his fingers out of his ears. "It's just an impersonator. You shouldn't be afraid of them, son. They're just men pretending. We've talked about this, remember?"

"Why don't you go for a walk, Aiden?" Mrs. Wylltson said. "Teagan and Abby will go with you." Even Aiden knew it was pointless to argue if Mom was sending them out of the house.

"Let's go," Teagan said. "I'll pull you in the wagon."

"It's a good thing that Ms. Skinner left before the Elvis thing set him off," Abby said as Teagan pulled the wagon down the street.

Teagan sighed.

"What?" Abby said. "I'm just saying. It makes your family seem a little *strange*, you know? I mean, who's afraid of Elvis impersonators?"

"I am," Aiden said. "So is Lennie."

Lennie was Aiden's professional consultant on scary and not scary. Teagan was sure they kept a secret list. Tooth fairy: scary, because she sneaks up and steals things. Bugs: not scary, even if they crawl on you. Worms: scary, because they have no eyes.

"I don't like that lady," Aiden said. "Why did she come?"

"To tell us our cousin Finn is going to be living with us."

"Is Finn a guy?"

"Yes."

"Is he a kid?"

"No," Teagan said. "He's almost a grownup."

"Does he know how to play Lego war?"

"Probably."

"Okay," Aiden said. "I guess he can come."

After dinner, Teagan started the dishes while Mr. Wylltson read aloud from *Peter Pan*.

Aiden's Tamagotchi made the special little *ping* that meant it had made a pile, and he showed Abby how to clean it up. After his electronic pet went to sleep, Aiden turned a lamp around so that he could cast shadows on the wall and act out the part of Peter's shadow.

"John, I'm on deadline," Mrs. Wylltson said the second time Aiden's shadow stretched across her painting.

"All right, bucko. Let's play war." Mr. Wylltson put down the book and scooped Aiden up.

"You're no good at war," Aiden said. "Mom's better. I'd rather play with her."

"It's a fact"—Mr. Wylltson swung Aiden over his shoulder— "that your father is a lover, not a fighter, and your mother's a blood-thirsty savage. But your mother has a book due. So set up your forces, and I will do my best." He carried Aiden giggling toward the alcove.

Teagan nodded toward the living room. Abby followed her to the computer desk and hung over her shoulder.

"You should go upstairs, Dad," Aiden said. "I'm not finished setting up my ambush. I got some ideas from the Lost Boys in that book."

"Perfect," Mr. Wylltson said. "Call me when you are ready to commence the slaughter."

"He's not coming back downstairs tonight, is he?" Abby said.

"Nope. Aiden will spend days setting up his forces for the attack. What did you say that guy's name was?"

"Which guy?" Abby said.

"The perv on the bus."

"Geoff Spikes."

It took Teagan less than a minute to find it. He had a video link with her picture on it on his Facebook account. It was titled "Shimmy, Shimmy, Ko-Ko-Bop."

"What's that about?" Abby asked.

"It's a song by Little Anthony and the Imperials."

"A Moldy Oldie," Abby said. "Why do you Wylltsons even have this stuff in your brains?"

Teagan shrugged and clicked play.

Geoff had looped it to make it longer and added a soundtrack. "*Shimmy, shimmy, ko-ko-bop*"—Teagan's shirt came up to her navel—"*shimmy, shimmy*"—her rib cage—

"No," Teagan said. "No, no, no!" Something blue and blurry shifted into view, filling the whole screen.

"Hey! That's my butt!" Abby leaned closer to the screen. "I'm famous!"

The camera phone bobbled as Geoff tried to get a better view, but Teagan had already pulled her shirt down by the time he had her on the screen again.

"Relax," Abby said. "No one is ever going to see it."

"What are you talking about? He's got three thousand friends linked. Probably everybody we know from school will have seen it. You just said your butt was famous!"

"Yeah, but there's lots worse stuff out there. Nobody's even going to care about your belly or your bra."

"You saw bra?"

"Just a peek. Run it again, and I'll show you."

"I'm not running it again."

"You should get a nice lace bra," Abby said. "That one is really boring. We have a padded number down at the shop that would help you out, if you know what I mean."

"Shut up," Teagan said.

"*Shimmy, shimmy, ko-ko-bop . . .*" The human iPod out in the alcove had picked up the tune.

Teagan put her head down and wrapped her arms around it.

Abby patted her shoulder. "I'll change the station. Then you and me are going to have a talk." She started humming, "*I kissed a girl, and I liked it . . .*"

"Abby!" Teagan jerked upright. Her mom would kill them if that one got stuck in Aiden's head. Abby switched to some boy-band thing that Teagan didn't know, but Aiden apparently did. He started singing along in his piping soprano.

"So, what are you going to do about it?" Abby asked once she had successfully sidetracked Aiden.

"Ignore it," Teagan said. "I have my last final tomorrow. Chemistry. I need to study, and you're going to help me."

"You always ace tests without studying."

"Not this time." College-level science classes only looked good on a college application if you kept a decent GPA.

"How am I supposed to help? I've never taken Chemistry."

"I made flash cards." Teagan pulled the thick stack of three-by-five cards out of her backpack. The rubber band that held them together was stretched to the limit.

"Of course you did."

"All you have to do is hold them up and read the back to see if I got the answer right."

"Fine." Abby folded her arms. "Right after we have the Talk."

"The talk?"

"Not 'the talk.' *The Talk!* The Guy Talk. I've been thinking about this Finn thing. Maybe you can ignore guys in school or on the bus, but one's moving in with you. There's things you gotta know if you're going to have a guy living here. Stuff can happen."

"What kind of stuff?"

"*Chemistry,*" Abby said.

"I'm immune, and you know it," Teagan said. "No boys until I've got my scholarship. Maybe not until I've got my degree."

Abby snorted. "No one's immune. You're just a late bloomer."

"And what do you know about a guy living in your house? You've never had a guy living in your house, unless you count Walter. All you've got is sisters."

"Walter wasn't a guy," Abby said. "He was so pathetic that his parents sent him on foreign exchange to get rid of him. But I've got the Turtles, right?"

Leo, Angel, Donnie, and Rafe were Abby's favorite cousins. They were really nice guys, too, unless you called them by their given names—Leonardo, Michelangelo, Donatello, and Raphael. Their mom had been a big fan of the Teenage Mutant Ninja Turtles.

"Actually"—Teagan shut down the computer—"I do need some relationship advice."

"Guy advice?" Abby looked shocked. "Really?"

"It's not for me. It's for a friend."

"Sure," Abby said. "A friend."

Teagan looked pointedly at Aiden. "It's kind of private."

"Like, the Thinking Place private?" Abby asked.

Teagan nodded.

"Let's go, then." Abby followed Teagan to her room.

Teagan shut the door behind them, then went to the window and slid it up. It was just a step down onto the gently sloping roof of the porch.

She'd first started coming out there when she was ten. She'd been doing it for weeks before her parents had caught her one evening. They'd crawled out the window and sat beside her, watching the people go by on the sidewalk and the insects spin around the streetlight.

"Almost as good as a tree house, isn't it?" Mr. Wylltson had said at last. "Maybe we should trade bedrooms. I could get used to this."

"It's Teagan's," her mom had said. "A girl needs a place of her own. Good night, dearie." She'd kissed Teagan's forehead, and they'd crawled back in the window. It had been Teagan's Thinking Place ever since.

Abby was the only other person Teagan had ever brought here. Aiden was strictly not allowed, though he liked to shout at Teagan from the sidewalk.

Teagan sat down in the square of light spilling from the window. Abby made her way gingerly across the roof.

"So talk already." She shivered as she sat down. "It's chilly out here."

Teagan hugged her knees. "I don't know if I should tell you. I don't think she's the kind of girl you could help."

"She's female, right?" Abby waved her hand. "Then I can help."

"Even if she's desperately in love with an . . . older man?"

Abby frowned. "How much older are we talking, Tea? Five years?"

"About . . . forty years, I think."

"Tea!" Abby shook her head. "I knew something like this was going to happen. It's because you don't date guys your own age."

"I told you it wasn't me. It's a friend."

"Who?" Abby demanded. "Give me a name."

"Cindy. She has a major crush on Dr. Max."

Abby's mouth dropped open.

"Gotcha," Teagan said.

"You dragged me onto the roof for that?"

"You dragged me into St. Drogo's," Teagan said, "with poop on my sweater, *and* made me walk six blocks home."

"I was saving your life." Abby stomped to the window and climbed through. Teagan caught it before Abby could shut it and lock her out.

"I can't believe you lied to me!" Abby grabbed a pillow off the bed and swung it at Teagan as she came inside.

"I didn't!" Teagan dodged.

Abby stopped swinging. "The chimp's seriously crushing on the bald guy?"

"Seriously."

"That's disgusting. He has *wrinkled lips!*"

"So, what's your advice, love doctor?"

"Bring her down to Smash Pad. We'll do a makeover. That girl could be hot!"

"Great." Teagan laughed. "I'll let her know. Now help me study."

"I'm getting my pajamas first," Abby said. "Studying always puts me to sleep."

They'd gone through the flash cards twice before Mrs. Wylltson came in.

"Will you pray with us, Abigail?"

"I don't do bedtime prayers anymore," Abby said.

"That's up to you, then." Mrs. Wylltson knelt by the side of the bed.

Teagan knelt beside her mother, took her hand, and breathed in the scent of paint, linseed oil, and turpentine. Her mom always smelled like creation.

"*I do not ask for a path with no trouble or regret,*" Mrs. Wylltson began. Teagan spoke the words with her. "*I ask instead for a friend who'll walk with me down any path.*

"*I do not ask never to feel pain. I ask instead for courage, even when hope can scarce shine through.*

"*And one more thing I ask: That in every hour of joy or pain, I feel the Creator close by my side. This is my truest prayer for myself and for all I love, now and forever. Amen.*"

"Amen," Abby echoed automatically. Mrs. Wylltson got up and turned the window latch before she drew the curtains.

"Good night, girls," she said as she closed the door.

"Why don't you pray like normal people?" Abby asked. "'No pain, God. Lots of money. Thanks.'"

"Because we're Irish." Teagan snapped the rubber band back around her flash cards. "Mom says things never go well for the Irish for very long. She says we've got to be realistic."

"And why'd she lock the window? Is she worried your hairy cousin will come sneaking down the back alley and climb up the drainpipe?"

"Hairy cousin?"

"Ms. Skinner said Finn was a fur ball, right? Maybe he should date Cindy."

"Feral." Teagan picked up the pillows Abby had thrown and tossed them back on the bed. "She said he was feral. Abby, you need to pay more attention to the words coming out of people's mouths."

"I pay attention. Is this my pillow?"

"What does it matter?"

"You drool like a mad dog." Abby ran her fingers over the pillowcase. "I hate crusty pillows. You're going to have a totally strange guy living in your house, Tea. It's going to be weird, even if you are blood related."

"We're not," Teagan said.

"Not what?"

"Blood related. Mamieo took Mom in when she was twelve or thirteen," Teagan said. "She brought her here from Ireland as part of their family."

"Was your mom an orphan or a runaway, or what?"

"I don't know," Teagan said. "I don't think Mom remembers anything before she was with the Mac Cumhaills."

"She can't remember being a little kid? Is something wrong with her brain? Sorry, Tea," Abby said quickly. "I didn't mean it like that. My mouth just says stuff sometimes, you know?"

"Yeah," Teagan said. "I know."

WE'LL be back in a couple of hours." Mrs. Wylltson looked from Teagan to Abby. "You'll make the spaghetti?"

"It's under control, Mom."

Abby had insisted on coming home with her after school again, even though Friday was one of her days to have the bedroom at the Gaglianos'. They'd helped Mrs. Wylltson finish preparing the guest room, then taken over in the kitchen.

"Mom?" Teagan pointed at her mother's feet—one pink running shoe, one blue. At least they were the same brand this time.

"Not again," Mrs. Wylltson said. "I should throw away the older pair. Well, I'm not taking time to find shoes now. Who looks at feet?"

"Put on some music for your brother," Mr. Wylltson said as they went out the door. "It will keep him out of trouble."

"You think Ms. Skinner will notice the shoes?" Teagan asked.

"She'll notice," Abby said.

Teagan sighed. "What do you want to listen to, Aiden?"

"Put on *Disney's Greatest Hits*," Abby said. "That's good for little kids."

"I'm not a princess." Aiden looked disgusted. "I want 'Bad, Bad Leroy Brown.'"

"Jim Croce it is." Teagan put it on and left Aiden twisting the lyrics around the story he was making up about his Lego castle.

Abby was watching the "Ko-Ko-Bop" video again, with the sound off so it wouldn't corrupt Aiden's mind.

"Do you think this makes my butt look fat?" Abby asked.

"Yes." Teagan pulled up a chair. "Do a search for Finn." It took about three minutes to figure out that "Finn Mac Cumhaill" didn't have a Facebook account, wasn't on MySpace, and didn't have a blog . . . at least, not any seventeen-year-old Finn Mac Cumhaill from Chicago.

"He's been living in a cave." Abby took the keyboard back, typed "Irish Travelers" in the Google box, and got 12,000 hits.

"Irish Travelers raided on fraud, other charges . . ."

"Cons, frauds, lies . . ."

She clicked on a video link titled "Irish Travelers Scam Chicago Couple."

"Police are seeking Angelica Roche, an Irish Traveler who allegedly scammed an elderly couple out of their life's savings," a grim-faced reporter said. "Mr. and Mrs. Gavin took Angelica Roche into their home . . . and into their confidence." He turned to the sad-looking couple. "Can you tell us what happened next?"

"She said she was a Seer." Mr. Gavin stopped to cough. Mrs. Gavin handed him a handkerchief.

"We'd been having a hard time," the old lady said. "Roof leaking, prescription costs going up. Angelica said it was because the money sitting in our bank account was dirty. Said the money had touched drugs and vile things, and evil clung to it. She said if it was cleansed, then everything would be fine."

"We took it all out." Mr. Gavin had recovered from his coughing fit. "She held a séance to cleanse it."

"I'd never seen one like that before," Mrs. Gavin said. "Never one with fresh vegetables and"—she blinked behind her thick glasses—"live lizards."

"And candles," Mr. Gavin added.

"They all have candles, dear." Mrs. Gavin patted his hand. "We wrapped the money up in a clean white cloth and put it in the center of the table, just like she said."

"I never took my eyes off that money." Mr. Gavin's lips were trembling. "When we were done, she said to put it under our bed for seven days, take it out on the Sabbath, and it would be clean. We did."

"But there was nothing in the cloth but cut-up newspaper," Mrs. Gavin said bitterly. "That's when we called the police."

"Mom would never do anything like that," Teagan said.

"Maybe that's why she doesn't have much to do with the Travelers." Abby stretched. "I got family, too, you know. It's called the Mob. I'm not proud of it, but what are you gonna do? Your family is what it is."

They gave up on the computer to start the spaghetti at four. Aiden came in to help, so Teagan put him up on a stool and let him watch her stir the burger while it browned. Abby chopped the vegetables for a salad. They finished the meat sauce and the noodles and set them aside.

"When are they getting here?" Aiden asked. "It's already been forever."

36

"Let's play Chutes and Ladders," Teagan suggested.

"No," Aiden said. "I'm going to work on my castle some more. I want to show it to Finn."

"I thought they said a couple of hours." Abby paced the floor while Teagan lay on her stomach in the alcove, helping Aiden. "It's, like, seven!"

"We'd better feed Aiden," Teagan decided.

"Good," Abby said. "I'll dish it up. I'm going to go nuts if I don't do something."

"Come on, Aiden." Teagan stood up.

"Just one more minute," Aiden said. "Just one more." She was about to drag him to the kitchen by his foot when she saw them coming up the walk.

Finn Mac Cumhaill was walking beside Ms. Skinner, with Teagan's parents following a few steps behind. Finn was taller than the social worker, five-ten at least. He was wearing a sleeveless T-shirt and jeans that hung on his wiry frame like they'd been bought for someone else. His blond hair was cropped short. An old green satchel hung from his left shoulder. His right arm was in a cast from just above the elbow to the fingertips and held close to his chest by a sling. Ms. Skinner marched beside him with the grimness of a prison guard as they passed the window and turned up the steps.

"Aiden, they're here," Teagan said. He scrambled to his feet, but Teagan caught his shoulder as the door opened. They were out of the line of sight in the alcove, and suddenly she wanted to stay that way, just for a minute.

Mrs. Wylltson came in first. Finn stepped inside, and his eyes went first to the kitchen door, then the stairs. Teagan had seen a wolf do the same thing—check a new habitat for exits as soon as it entered. But the wolf had been frightened, and Finn was not. It took her five seconds to figure out that Ms. Skinner was wrong. He wasn't feral. You had to be tame before you could turn feral. Finn Mac Cumhaill did not look like he had ever been tame.

Ms. Skinner came in the door behind him.

"I don't usually escort a ward all the way to the house," she was saying, "but in this case I thought it might be best. Just to be sure, once you'd had a chance to see him—"

"We're not changing our minds," Mr. Wylltson said.

"At least take my card, John."

"Thank you." Mr. Wylltson took it gingerly. "I'll be sure to file it."

The social worker turned to Finn. "You cause any kind of trouble, I'm just a phone call away." She lowered her voice. "We can come pick you up at any time. Pick you up and take you somewhere more appropriate."

"That would be cheaper than a taxi, then," Finn said lazily, "wouldn't it?" His accent was stronger than Teagan's mother's, even though he'd been born in the States.

"I'll leave you to get to know each other," Ms. Skinner said. "I'll be waiting for the call, Mr. Mac Cumhaill."

"Goodbye," Mr. Wylltson said as he shut the door behind her.

"Good Lord, that woman grates." Aileen Wylltson snatched the card from her husband's hand, ripped it in half, and threw it in the recycling bin by the door. "There," she said. "It's filed. Welcome home, Finn."

Teagan let go of Aiden, but Abby came in from the kitchen before he could move.

"Tea," Abby said, "where did you put—" She saw Finn and sucked in her breath.

"What the crap are you looking at?" Finn asked.

"Finn," Mr. Wylltson said, "we don't use vulgarity in front of ladies."

"Didn't consider it vulgar, John." Finn flushed. "I'll remember it."

"I was just about to make introductions, Abby," Mrs. Wylltson said. "Finn Mac Cumhaill"—she touched his shoulder lightly to turn him—"I would like you to meet your cousins Teagan and Aiden Wylltson."

Teagan smiled.

Finn swayed, and Mrs. Wylltson grabbed his good arm to keep him from falling. His face had gone paper white.

"Finn?" Mr. Wylltson said. "Are you all right, son?"

"What kind of painkillers did they give you?" Mrs. Wylltson asked.

"None today," Finn said. "I'm all right."

"Nice to meet you." Aiden marched over and stuck out his hand.

Finn leaned down to shake it. "Nice to meet you, my man," he said. "That's a fine castle you have there."

Aiden beamed.

Finn nodded at Teagan. "Nice to meet you, as well."

Abby made a squeaking noise.

"This is my friend Abby Gagliano." Teagan waved toward her.

"Her best friend," Abby said. "I'm over all the time."

"Gabby." Finn nodded.

"Let's get your things into your room," Mr. Wylltson said. "We'll have a talk as you settle in."

Mrs. Wylltson and Aiden followed him up the stairs.

"It's Abby," Abby said as Finn went past.

"Oh. My. God." She collapsed against the wall as soon as they were out of sight. "Brad Pitt just moved in with you. I swear, Tea, he looks just like a young Brad Pitt, and you get to keep him! This is so not fair. Walter looked like Jack Black. You know he did."

She stopped and looked at Teagan. "Tea? What's wrong with you? You're face looks all . . . funny."

"It does?"

"Not funny ha-ha," Abby said. "Funny sick."

"Yeah," Teagan said, and bolted for the bathroom.

"Oh, my god." Abby was waiting in the hall when she came out. "You threw up, didn't you? Just like you used to do before spelling bees. Oh. My. God!"

"Will you stop saying that?" Teagan wiped her mouth. "It's blasphemy or something."

"You're in love," Abby said.

"Sure," Teagan said. "Like I was in love at the spelling bees. I'm just . . . nervous."

"*Nervous*," Abby said knowingly. "You ever meet a boy who made you *nervous* like that before? You know what? I don't think I like this guy."

"You just said he looked like Brad Pitt. You said it was unfair that he was going to live with us."

"That was five minutes ago. Now my hair is standing on end. There's something about him, Tea, I swear."

"It's the way he smells," Teagan said. She'd noticed it as soon as he stepped in the door.

"Smells?"

"Didn't you think he smelled . . . really good?" Teagan could tell by the way Abby frowned that she didn't.

"Like what?" Abby looked puzzled. "Cologne? I didn't smell anything."

"No, it was more . . ." Teagan shook her head. "I don't know how to describe it." Finn smelled *wild*. Abby would never let her live it down if she said that.

"Oh, my god," Abby said. "That's how Bartholomew Dark seduces his victims . . . they're drawn to his smell. Lock your door tonight, okay? I'll get some holy water from the font at Drogo's tomorrow."

Teagan sighed. "How long has it been since you read a book that didn't have vampires in it?"

"They write books with no vampires? Wait . . . the penguins made us read that Shakesrear guy, right?"

"Shakespeare," Teagan said.

"Whatever. I'm pretty sure Mercutio was a vampire. He had the attitude, you know? He just never got a chance to show his fangs."

"Did I hear you referring to the Sisters of Mercy as penguins, Abigail?" Mrs. Wylltson came down the stairs, towing Aiden behind her. "You'll be respecting godly women in this house."

"Sorry, Mrs. Wylltson," Abby said contritely. "I'll confess it next time I go to Mass. Can I spend the night again?"

"Not tonight," Mrs. Wylltson said. "You'd best head home."

"But . . . I helped cook dinner! Can't I help eat it?"

"We need to give Finn a chance to settle in." She ushered Abby toward the door.

"I think the spaghetti sauce needs more garlic," Abby said as Mrs. Wylltson herded her onto the porch. "Lots more!"

"I'll consider it," Mrs. Wylltson said.

Abby made a pinky-thumb phone and held it to her ear. *Call me*, she mouthed to Teagan as Mrs. Wylltson shut the door.

"Garlic?" Mrs. Wylltson asked.

"Vampires," Teagan said.

"Abby thinks . . . ?" She shook her head. "You can call her later and tell her Finn has no fangs. The boy has a broken arm. That would make anyone pale. Let's get supper heated before they come downstairs."

"I'll be the lookout," Aiden said as he stationed himself at the foot of the stairs, "and tell you when they're coming."

Mrs. Wylltson set plates on the table, while Teagan poured milk for herself, Aiden, and Finn, and wine for her parents.

"They're taking their time up there," Teagan said.

"Your da is explaining the house rules," Mrs. Wylltson said. "Ms. Skinner was hovering at the hospital. She didn't even let Finn ride with us on the way over. That woman knows nothing about the boy. He's a Mac Cumhaill through and through."

"What does that mean?"

"It means he's a Traveler. He wasn't meant to live by Ms. Skinner's rules."

"They're coming." Aiden scooted around the corner on his hands and knees.

"Good," Mrs. Wylltson said. "Now go wash your hands."

"I don't want to wash my hands. I want to stay here and see Cousin Finn."

Mrs. Wylltson tipped her chin down and gave him the Look.

"Yes, ma'am." Aiden ran for the bathroom.

Finn still had the satchel strap over his shoulder when he came into the kitchen. Teagan turned so she could just see him from the corner of her eye as she arranged the napkins. There was a moment of awkward silence, Finn studying the painting of Ginny Greenteeth and the older Wylltsons studying Finn, before Aiden came back, his hands still dripping.

"How'd you break your arm?" Aiden asked.

"Fell out of a tree," Finn said.

"What were you doing in the tree?"

"Being foolish."

Aiden poked the satchel. "Is that a man purse?"

"It's my kit."

"What's in it?"

"A change of clothes," Finn said. "An extra pair of socks, the sort of things you need when you travel. Do you want to see?"

"Yes." Aiden reached for it, but Finn caught his arm. "Dry your hands first."

Aiden dried his hands on his shirt while Finn set the satchel down and opened it. Aiden dug into it and pulled out a pair of clean socks, then a roll of duct tape.

"What's this?"

"Duct tape. It's the most useful stuff on earth," Finn said seriously. "You can fix anything with duct tape."

"Not animals." Aiden shoved the tape back in the bag. "Teagan fixes hurt animals at the zoo."

"Does she, then?" Finn said. "What kind?"

"Naked mole rats." Aiden shrugged. "Ugly things like that. Tea thinks apes are just ugly people."

"Not really." Teagan was surprised to find that her voice wasn't shaky. "Not exactly. But I think they are more than we give them credit for, and they should be given space to survive. To live free."

"How can you like the zoo, then?" Finn asked.

"I don't have to like the cages to love the animals." She set the noodles on the table.

The Wylltsons sat down, and Finn took his place across from Mrs. Wylltson. Teagan bowed her head.

"*May the blessing of the five loaves and the two fishes be ours,*" they all spoke the prayer together. Finn clearly knew it—he didn't miss a word. "*May the King who did the sharing bless our sharing and our co-sharing. Amen.*"

He had a little difficulty using his left hand for the silverware, and it was obvious he wasn't used to eating at a table. But he wasn't embarrassed or awkward, just . . . observant.

He took a portion of every dish that was passed to him, just like Mr. Wylltson did.

Teagan was sure the spaghetti would defeat him. He studied Mr. Wylltson's method of twirling a neat knob of noodles on the end of his fork, using his spoon for support, and Aiden's capture-and-slurp-the-worm method. Since he couldn't use the spoon, he settled for a twirl and slurp and managed to get tomato sauce on his chin.

Mr. Wylltson picked up his napkin and wiped his lips and chin, and Finn immediately did the same. Teagan looked away quickly to hide her smile. Her father had figured out what Finn was doing and was giving him cues.

"Where is Mamieo?" Mrs. Wylltson asked.

"Around," Finn said. "You didn't mention her to Ms. Skinner?"

"Finn Mac Cumhaill," Mrs. Wylltson said. "I've lived the Traveler way. Of course I didn't."

"I don't know where she is, exactly," Finn said, relaxing a little. "I didn't know you were still in Chicago, either, Aunt Aileen. Not when I gave them your name. Mamieo has scattered the family."

"Why?" Mrs. Wylltson asked. "Why would she do that?"

"I don't know. It was years ago."

"How long have you been living on your own?"

"Five years," Finn said. "I was in a foster home for a year after my parents died. They were good people, for rooters. It's why I had to leave. I stayed with Mamieo for a year. I've been on my own since then."

"You've been living on the streets since you were twelve?" Mr. Wylltson asked. "How did you manage?"

"Let the boy eat in peace," Mrs. Wylltson said. "He's home now."

"This is how it works around here, Finn," Mr. Wylltson said when the meal was finished. "Teagan cooked, Aileen's on a deadline with her painting, so that leaves you and me to clean up. Do you want to do the dishes, or read aloud while I do them?"

"Never been much for books." Finn eyed the pile of pots in the sink.

"The boy's injured, John," Mrs. Wylltson said.

"I can manage well enough," Finn said. "I'll do my share."

"Think before you make your move, Finn," Mrs. Wylltson advised. "You should never take the first deal offered. This is where negotiation comes in."

"Negotiation?"

45

"For instance"—she pushed back her chair and stretched—"I could delay my deadline just a little, and you could play me a game of chess while John reads. I'd wash the dishes when we're done. You could rinse. Everyone's happy."

"As a fellow male, I feel it only fair to warn you, Finn," Mr. Wylltson said, "my blushing bride has never lost a game of chess. Or Monopoly, or checkers, or Risk. She's luring you like a lamb to the slaughter, boy."

"John! I'm doing no such thing!"

"Yes, she is," Aiden said. "Mom doesn't lose."

"Right." Finn stood and picked up his plate. "It'll be the dishes, then."

"I'll help." Teagan stood as well. It would take him forever to do the dishes one-handed. "Abby helped me cook, after all."

"Excellent," Mr. Wylltson said. "That means I read. When I meet someone who says they're not 'much for books,' I can guarantee that they haven't met the right book yet." Mr. Wylltson stood up. "I'd be happy to make some introductions."

Finn jumped right in as soon he had figured out the proper way to do things, rinsing while Teagan washed. Her arm tingled every time she leaned close to hand him a dish, like he was carrying some kind of electric charge.

Mr. Wylltson came back in with two books. "I'm feeling poetic. My first choice for the evening: *Songs of Experience*, by William Blake!"

"I don't think so," Mrs. Wylltson said.

"Why not?"

" 'The Tyger' is tucked into that book, isn't it? That poem gave Aiden nightmares the last time you read it."

"I'd forgotten that." Mr. Wylltson set the book down reluctantly. "The Boyhood Deeds of Fionn, then, by James Macpherson. I expect Finn knows this story." Mrs. Wylltson went back to selecting a brush. "But he'll enjoy Macpherson's version."

"Why would he know the story if he hasn't read the book?" Aiden asked. It was past his bedtime, and he was starting to get grumpy.

"Because," Mrs. Wylltson said, "Fionn is another way of saying 'Finn.' Your cousin Finn is named after the great Irish hero Fionn Mac Cumhaill."

"This is the story of Fionn's parents," Mr. Wylltson said. "And how he came to be."

The story was all in poetry, the kind of old words Teagan's father liked best. He read how Cumhaill, the leader of the fierce Fianna of Éireann—as Ireland was called in those days—fell in love with Muirne, the beautiful daughter of Tadg Mac Nudat. Tadg's veins were blue with royal blood, and his heart black with royal pride.

When he found out that Cumhaill came from the Travelers Clan, a people who owned nothing but what they could carry on their backs and went about the country practicing the tinker's trade, Tadg forbade the marriage. Cumhaill and Muirne went to the Druids of the deep wood and were married there.

Teagan tried to slide the dishes into the suds without allowing them to clink or clatter—then tried to hand them to Finn without touching him. Or looking at him. Because every time he caught her looking, he smiled, and she got goose bumps. It was a good thing her dad was reading and her mom painting, because she was sure they would notice. She focused on her father's voice.

Tadg learned of the marriage and made a blood covenant with Fear Doirich, the goblin god, known as the Dark Man. The Dark Man cursed the lovers, sending goblins after them and their children through all eternity.

Cumhaill was betrayed to his death, but Muirne, heavy with child, fled into the deep woods. There she gave birth to a baby boy and died soon after. The boy was raised by a druidess and a warrior woman. They named him Fionn Mac Cumhaill and taught him the skills he would need to fight against all goblinkind.

"That's not a happy ending," Aiden said when Mr. Wylltson stopped reading. "I don't like it."

"It's an Irish story, love," Mrs. Wylltson said. "We don't do happy endings."

"Still, you're a very good reader," Finn said. "You read it almost as well as Mamieo tells it."

"Thank you." Mr. Wylltson took a bow. "I have sworn to use my great powers of literacy for the good of all mankind. That is why I became a librarian."

"Don't tease the boy, John," Mrs. Wylltson said. "It's not his reading, Finn. It's his voice. I married him for that voice."

"I thought you married me for my good looks," Mr. Wylltson said.

"Now, dear," Mrs. Wylltson said. "Be realistic."

"Women can tear the heart right out of you, Finn," Mr. Wylltson said. "Never forget it."

"Is Finn really named after that guy?" Aiden asked.

"Finn's not only named after him," Mrs. Wylltson said. "He's a descendant of Fionn himself."

Finn shrugged. "Everyone from the isles is descended from

someone if you go back far enough. My da used to say there was a king or hero under every family tree."

"That's true," Mrs. Wylltson agreed.

"Am I descended from a king or a hero?" Aiden was half lying on the table.

"Neither." Mrs. Wylltson winked at her husband. "Just a ratty old wizard named Merlin."

"*The* Merlin?" Aiden actually sat up. "Like in the movie?" *The Sword in the Stone* had been his favorite video for weeks.

"Myrddin Wyllt, actually," Mr. Wylltson replied. "He was a Welsh bard who saw his king slaughtered in battle. The horror turned him into a madman or a prophet, depending on whom you believe. Lived alone in the woods, talked to trees. It was a writer who turned him into Arthur's Merlin and gave him the magic. Which just goes to show that if you want to be remembered well in history, you should be kind to writers."

"That stinks," Aiden said. "I wanted him to be magic."

"It's past your bedtime, son," Mr. Wylltson said.

"Just a little longer." Aiden opened his eyes very wide. "I'm not sleepy at all. I want to talk to Finn."

"Nope," Mr. Wylltson said. "And no arguing. Finn will be here in the morning."

The doorbell rang.

"I swear, if that's Ms. Skinner..." Mrs. Wylltson marched into the front room, gripping her paintbrush like a weapon. Mr. Wylltson followed her as far as the kitchen door, then peeked around.

"It's Mrs. Santini," he said in a stage whisper.

Aiden jumped up. "Is Lennie with her?"

"Sorry, son. It's past Lennie's bedtime, too. Don't worry." He turned to Teagan. "Your mother will hold her off in the living room. I'll toss this one into bed and be right back down." He scooped Aiden up and carried him kicking and giggling from the room.

Teagan focused on finishing the last pan, then passed it to Finn. He rinsed it, and she held out a dishtowel so he could dry his hand.

"You're a quiet one, aren't you?" he asked.

"Not usually." She tossed the towel on the counter.

"Then I'm thinking you've noticed it, as well."

Teagan felt warmth flood her face as she looked away. So he'd felt them, too. The . . . sparks. If this was how Abby felt around boys, it was no wonder she had a hard time studying.

Teagan turned back to Finn, but he wasn't looking at her anymore. He had leaned over to peer out the window.

"I'm glad I'm not the only one noticing. There's something strange afoot all right. I haven't seen one *cat-sídhe* around the place all night, neither outside nor in. Not one."

He hadn't been talking about the sparks after all. Teagan blushed redder. "You haven't seen a what?"

"A *cat-sídhe*." Finn gave her an odd look.

"What is that?"

"Like the *bean-sídhe*. They're cattish and small. They're always around Travelers' camps, or houses, always watching. Setting traps and causing trouble."

"*Bean-sídhe*?" Teagan asked. "You mean 'banshee'?"

Finn frowned. "That's what rooters call the hussy."

50

"Rooters?" It was like talking to someone from a different planet.

"Folk who put down roots. You've never seen a *cat-sídhe*, girl?"

"I . . . don't think so. What do they look like?"

"Cat goblins that walk upright. You'd know it if you'd seen one. About two feet tall, half dead and half alive. They're some of the goblins from your da's story."

Goblins? Finn hadn't had any time to talk to Abby, so it couldn't be a setup.

"What do these *cat-sídhe* do?" Teagan asked. "Other than walk around like zombies?"

"I've seen one squeeze the life out of a baby bird," Finn said. "Just to hear it squeak. I hate the little bastards."

Mr. Wylltson's Welsh baritone rang out from the laundry chute. Finn jumped and whirled to look at the hole in the wall.

"It's Dad." Teagan tried not to laugh. "He's singing the monsters away. You know, out from under the bed, out of the closet. That's the only way Aiden will go to sleep."

"What kind of monsters?" Finn asked.

"Imaginary ones," Teagan assured him. "Aiden has a wild imagination. He's scared of all sorts of things. Like Elvis impersonators, and the tooth fairy. He's terrified of the tooth fairy."

"Poor kid." Finn leaned back against the counter, studying her. "You have a heart for the injured, don't you? That's why you offered to help with the dishes."

Perceptive, as Dr. Max would say. Even if he did think zombie cats were stalking him.

"Do you have a boyfriend?"

Teagan's face went warm again. "I'm working on getting a scholarship to Cornell's vet-med school."

"So?"

"So it's the best school in the nation. Getting in is tougher than getting into med school. I have to focus. I have a plan, and a boyfriend is not a part of it."

Finn tipped his head and nodded.

"Mamieo told me once that Aunt Aileen was the prettiest child she'd ever seen. But she hasn't seen you, has she? Not since you were a baby. I'm glad you're not my blood cousin, Teagan Wylltson."

"Why?" Teagan felt foolish even as she asked it. She'd seen that look in a guy's eyes before. It meant they were never going to be friends, because he wanted . . . *more.* A lot more. When a guy looked at her that way, it was time to walk away.

But she couldn't walk away this time. This one was going to be living in her house. And if it felt like fireworks standing next to him, then touching him would be—

"Tea"—he leaned toward her, and Teagan took a step back—"I'm going to change that plan of yours."

Her face flashed from warm to very hot, and her knees felt . . . wobbly. And Finn could tell, because he grinned.

She stomped across the kitchen and jerked open the door to the maid's stairs. "Here. If you go up this way, Mrs. Santini won't see you. She's dying to get the gossip—that's why she's here. Your room is right at the top."

"Sending me to my room, eh?" Finn laughed. "Mamieo would like you, girl. Good night, then." He grabbed his satchel and disappeared up the stairs.

FOUR

I'M *going to change that plan of yours'?* He *said* that?"

"Yeah." Teagan shifted her cell phone to her other ear and leaned her head against the bus window. "Maybe you were right, Abby." She was glad she had to work early on Saturdays. She'd left the house before Finn was awake.

"I'm going to have a talk with him," Abby said.

"A talk? I thought you were bringing holy water."

"First I'll talk. Then I'll hit him with the holy water. Drogo was trying to *tell* me something, Tea, I swear. And Finn shows up, like, the next day."

The bus was passing St. Drogo's at that moment. What were the odds? Teagan half expected Drogo to drop his hoe and wave.

She'd woken up with the kind of headache that makes things jiggle and blur at the edges of your vision, as if your brain were just too tired to process the information sent along by your eyes. That's what she got for staying up half the night thinking about Finn. Trying to get him out of her head.

"Tea?" Abby said. "Are you there? I said Saint Drogo was trying to tell me something."

"Maybe he wanted to tell you not to run away from Father Gordon."

"Yeah, yeah," Abby said. "Saints don't go to any trouble unless it's *important*. Like, your best friend's falling for some—" Abby's voice was drowned out by a furious banging.

"What's that noise?" Teagan asked.

"Sheila's banging on the bathroom door. WHAT?"

Teagan jerked the phone away from her ear. Abby's voice was loud enough that people three seats away turned to look.

"I'M TAKING SOME PRIVATES TIME HERE!"

"Private time," Teagan explained automatically. "She means private time. The whole bus heard that," she said, putting the phone back to her ear and sinking a little lower in her seat. Public transit was becoming *way* too public lately.

"Sorry," Abby said. "We're having a sale, and I'm supposed to be on the register. See ya."

"See ya," Teagan said, but Abby had already hung up.

Teagan took a shortcut through the Primate Research House on her way to the clinic, to see if Cindy had forgiven her for shoving Dr. Max. The chimp shrieked and covered her eyes as soon as Teagan came in.

"I'm the one who should be screaming," Teagan said. "You ruined my sweater. That stain's never coming out."

Cindy shook her head and puckered her lips.

"I'm not after your Dr. Max, I promise. I have a problem of my own." The wiggles at the edges of her vision were getting worse. "It seems he's going to be around awhile. Maybe I'll bring him by so you can meet him."

Cindy peeked out between her fingers and screeched even louder. The rest of the apes decided to join in, so Teagan retreated to the clinic.

The office was empty when she got there. "Hello?" she called.

"Back here." Teagan followed Agnes's voice into the exam room.

"We've had some excitement this morning." The vet tech was wiping down the table. "Apparently a hyena ate a rubber boot two days ago."

"Buster?" Teagan asked. Buster was eight years old and would shred and swallow anything he could latch his powerful jaws on.

"The Hyaenidae garbage disposal himself," Agnes said. "He's going to need surgery. The groundskeeper who was wearing the boot when Buster got it didn't tell anyone it had happened until Buster was down and hurting. He was afraid of getting in trouble."

"Buster took it off his foot? I'd be afraid of losing more than my job."

"He'll check the enclosure more carefully before he goes in next time, for sure—if there is a next time. Dr. Max is taking a short walkabout to calm himself before we start. I pity anyone who gets in his way today. Oh—I haven't had time to feed anybody this morning, much less clean cages."

"I'll do it."

Teagan had finished the cages and was heating the goat's milk for the tiddlywinks' breakfast when Dr. Max came in.

"Were you in the primate house?" he asked.

"Yes," Teagan said. "I came through there."

"Did you see a stray cat?"

"A cat?"

"I heard a commotion and went over there. Cindy told me you had a 'scary kitty' with you. I wondered if a stray might have gotten in."

"I don't think so," Teagan said. "I didn't see one, at any rate."

"Well, keep your eyes open," Dr. Max said. "Strays carry all kinds of diseases. I've got to scrub up. I can't observe in the primate house today, so stay a good distance from the enclosure. Ms. Hahn is still having fits."

Teagan mixed the hedgehogs' food, then tapped on their box to wake them up. They had to be hungry if they hadn't been fed yet, but they huddled together in their little ball, their black eyes blinking at her.

"What's the matter with you?" Teagan picked up Tiny Tiddly gently and offered him the eyedropper of milk. His little heart was beating like a trip hammer.

"What's wrong?" Teagan stroked him with a fingertip. "It's just me." She coaxed him into eating. The other hoglets finished their bowl of food, and she took it away. They huddled together again, trying to burrow deeper into their nest.

Dr. Max was still in surgery when she opened her locker and took out her baby chimp doll. She always felt foolish carrying it across the zoo grounds. Little girls stopped to point, and their mothers stared.

Cindy seemed to have forgotten about Dr. Max or any scary kitties. *Out,* she signed when she saw Teagan. *Out, please.* Cindy always asked to come out. It broke Teagan's heart. Cindy was never going to get out.

Where is your baby? Teagan signed. The chimp shook her head.

Cindy had been stolen from the wild as an infant, sold on the black market, and raised by humans until she was too big to be a plaything dressed in human baby clothes anymore.

She was too confused to ever live in the wild. She had no chimp social skills at all and would attack other chimps if they were allowed in the same enclosure.

Dr. Max hoped that would change. He had arranged for a male chimp, Oscar, who had been raised in similar conditions, to come to the Lincoln Park Zoo as a companion and possibly a mate for Cindy. Oscar was supposed to arrive in the fall, but they would be kept far apart until Dr. Max thought Cindy was ready to meet him.

The fact that the chimp was crushing on the primate research scientist did not bode well for Oscar.

Where is your baby? Teagan asked again.

Dr. Max thought that play therapy might help Cindy remember her few months in the wild with her mother. It might help her remember that she was a chimpanzee.

Teagan had studied hours of footage of mother chimps and their babies before they started their creative play.

Cindy ignored the question, so Teagan sat down and started searching through her doll's hair for fleas. She pretended to find one, pick it out, and pop it between her teeth. Cindy jumped up into her swing. She brought her own doll back down, and started searching it for fleas, too.

Teagan cuddled her doll. Cindy cuddled her doll for about a minute. Then she threw it on its head, jumped up to her swing, and lay down, one foot dangling over the side.

"Don't want to play today, huh?" Teagan spent the rest of the hour pretending to be a mother chimp, while Cindy peeked at her over the edge of the tire swing.

When she got back to the office, Dr. Max and Agnes were standing in the middle of the floor. Agnes cradled something in her hand.

"Is everything all right?" Teagan asked. "How'd surgery go?"

"Buster should be fine," Dr. Max said.

"Tiny Tiddly's dead," Agnes blurted out. She was holding the small body.

"He was fine just an hour ago." Teagan took him. The *wrongness* she always felt when she touched death spread through her, and then the anger. "Who did this?"

"He was in the middle of the floor," Dr. Max said.

"He couldn't have been," Teagan said. "I put him in the nest box myself." There was a froth of blood on his snout, and his mouth gaped open. "Who else has been in the office?"

Agnes met her eyes then looked away. "No one else has come in, Teagan. Just you."

Someone had to have come into the lab. Teagan shook her head. No one here would do something so . . . evil.

I've seen a cat-sídhe *squeeze the life out of a baby bird. Just to hear it squeak. . . . Cindy told me you had a "scary kitty" with you. . . .*

Teagan shook her head. There had to be a logical explanation.

"Agnes will take over the feedings from now on." Dr. Max took the little body from her. "I'll dispose of this."

"Dr. Max, I—"

"Let's follow Ms. Hahn's rules for a while," he said. "No animal contact without supervision. None. I have some paperwork to do."

Agnes turned her back on them and pretended to be busy with paperwork of her own.

Teagan held back the tears until she was at the bus stop. Her vision blurred as they welled up, and the jiggles she'd been catching out of the corner of her eye all morning seemed to swim together into . . . a *creature* about a foot and a half tall. It leaned against the wall of the bus-stop shelter, its cat mouth open in horrible laughter.

None of the other people at the bus stop seemed to see it. *It's just tears twisting things around.* Teagan squeezed her eyes shut and rubbed them hard enough to make little stars appear. When she opened them again, there was nothing strange in the bus shelter, just the usual trash and graffiti on the back wall.

When she got home, Abby was waiting for her on the front steps of her house.

"Nobody's here," she said as Teagan walked up.

"They've gone to the library," Teagan said. "Mom's signing books at the Spring Book Fest. Dad is in charge of the whole thing. I'm supposed to go right down to help watch Aiden."

"What's the matter? You look like you've been crying."

"You can tell?"

"Salt puckers your cheeks. You need some moisturizer." She started digging through her purse. "If it's that Irish idiot making you cry, I swear I'm gonna call *my* cousins. He thinks he's got family? I'll show him Family."

"Finn didn't make me cry." Teagan unlocked the door.

"He's trouble." Abby pulled some lotion out of her bag. "I've got instincts about boys, and they're telling me something is wrong with this guy. Something is . . . *wrong*."

Teagan washed her face with cold water before she told Abby about Tiny Tiddly. The tears started to well up again, but she pressed the washcloth to her eyelids.

"Dr. Max thinks you left one of those babies out on the floor and then stepped on it? What, is he an idiot or something?"

"No," Teagan said. "He's my boss. It's like everything I've worked for this whole year . . . all the trust . . . just went away." She threw the washcloth in the sink and put some of Abby's lotion on her face. "Come on, I'm late already."

The five acres tucked behind the old brick library building were half library grounds, half city park. Houses had grown up against three sides of the wrought-iron fence, hiding the park from the street. Teagan checked behind the gate as they went in. It was rusted open, making a little triangle-shaped corral full of weeds and completely covered with trumpet vines. Aiden liked to squeeze through the narrow opening and pretend it was his wild house. He wasn't in residence right now, though.

The library lawn was in chaos. Kids dressed as characters from their favorite books ran around under banners that read, Let Your Imagination Run Wild—at the Library! and Spring Fever Madness: Expand Your Mind. There was a crowd of tiny princesses and strange creatures from her mother's books waiting to have their copies signed.

Her dad was lining up the older middle-graders on the far side of the lawn for the costume contest. A few wore the predictable

Harry Potter themes. A bespectacled girl with a notebook was sitting on a tree branch; Harriet the Spy, Teagan decided. A boy who had a pair of sneakers hung over his shoulders by their laces could have been Maniac Magee or Stanley Yelnats. Stanley, she decided when she saw the shovel he was carrying. A diminutive Jack Sparrow swung a fake sword. He wouldn't get any points from her dad, even if the movie had been turned into a book. John Wylltson was a purist.

Closer to the trees, teen vampires mingled with High Elves and angels. A lone werewolf wandered the grounds, seemingly torn between the cake table and a group of girls gathered around the old willow.

"There he is." Abby pointed.

Aiden, in a wolf suit like Max from *Where the Wild Things Are*, was riding on Lennie's shoulders.

Lennie's face was painted like the biggest, toothiest Wild Thing, and he had pinned a feather boa to his pants for a tail. Aiden was bouncing on his shoulders, swinging a stick at a banner.

"What's he doing this time?" Abby asked.

"Making mischief of one kind and another," Teagan said.

"Is he carrying a purse?" Abby asked.

"A kit," Teagan said. "It has socks and Scotch tape in it."

"Scotch tape?"

"We didn't have any duct tape," Teagan explained.

"What?"

"Never mind. Aiden! Stop that!" Teagan said as they walked up. "Hi, Lennie. You have to put Aiden down now."

"Okay." Lennie pulled Aiden off his shoulders and set him down gently. "Hi, Ab-by. Are we in trouble, Tee-gan?" He looked like he might cry.

"No," Teagan said. "But you almost were. You shouldn't help Aiden tear things down."

"No." Lennie stared at his feet. "That would be bad."

"That's right," Teagan said. "Is your mom here?"

"I came by myself," Lennie said proudly. "I'm going to get cake. Mom said to come home after cake. And not to eat too much. She's making lasagna."

"Lasagna!" Aiden shouted. It was his favorite food. He'd probably try to sneak over to Lennie's for supper.

"If you want cake, Lennie," Abby said, "you'd better get some now. It looks like it's going fast."

"Okay," Lennie said. "Want some, little guy?"

"I already got some." Aiden patted his purse. "I put it in my kit."

"Okay," Lennie said. "See ya."

"Wouldn't want to be ya," Aiden said, and they both laughed.

"Where is Finn?" Teagan asked Aiden.

"By the willow." Aiden pointed. "With the *girls*."

Finn's back was to a tree. A teen vampire—the sexy kind—looked like she was getting ready to sink her teeth into him. Molly Geltz, Teagan's lab partner from Chemistry class, was there, and several girls that Teagan didn't know. None of them was close enough to talk to Finn, though, except the Queen of Darkness.

"Oh, my god," Abby said. "Like attracts like."

"Finn's not a vampire," Teagan said.

"He's a good guy," Aiden agreed.

Abby wasn't listening. "Is that walking wardrobe malfunction Kiera Jones? That girl is so skanky. I swear that vamp costume's about to fall right off her. He shouldn't even be talking to her, after what he said to you!"

"What did he say to you?" Aiden asked.

"Nothing important," Teagan said.

Abby snorted. "We'll straighten him out now and put a stake through his heart later. Nobody messes with my best friend like that." She started toward the trees.

"Abby, don't . . ." Teagan pulled Aiden after her.

Abby pushed her way through the girls and stood between Kiera and Finn. "So. You're into trash, huh?"

"*Abby!*" Teagan said.

"Teagan!" Finn smiled at her, completely ignoring Abby. "I was wondering when you'd get here."

"Yeah, you looked like you were wondering real hard." Abby folded her arms.

"Did you just call me trash?" Kiera asked Abby.

"I was talking to lover boy here"—Abby jerked her head toward Finn—"but if the foo shits . . ."

"Abby!" Teagan said. "*Stop it.*"

"Do you eat out of garbage cans?" Abby had Finn's attention now. "That's what I heard."

"Skinner tell you that?" Finn said. "She needs to mind her own business."

"Did you really *scavenge?*" Molly had gathered enough courage to join the conversation. "That's so cool."

"I think trash is disgusting." Abby looked at Kiera. "All kinds of trash."

"Maybe some people don't think it's disgusting." Kiera adjusted her top to show a little more flesh. "Maybe they think it's *tasty.*"

"Why shouldn't people use things that have been thrown out?" Molly asked. "Some people never buy anything in the stores. They collect it from garbage cans and recycle it. They're called 'freegans.' I . . . I would totally live like that." She smiled wistfully at Finn. "I'd be a freegan."

Abby and Kiera both looked at Molly.

"I would." Molly pushed her glasses up defiantly.

"You don't have any idea what we're talking about here, do you?" Abby asked.

"Of course I do." Molly's glasses were slipping down again. "I did a report on recycling."

"Oh, my god," Abby said.

"You want some cake, Finn?" Aiden asked. Everyone turned to look at him. "It's going fast."

"That I do." Finn stepped past Abby and took Teagan's arm. "I think Teagan does, too."

"What?" Molly was saying as Finn pulled Teagan away. "It was a great report. Tea proofread it for me . . ."

FIVE

"THANKS, my man," Finn said. "That was quick thinking."

"I know," Aiden agreed solemnly. "You might not have gotten any cake at all."

Abby caught up with them halfway across the lawn.

"No bite marks," Finn observed. "Did you put a stake through her heart?"

"I wasn't talking to her," Abby said. "I was talking to you. And I still have some talking to do. But first, I've got something for you." She pulled a squirt gun out of her purse and squirted him in the face.

"What the cr—" Finn glanced at Teagan. "Heck . . . was that?"

"Holy water," Abby said. "Does it sting?"

"You're crazy." Finn wiped his face.

"Is heck better than crap?" Aiden asked.

"A lot better," Teagan said.

"Why?"

"I don't know why. Ask Dad."

Abby and Finn were having a stare-down.

"Abby!" Abby's older sister Deirdre was standing at the park entrance, her cousins Angel and Donnie on either side of her. Leo leaned against the hood of a stretch limo pulled up at the curb.

"Abby!" Deirdre yelled again. "Get over here."

"I'm busy," Abby bellowed back.

Rafe, the youngest of the brothers, got out of the passenger side of the limo. While the rest of the Gaglianos were dressed in everyday clothes, Rafe was wearing a three-piece suit that made him look like a mini-mobster from a bad TV series. Mrs. Gagliano said it was some kind of phase he was going through. He stood on tiptoe to whisper in Deirdre's ear. She nodded.

"Ab-i-gail Gagliano!" Deirdre screeched. "Your mother's in this car. She says to get your butt over here! You're late for Uncle Vito's party, and we're not going without you!"

"Your butt is being paged," Finn said.

"I swear I'm moving out the day I turn eighteen," Abby said. "Tea . . . are you going to be all right?"

"I'm fine," Teagan said. "Really."

"Why wouldn't she be all right?" Finn asked.

"She's having a bad day." Abby glared at him. "You and me are going to finish our conversation later."

"We were having a conversation?" Finn said. "I thought you were washing me down with holy water."

"ABIGAIL GAGLIANO!"

"I'M COMING!" Abby screamed back. "Then you should have been listening a little closer. We're going to talk." She stalked off toward the limousine.

"She's your best friend?" Finn asked.

"We're like sisters," Teagan said.

"They always drive around in a limo?"

"One of her uncles owns the company. Abby's cousin Leo drives for him, and sometimes he takes the limo home."

There was no cake left when they reached the table. Mrs. Wylltson had finished signing books and was packing her extra copies, fliers, and props into Aiden's red wagon.

"I forgot to feed my Tamagotchi," Aiden said.

"You can feed it when we get home," Mrs. Wylltson told him.

"No, I can't wait. If I don't feed it now and clean up its poop, it will *die*."

"I'll walk him home, Mom," Teagan said. She couldn't take any more death, not even pixel death, today.

"You might as well take the wagon, then. One less thing I have to keep an eye on. Dad and I will be home as soon as we have this cleaned up."

"I'll bring it along." Finn took the handle.

Great. She was going to have to walk home with him. It had been fine with Abby in between them, but she didn't want to have to deal with the sizzle. Not today.

Teagan tried to walk quickly enough that she'd stay ahead of him, but it didn't work. His legs were longer, and he wanted to walk beside her. That didn't mean she had to be talkative, though. He kept glancing sideways at her, and Teagan pretended she didn't notice.

"Go this way," Aiden said when they were halfway home. He made a bee-boop-boop video-game noise and pointed at an alley. "It's faster."

"Are you sure?" Finn asked.

"Yes, I told Dad once, and now that's the way I go with Dad and Lennie. It's our shortcut. We've got to hurry."

"Doesn't seem to head the right direction," Finn said.

"It will if Aiden says so," Teagan said. Getting home faster would be good. If Finn didn't go to his room, she could go to hers. And stay there until she figured out how to deal with this chemistry thing. "We call him the human homing pigeon."

"I'm not a pigeon!"

"Human GPS, then. He never gets lost."

"Yeah," Aiden said. "I never get lost." He led the way, his wolf tail wagging behind him.

The alley ran behind the trendy shops on Clark Street, but the buildings looked different from back here. A few windows were broken, and others boarded up. There were big Dumpsters, some gaping open like mouths too full to chew, showing boxes and scraps, some with their lids down, lips tight. All of them smelled bad. Aiden marched ahead as if he knew exactly where he was going.

The alley crossed a back street and another alley, where a stray cat growled over a pile of chicken bones.

Teagan glanced sideways at Finn. "Will you tell me more about the *cat-sídhe*?"

"Does this have something to do with your having a bad day?"

"Maybe." Teagan told him about Tiny Tiddly, and the scary kitty in the primate house.

"Sounds like a *cat-sídhe*, sure enough. Travelers are blamed for many a thing a *cat-sídhe* has done. They delight in ruining our lives. But it's never happened to you before? That's surprising."

"Can Travelers see these . . . cats?"

"Most don't have the second sight," Finn said. "But they know the creatures are about. Like I said, *cat-sídhe* cause trouble. Set traps."

"But you see them?"

"I'm the Mac Cumhaill." Finn shrugged. "It's part of the curse."

"What curse?"

"Your da just read you the story," Finn said. "Fear Doirich cursed my family for all time. It's surprising that you've never seen one before if you have the second sight, though. And if you don't, then how did you see the creature at the bus stop?"

Aiden had stopped, and Teagan was so focused on Finn that she almost ran into him.

"Lennie?" Aiden whispered.

Twenty-five feet ahead, three guys had Lennie backed against a brick wall. Teagan had seen one of them at school in the senior lobby and the others around the neighborhood. The senior wore his football jersey; one of the others had a goatee, and the third wore a baseball cap turned backwards. They looked like Football Jersey's older brothers.

Lennie hadn't washed the face paint off before he'd started home, and his feather-boa tail was draped over his arm. He looked more like the Cowardly Lion than a Wild Thing.

"I was talking to you." Jersey slapped him. "You think that paint makes you scary?"

Teagan saw a dark stain spread across the front of Lennie's pants.

"Pee yourself, retard?" Baseball Cap shoved Lennie. "Your mama never teach you what a potty's for?"

Teagan took out her cell phone. These were college kids, and they were going to hurt Lennie.

"What are you doing?" Finn asked.

"Calling the police."

Finn snatched the phone out of her hand, dropped it in his pocket, and pushed her and Aiden behind the nearest Dumpster.

"What are *you* doing?" Teagan demanded.

"Keeping you and the boyo out of it," Finn said. "Cops won't get here in time to help. Go on home the long way. I'll meet you there."

"Finn!" Teagan whispered. "Your arm's broken. What do you think you *can* do?"

"I told you," Finn said. "I'm the Mac Cumhaill. I'll do what needs doing. Go on, now. I don't have time to argue. Get your baby brother out of here."

He strolled around the corner of the Dumpster.

Teagan took Aiden's hand to pull him back down the alley, but he jerked it away.

"I'm not a baby! I want to go with Finn!"

She caught his collar and dragged him back behind the Dumpster, just as Baseball Cap shoved Lennie again.

"You'll be stopping that now," Finn said.

All three bullies turned to look at him, and Lennie whimpered.

"Do I know you?" Goatee asked.

"We're about to get acquainted," Finn assured him. "You can go on home, Lennie."

"He can what?" Jersey asked.

"I said he could go home. You're done with him."

"You did?" Goatee laughed. "Well, we're not done. It's just starting to get entertaining."

Finn hit him in the mouth with his left hand.

Lennie looked confused. So did Goatee.

"Go on, Lennie," Finn said.

"What the f—" Goatee started. Finn hit him again.

Lennie started shuffling away.

Goatee looked at his brothers. "What the hell are you waiting for?"

Finn was fast. He kept them all in front of him, and Teagan could hear the impact every time his fist connected. She wrapped her arms around Aiden, who had gone very still. *Run.* They should run for help. But her muscles weren't moving. She'd never been this close to a fight before. The sound of fists on flesh made bile rise in her throat.

Aiden put his hands over his eyes. "No bad guys, no bad guys," he chanted.

Teagan pulled him close. "Lennie is getting away," she whispered.

Finn was buying Lennie time. But with his cast strapped to his side in a sling, he couldn't even use his right arm to deflect their fists. He made up for it by striking twice for every blow they threw at him.

Jersey didn't get behind Finn until Lennie was half a block away. He jumped in as Finn was punching and caught his left arm.

Teagan looked around wildly, hoping to see someone peering out of a window or standing in a doorway, anyone she could call to for help, could ask to call the police. There was no one.

Jersey Boy and Baseball Cap held Finn while Goatee used him for a punching bag.

When they let go, Finn collapsed. Goatee aimed a kick at Finn's broken arm, but Finn twisted and took the boot in his side instead. It lifted him off the ground, and Ball Cap and Jersey laughed.

"This leprechaun's done," Ball Cap said.

Please let it be over. Teagan rocked Aiden. *Let Finn stay down until they leave. If he gets up again . . .*

Finn shook his head like he was trying to clear the sweat and blood from his eyes and turned to look the way Lennie had gone. Lennie was shuffling as fast as he could, one hand holding his wet pants up, his tail dragging in the dirt behind him. He was almost at the end of the alley. If he made it out onto the street there would be people to help him. Everyone in the neighborhood knew Lennie.

"So if the leprechaun's done," Goatee said, "let's go get the retard."

Nausea washed over Teagan. *It wasn't over.* They were going to hurt Lennie the way they'd hurt Finn.

"Hey, asshole." Finn had pushed himself up.

Goatee turned back as he struggled to his feet.

"What did you call me?"

Finn spat blood against the wall.

"Asshole," he said. "And you answered."

"You Irish shit," Jersey said. "We're going to kill you."

Finn got in a couple of good swings before Ball Cap and Jersey caught his arms again.

"Aiden." Teagan pulled his hands away from his eyes. "Stay here. I mean it." He nodded, then covered his eyes again.

Teagan grabbed the first thing she could find from the pile of trash—a flat bicycle tube—and ran at the bullies swinging it as hard as she could. The tube made a loud *twok* when it hit Baseball Cap on the side of the face.

He let go of Finn and jumped back. "What the hell?"

"Hey! It's Spikes' friend Ko-Ko-Bop." Jersey let go, too, and Finn slumped against the brick wall. "What's she doing here? Show us some shimmy, babe."

Teagan swung the inner tube backhand, slapping him across the face. "Shut up!"

"The little bitch wants to play." Jersey started to circle around behind her, but Finn came off the wall and stepped between them.

"Don't you know when you're beat?" Goatee asked.

Finn wiped his mouth with the back of his good hand. "I'll let you know when I am. Go on, Tea. I told you to go home."

A horn blared, and everybody jumped. Lennie must have made it out of the alley, because a rusted old pickup truck had turned in from the street and was almost on top of them. The driver was leaning forward, peering at them over the steering wheel through John Lennon glasses. "American Pie" blared from the radio. He leaned on his horn again.

"Let's get outta here," Jersey said. He shoved Teagan's shoulder on his way past.

Teagan and Finn pressed up against the wall. The driver stared disapprovingly at the blood on Finn's shirt as he went past. The pickup stopped and the driver got out. He pulled the red wagon from behind the Dumpster, then reached behind it again and pulled Aiden out as well. He held him up and examined him.

"Hey!" Teagan yelled. "Put my brother down!"

The man looked at the inner tube in Teagan's hand, then dropped Aiden beside the wagon, climbed up into the Dumpster, and started rooting through the contents. Aiden grabbed the wagon's handle and ran toward them as fast as he could over the bumpy alley ground.

"That freegan almost recycled me," he said, and started to cry.

Teagan picked him up and hugged him. She was still shaking inside and out.

"I'm *not* a baby." Aiden sobbed.

"I was wrong to say it," Finn said. "I might cry, too, if that freegan had caught me. He was scary."

"Really?" Aiden gulped. "Scarier than those big boys?"

"I don't lie, my man." Finn was still leaning against the wall. "He was a lot scarier." He turned to Teagan. "Who's this Spikes?"

"He was just some jerk on the bus," Teagan said. "I don't even know him. Can you walk, or do you want to ride in the wagon?"

Finn eyed the wagon. "I think I can stagger along if you help me."

"I'll pull the wagon." Aiden took the handle again and started down the alley. The wheel caught the tail of his wolf suit, but after Teagan tucked it up, he did just fine.

Teagan put her arm around Finn's waist to hold him up, and he draped an arm over her shoulder. Even the adrenaline that was making her shake inside hadn't cured the chemistry. Touching Finn didn't feel good. It felt really good.

"You're just the right size for hugging." Finn pulled her closer. "That's nice to know."

"You can walk by yourself." Teagan started to step away.

"Ouch! Don't let go," Finn said. "I'll fall over, really. You can send me to my room when we get home, girl."

"You're sure you can't walk?"

"Finn doesn't lie," Aiden assured her. "He saved Lennie. He's *the Mac Cumhaill*."

"I get it," Teagan said. "You're some kind of cursed Irish Robin Hood."

"Nah," Finn said, and winced. "I never steal from the rich. That's a goblin game."

STREET fighting?" Mr. Wylltson examined Finn's swollen eye. "You need to talk your way out of these things. Use your head!"

"Sorry, John," Finn said. "If I were a book man like yourself, I might have tried it. I never meant to get your daughter involved, though. I told Tea and Aiden to go on home."

"I got myself involved." Teagan handed Finn a fresh ice pack. "And they were beyond talking when we got there, Dad."

"You did just fine." Mrs. Wylltson's eyes flashed. "Both of you. I'd have given them something myself, if I'd been there. Picking on that poor boy! Next time, put a rock in the inner tube, Tea. It'll be more useful. You have to think your way through things, even in the midst of it. Use your brain, girl."

"Aileen!" Mr. Wylltson said. "Don't encourage violence. There are civilized ways to deal with things like this."

"I'd have civilized the hooligans on the spot," Mrs. Wylltson said, pulling Finn's shirt up to look at his ribs. "It was the right thing they did, and you know it, John."

"You said you don't know their names, Tea?" Mr. Wylltson asked.

"I've seen one of them around school," Tea said. "But I don't know any names."

"You don't have any broken ribs," Mrs. Wylltson said.

"Na." Finn touched his side gingerly. "I thought I did, but it was only the wind they kicked out of me. I'll have some bruises for certain." He had just pulled down his shirt when Mrs. Santini burst into the room.

"Lennie and his mom are here," Aiden said as he came in behind her. "I let them in."

Lennie had changed his pants so he no longer had a tail, but he was still wearing his Wild Thing face paint. He leaned against the wall and slid down until he was sitting on the floor. Teagan knew just how he felt. Her legs still felt weak. Aiden put his arms around Lennie and started whispering to him.

Mrs. Santini stood in the doorway, looking at Finn, her hand over her heart for half a minute before she rushed across the kitchen, wrapped her arms around him, and pressed him to her large bosom.

"Ouch," Finn said.

"My Lennie told me. He told me what you did."

"Ouch." Finn's voice squeaked this time.

"I think you're hurting the boy, Sophia," Mrs. Wylltson said.

Mrs. Santini released him.

"You need anything, you come to me," she said. "You need a kidney? I got two. You need money . . . ?" She hesitated. "I don't got any. But anything else, you just come to me—"

"You could give them lasagna," Lennie said. "Aiden likes lasagna."

Mrs. Santini's mouth fell open. "Of course I could! What was I thinking? Aileen! Don't cook supper! I've been cooking all day, because my bum of a brother Jordy said he might come over. I'm telling him not to come. I'll bring the food here."

"You don't have to do that," Mrs. Wylltson said.

"Of course I don't have to. I want to, all right? Jordy eats like a pig, so I cooked plenty."

"Sophia," Mrs. Wylltson said, "we don't really need—"

Mrs. Santini drew herself up. "Finn saved my Lennie. I don't have much, but you gotta let me do this."

Mr. Wylltson looked at his wife and shrugged.

"Then it's settled," Mrs. Santini said.

Aiden gave Lennie a high-five.

"Come on, Lennie." Mrs. Santini pulled him to his feet. "I'll make some calls while I finish the salad. I'm going to tell everybody there's a hero on the street. A hero!"

"Sophia," Mr. Wylltson said, "there is one thing that Finn needs."

"You name it," Mrs. Santini said. "It's yours already."

"He needs this whole thing kept quiet. If his caseworker finds out he was fighting, it won't matter that he was saving Lennie. They'll take him to Juvenile Hall."

Mrs. Santini's broad face went slack with shock, then stretched and reddened into outrage. "They'd throw a saint into juvie?"

"Yes," Mr. Wylltson said. "They would."

"My lips"—Mrs. Santini pretended to zip them shut—"are sealed forever. Don't cook, Aileen. I'll be back."

"How long is forever?" Aiden asked after she had gone.

"In this case," Mr. Wylltson said, "probably a week."

Finn was cleaned up before Mrs. Santini came back with lasagna, calamari, eggplant Parmesan, breadsticks, green salad, tiramisu, and Lennie, with every trace of Wild Thing washed from his face. He was carrying a man purse like Aiden's. He and Aiden settled at the table and compared contents. Aiden must have shown Lennie what he carried in his kit at the park; Lennie had the requisite socks and tape, but Aiden pulled out a bottle of perfume from the bottom of Lennie's kit.

"That's not right," he said. "That's for girls. You only carry guy stuff. See?" He dumped his kit out on the table. He had a pair of socks, his Scotch tape, a dull pocketknife, two rubber bands for making traps, a rock that looked like an egg, and his Tamagotchi, which had been sick but still alive when they finally got home.

"Take it off the table, Aiden," Mrs. Wylltson said. "We're getting ready for dinner here." They put out the fine china to match the cut-glass salad bowl and serving pieces Mrs. Santini had brought. Teagan and her mother set the table, and Mr. Wylltson blessed the company and the food, giving thanks for the hands that made it. As soon as he was done, Mrs. Santini took over.

She passed each plate as if she were a conductor and the meal her symphony. Lennie reached across Aiden for a breadstick, and she slapped his hand.

"Mind your manners! You pass the food."

Mrs. Wylltson stopped in the middle of lifting a piece of calamari to her mouth, put it back on her plate, and frowned at the picture of Ginny Greenteeth in the corner.

"Aileen," Mrs. Santini said, "is the food all right?"

"It's wonderful. Excuse me for just a moment." She got up and started searching through the kitchen drawers.

"What's so important you have to leave the table?" Mrs. Santini asked.

"Inspiration," Mrs. Wylltson said. "The words started bouncing around in my head while I was at the book signing, and I thought I'd lost them. They're back. Ah!" She'd found a pen. "You go ahead." She was already writing. "I just want to get this down."

The corners of Mrs. Santini's mouth turned down. "Lennie, pass the salad to Finn. His plate is empty. I don't think he likes my cooking—"

Aiden screamed.

Lennie, who had just picked up the salad bowl, threw it in the air. Finn came out of his chair and caught the salad bowl with one hand, but the lettuce and sweet onions rained down on the table.

"Holy Mother of God." Mrs. Santini crossed herself. "What is wrong?"

"A shadow." Aiden pointed. "There was a shadow by Mom."

"A . . . shadow," Mr. Wylltson said. Aiden nodded, clearly terrified.

"Like the Peter Pan shadow you were making a couple of nights ago?" Teagan asked.

"No," Aiden said. "Scarier. It had ears like this." He held his hands to his head, fingers together and thumbs folded across his palms.

"A rabbit shadow?" Mrs. Santini asked.

"It wasn't a rabbit," Aiden said. "Rabbits aren't scary."

"Nope," Lennie agreed. "Not scary."

"There's no shadow," Teagan said. "What would have made it?"

"There was," Aiden insisted. "And nobody made it. It was just a *shadow by itself.*"

Finn was clutching the salad bowl to his chest, studying Aiden. Mrs. Santini was plucking lettuce from her lap, and Lennie looked like he might cry.

"Somebody has had a very busy day." Mrs. Wylltson put her pen down. "Full of Wild Things, freegans, and shenanigans. I'm thinking he's tired."

"I'm not," Aiden said. "Don't talk about me like I'm a baby. I'm not a baby."

"Of course not," Mr. Wylltson said. "And that's why I think you should practice a more manly scream. A . . . Tarzan scream. Like this."

Teagan put her hands over her ears as he demonstrated.

"John Paul Wylltson," Mrs. Wylltson said, "you'll not be calling elephants to my table."

Mr. Wylltson looked offended. "Street brawling is acceptable, but calling elephants is not?"

"Not at the table." She came back to her chair, picked up a lettuce leaf, and took a bite.

"Why, Sophia," she said, "I believe this is the best tossed salad I've ever tasted."

"Heh." Lennie looked at his mom.

"My special recipe." Mrs. Santini waved her hand. "More toss than salad."

"That was an amazing catch." Mr. Wylltson took the salad bowl from Finn.

"Thank you, John."

"I did see it," Aiden said as Finn took his place at the table. "But no one believes me."

"Because it's impossible," Mrs. Santini said.

"Don't be so hasty." Mr. Wylltson patted Aiden's head. "To quote the Bard, 'There are more things in heaven and earth, Horatio, than are dreamt of in your philosophy.'"

"What does that mean?" Aiden asked.

"It means that you might see a shadow that no one else sees."

"Really?" Aiden asked.

"You would have to look for further evidence, of course," Mr. Wylltson said. "Extraordinary claims demand extraordinary proof."

"I think this extraordinary food demands our attention." Mrs. Wylltson picked up another piece of lettuce. "I apologize, Sophia."

They gathered the rest of the greens from the table, and by the time the last leaf was collected, everyone was laughing.

Everyone but Finn. He ate quietly, studying each face at the table in turn. He didn't look away or even blush when Teagan caught him staring at her. His face was still and somehow sad.

After the Santinis had gone home and prayers had been said, Teagan lay in her bed with the covers pulled up to her nose. It felt like she had lived three weeks in one day, and they hadn't been good weeks. Her eyes welled as she remembered Tiny Tiddly and the blood on his little snout. She kept coming back to the figure she'd seen at the bus stop, with its awful mouth open in laughter. The longer she thought about it, the clearer the picture became. But it couldn't have been real, could it?

There are more things in heaven and earth, Horatio, than are dreamt of in your philosophy.

Wasn't Tiny Tiddly's crushed body extraordinary proof of . . . something?

It was past midnight when Teagan came fully awake, cold with sweat and shivering from her dreams. She had dreamed of running, hunted by something with a bloody muzzle and ember-bright eyes. A sound from inside the wall made her jump. It took her a moment to figure out that Finn was going down the maid's stairs hidden behind the paneling. She listened for the door to open in the hall by the bathroom, but it didn't. He wasn't headed to the bathroom.

Teagan threw her sheet off and ran down the stairs.

Finn was at the back door, his kit strap over his shoulder.

"You're leaving?"

"I am."

"But . . . why?"

"Because the *cat-sídhe* are not the worst of the things that follow me, Tea. I'm sorry I brought them here."

"So there *are* shadows with nothing to cast them?"

"There are, and I'm hoping your brother didn't really see one. The best thing I can do for Aiden . . . for you . . . is leave. The way Mamieo talked about Aunt Aileen, I thought you would have dealt with the goblins before. If I'd known you hadn't, I'd never have come."

"You think they'll follow you away?"

"They will. I'm making it easy for them, going at night through the alleys and darkness. They'll come after me. You're not going to wake anyone?"

"No."

"You're a corker, aren't you?" He brushed her hair back from her face with his fingertips and tucked it behind her ear. Teagan felt electricity arc, rippling across her skin where his fingers passed. "Can I kiss you, girl?"

"No," Teagan said.

"No?" He sounded surprised.

"My plan hasn't changed."

Finn nodded. "Probably for the best. It's been nice knowing you, Teagan Wylltson."

"Finn!" Teagan said as he opened the door. "What happens if the goblins catch you?"

"They won't." Finn's smile flashed, white in the darkness and crooked from his swollen lip. "I'm the Mac Cumhaill, remember?"

"You have no idea where he went?" Ms. Skinner glanced at the police officer who was taking notes.

"None," Mr. Wylltson said.

"The state will decide what is best for the . . . child." Ms. Skinner sniffled. "I had reservations about allowing him to come here in the first place. They are on file."

"A Mrs. Gillhelm called us," the officer said. "It seems her sons were beaten up by a street gang yesterday afternoon. It happened not far from here."

"They were hitting Lennie," Aiden said. "Finn saved him."

"He was involved in a fight and you didn't call me?" Ms. Skinner did not look pleased.

"Finn gave the hooligans what they deserved," Mrs. Wylltson said.

"Who's Lennie?" the officer asked.

"He's the boy who lives across the street," Teagan said. "His mom, Mrs. Santini, is always home. I'm sure she'd be happy to talk to you."

"Right across the street?"

"Yes, sir." Teagan pointed out the house through the front window.

"If Finn contacts you," Ms. Skinner said, "you are to call me immediately."

"It's a police matter." The cop glanced at Ms. Skinner, then handed Mr. Wylltson a card. "We'll take care of it. Call my cell."

Teagan watched the policeman and Ms. Skinner cross the street and knock on the Santinis' door. Lennie opened it, and they went in.

"Tea," Mr. Wylltson asked, "did you do that on purpose?"

"Yes," Teagan said.

Two minutes later, the Santinis' door opened again. Ms. Skinner and the cop hurried out, practically scrambling down the steps. Mrs. Santini followed them, her arms waving and housecoat flapping in the wind, exposing thunderous calves and dimpled knees above fuzzy pink slippers. She was still waving her arms as they retreated to their cars.

Mr. Wylltson sighed. "Do you think we can find Finn before they do?"

"Nobody's going to find Finn." Mrs. Wylltson rubbed her temples. "Not unless he wants them to. I ache in my very bones this morning. I'm going back to bed for a little while."

Mr. Wylltson made himself a sack lunch, then took a cup of cocoa to his wife.

"Can you call in today, Tea?" he asked when he came out of the bedroom. "I think your mother has a migraine coming on. She'll need some help with Aiden, and I have to work all day."

Mrs. Wylltson came into the living room an hour later, walking a little unstably.

"I hurt, and . . ." Her words slowed, slurred, and seemed to re-arrange themselves. "Tá . . . tá mé tuirseach."

"Mom?" Teagan said.

"I remember. Oh, my god, Roisin. I promised! Tá áthas fearg, Roisin. Tá áthas fearg!" Her knees buckled, and she pitched forward.

"Mom." Teagan knelt on the floor beside her. "Mom!" She wasn't moving. "Aiden!" Teagan yelled. "My phone's in my room. Get it!"

She dialed 911 while Aiden crouched beside his mother, smoothing her hair. As soon as the ambulance was on its way, Teagan called her father at work and told him what had happened.

When the paramedics carried Mrs. Wylltson out on a stretcher, Aiden leaned into Teagan and buried his face in her shirt. She put her arms around him.

"It will be all right."

"No, it won't, Tea," Aiden whispered. "The shadow man touched her. Last night while she was writing, it touched her. I should have made it stop."

"How could you stop a shadow?"

"I don't know," Aiden said, and started to cry.

PART II: MAMIEO

SEVEN

EAGAN?" Molly passed the calculus handout to her.
"Are you all right?"

Teagan nodded. She couldn't take her eyes off the
window on the other side of Molly's desk. Teagan held her breath as
the woman walking past turned . . . and then she breathed again.

"Oh." Molly had turned to follow Teagan's gaze. "She looked like
your mom, didn't she?"

"Only from the back."

"You're not crazy," Molly said softly. "After my brother died, I
thought I saw him on the street all the time. Sometimes I still do.
It's like that when you lose someone."

Teagan nodded.

Aileen Wylltson had been in a deep coma by the time the ambulance arrived at the hospital. She died three days later, with Tea
and Aiden sitting by her bed, and John Paul Wylltson holding her
hand. She'd never even woken up to say goodbye.

The final bell rang, and Teagan picked up the papers and tucked
them into her notebook. She didn't have zoo hours this afternoon,
so she might be able to catch up on some homework. It was hard to

get her brain around homework again after spending the summer taking care of Aiden and her dad.

Her cell phone vibrated, and Teagan pulled it out of her pocket. Aiden. Her life would be so much easier when he learned to spell well enough to text.

She flipped it open. "Aiden? What's up?"

"Tea?" His voice was barely a whisper. "I need you. Come quick!"

"Are you at Mrs. Santini's house?"

"I'm at home."

"Where's Dad?"

"I don't know. I'm hiding in the closet."

"Get out of the closet and go back to Mrs. Santini's house."

"I can't. *The Skinner is here.*"

"You're sure Dad's not home?" Teagan glanced at the clock. He was supposed to be home for this meeting with Ms. Skinner.

"He's not. I need you, Tea!"

"Trouble?" Molly asked. "I can give you a ride home if you need one."

It would only take fifteen minutes to get home if she had a ride.

"Okay, I'm coming, Aiden. Just wait. I'll be there soon." Teagan hung up. "Thanks, Molly."

"Is everything all right?"

"Dad just missed a meeting," Teagan said as she dialed her father's cell. "I have to get home to take care of my brother." The call went directly to voicemail. She hung up and dialed the library number.

"Mr. Wylltson hasn't returned from lunch, Tea," the library aide said. "We were expecting him hours ago."

She started to dial Mrs. Santini, then stopped. Mrs. Santini would be worried if she found Aiden gone. And she would explode if she found Ms. Skinner waiting on their doorstep. She'd never forgiven the woman's attitude toward Finn.

Molly finished loading her backpack. "I have to drop off some books. Meet me in the parking lot."

Teagan pushed her way through the press of kids in the hall. The school crowding was so bad this year that even seniors were sharing lockers. Abby was already at the locker when Tea got there.

"You want to come down to Smash Pad? I'm giving an art show. We're hanging fake nails, just like it was a real art gallery."

"Can't." Teagan reached past Abby and grabbed her Literature book. "I've got to get home."

"Choirboy's in trouble again?"

Aiden had been in first grade for a whole month, and he hadn't spoken in class. Not once. His teacher said he wouldn't follow instructions. He sat and hummed to himself or wandered around the classroom. Teagan wasn't sure how Ms. Skinner got involved, but she had called to make an appointment with Mr. Wylltson to discuss the situation. The appointment he'd just missed.

"Yeah," Teagan said.

Abby frowned. "Angel's got his car. He could give you a ride."

"Thanks," Teagan said. "I've got one. Molly's going that way. Gotta run, but I'll call you."

"Hey," Abby shouted after her, "I need some shoes to wear to the dance. Can I borrow your baby dolls?"

"Sure." Teagan waved. "Come over after work."

"Thanks for the ride," Teagan said as Molly's sunshine-yellow Volkswagen pulled up outside her house. "I owe you."

"You can help me with calc." Molly laughed. "See you tomorrow."

Ms. Skinner wasn't sitting on the porch. Teagan used her key out of habit, but the door wasn't locked.

When she stepped inside, Teagan could hear a voice in the kitchen.

"Did your father lock you in that closet?"

What was Ms. Skinner doing in the house?

Aiden jumped up and ran to Teagan as soon as she entered the room.

"She caught me, Tea," he said. "I sneezed."

"You shouldn't have left Mrs. Santini's," Teagan said.

"She's cooking cabbage!" Aiden gagged. "It stinks."

"This child was locked in a closet. And he refuses to speak to me. Has he been told he will be punished if he does?"

"Aiden, did you lock yourself in the closet?" Teagan asked, still trying to figure out what was going on.

"It's the best place to hide when there's an *Elvis impersonator* in the house."

Aiden glared at Ms. Skinner. He had moved from terror of Elvis impersonators to complete disdain of the pretenders who had no music of their own. It was the vilest insult he knew.

"She came into the house? You didn't let her in?"

"I told you, the Skinner was here."

Teagan turned to Ms. Skinner. "How *did* you get in?"

"I'll ask the questions." Ms. Skinner had the decency to turn slightly pink. "Why would a closet have a lock on the door, anyway? How long have you been locked in there, Aiden?"

"It's an old basement door that Dad hung there," Teagan said. "You can work that lock from either side. Aiden locked himself in."

Ms. Skinner ignored her.

"And why aren't you in school, young man?"

Aiden's eyes slid away from her, and he started humming. Teagan bit her lip. His personal playlist selection was Pink Floyd's "Another Brick in the Wall."

"Come back over here and sit down," Ms. Skinner commanded. Aiden hummed louder.

"Aiden is never left alone, Ms. Skinner." Teagan forced herself to smile. Whatever was going on, her dad would sort it out as soon as he got here. But it would be better if she could calm things down before he arrived. *Or before Aiden started singing out loud.* If Ms. Skinner didn't already know the words to the song, Teagan was sure she would not be pleased.

"His school has an in-service today. He is supposed to be across the street at Mrs. Santini's. She probably hasn't noticed that he's missing."

"This child needs intervention," Ms. Skinner said, as if Aiden weren't even in the room. "Something is clearly amiss. With your family history . . . he needs to be evaluated."

So much for making nice.

"Did you let yourself in?" Teagan asked. "I know Aiden didn't leave the front door open."

Ms. Skinner pressed her lips together. "Mr. Wylltson and I had an appointment today. When he didn't answer the bell, I thought something might be wrong. Apparently, my professional intuition was correct. Do you know where your father is?"

"He should be at work."

"I have been calling his work number. They don't know where he is."

"I'll let him know that you came by." Teagan motioned toward the door. "Since he is not here now, I think you should leave."

"This child was unattended."

"He's attended now. And I'm sure Mrs. Santini would be happy to verify where he was supposed to be."

Ms. Skinner gave her a sour look. "Tell your father that I will be here at exactly two tomorrow. And I would watch my tone if I were you, young lady."

"I would watch breaking and entering if I were you," Teagan said. "You had no permission to enter our home."

"I didn't break anything. The door was unlocked, and I am on official business. You're seventeen, as I recall. I can have your brother *and* you removed with one phone call."

"There is no reason to remove anyone."

"You could spend a year in a foster home waiting for your father to prove that. Tell him not to make me wait tomorrow. I don't like what I've seen here."

Teagan showed her to the front door and resisted the urge to slam it after her.

"The Skinner said Mom's paintings were bad," Aiden said.

"She went into the basement? What for?"

Aiden shrugged. "Where's Dad?"

"I don't know," Teagan said. "Let's go find him." She made sure both the front and back doors were locked before they left, just in case Skinner decided to come prowling around again.

"I don't want to go into the park," Aiden said. "The trees are still crying."

"That's all right," Tea assured him. "We'll go up into the library stacks. We can look out the window to see if he's in the park. But first we've got to talk to Mrs. Santini."

Lennie let them in when Teagan knocked. Mrs. Santini's cheeks were flushed from the heat of her kitchen, but they turned redder still when Aiden explained what he had done.

"I thought you were taking a nap," she said. "I don't know what I am going to tell your father."

"He won't blame you," Teagan assured her. "I'll let Dad know what happened."

Aiden stomped on every crack in the sidewalk all the way to the library and gave his foot a twist on the bigger ones. "Are you trying to call up *'the masses of bears/Who wait at the corners all ready to eat/The sillies who tread on the lines of the street'*?" Teagan asked, quoting one of Aiden's favorite Milne poems.

"Yes," Aiden said. "But they won't eat *me*. I'm going to send them after the Skinner."

"Don't worry about her. Dad will talk to her, and everything will be all right."

"You should stop saying that," Aiden said. "It's never going to be all right."

"It will," Teagan said. "But you have to look people in the eye when they talk to you. Even people like Ms. Skinner, or your teacher. If you don't, they'll think something is wrong with you."

95

"I'm not like them," Aiden said.

That was true enough. Aiden was definitely his own creature. Her dad said he was a lot like Aileen had been when they first met, following only rules that made sense to her. Apparently nothing about school made sense to Aiden.

"Can you pretend to be like them at school? It could be a game. I'll bet there are things at school you would really like if you tried them."

"Nope." Aiden stomped hard on another crack, and Teagan studied his curly blond head. There had to be some way to convince him to give school a chance.

Suddenly, the hair rose on her arms. *Finn.* It wasn't a question. She knew he was somewhere close. *Close enough to make her shiver.* He wasn't on the library steps, or the street. She turned to the bushes under the windows and saw him sitting very still in the shadows there.

He was wearing jeans, lace-up boots, a T-shirt with the sleeves ripped off, and a blue bandanna tied pirate-style. A Celtic tattoo curled around his biceps. He hadn't had that before. Or the scar along his jaw.

"Finn?" Teagan grabbed Aiden's shoulder.

"In the flesh."

Finn's right arm was sun-browned where the cast had been, and he looked older. Older and a little . . . dangerous. Teagan glanced around.

"If it's goblins you're looking for, there's none about." He stood up, brushed the dirt from his pants, and stepped into the sunshine. It was Finn, but not the same Finn. His easy smile was gone, and there was a different look in his eyes. A wary look.

"I remember you," Aiden said. "You're the Mac Cumhaill. What happened to your face?"

Finn ran his thumb along the scar. "You mean this? Got into a disagreement with something ugly."

"The night you ran away?"

"It was. I'm more sorry than I can say about your ma, Tea. The news just reached Mamieo. She sent me to talk to John. When did it happen?"

"The day after you left," Teagan said. "Mom collapsed the morning after you left."

"You're all right, though? You and Aiden and John?"

"We haven't seen any more bad guys," Aiden said.

"That's good."

"The doctors said it was acute leukemia." Teagan shivered again. "They said she must have had it for weeks."

Finn studied her. "Did they?"

"Yes."

"And you believe them?"

She pulled Aiden closer.

Finn nodded. "I'll be gone before sunset, and I won't come to the house. But I need to speak to John. It's very important. I asked inside, but they said he wasn't in."

"We're looking for Dad, too," Aiden said. "Because the Skinner's going to take me away."

"Skinner?" Finn spat. "What's this about, then?"

"Aiden's had some trouble at school," Teagan explained. "Ms. Skinner set up a meeting with Dad, but he didn't show up. We came to look for him."

"Mind if I come along?"

"You might as well." Teagan started up the steps. More than Finn's looks had changed. He was keeping his distance from her, almost like the wolf that had shadowed the Wylltsons as they hiked in the woods one summer. Curious, cautious.

"Where have you been?" Teagan asked.

"Living with Mamieo." Finn jumped up the steps and held the door open for her. "Asking her questions I should have asked before, Cuz."

"So I'm your cousin now?"

"You are."

"Good," Teagan said. That would make it easier to ignore the sparks. Because they were there, all right. Stronger than ever.

"We're closing in five minutes, Tea," the woman at the desk said.

"We'll be gone," Teagan assured her. The woman gave Finn and his bag a suspicious look but didn't suggest he leave it behind.

They went up the wooden stairs to the third-floor window that looked out over the park.

"You think your da is up here?" Finn asked.

"No," Teagan said. "I think he's walking in the park, but Aiden doesn't like to go there. We can see most of it from this window." Aiden climbed into the window seat and pressed his nose against the glass.

"Nope," he said. "Not there."

Teagan sat down beside him and leaned over to look. The park had gone wild over the summer. Morning glories had escaped from some city garden and planted themselves, and their vines grew up the walls, mixing with the trumpet vines. First frost hadn't touched them yet. It was beautiful, but Aiden was right. There was no one in the park.

She turned to Finn. "He might be at the very back, under the trees. You could check . . ."

"Poof!" Aiden shouted. "There he is!"

Mr. Wylltson was walking toward the park gate, almost all the way across the lawn that had been empty a split second before.

"Poof?" Finn leaned over and looked out the window. "Something went poof?"

Teagan was already following Aiden to the stairs. She waved at the librarian behind the desk as they went past. Aiden slammed through the doors and ran to his father.

"Dad!" Aiden threw his arms around him. "Don't let her take me away!"

"Who?" Mr. Wylltson asked.

"Ms. Skinner came by," Teagan said. "You missed your appointment."

"Missed it? What time is it?"

"Past five," Teagan said.

"That can't be right. I've only been in the park for a few minutes." His speech was slightly slurred, and he brushed one hand across his eyes.

"Did you fall asleep?" Teagan asked.

"I don't think so . . ." He was coming more awake. He looked at his watch and frowned. "Good Lord, I must have. I wonder why someone didn't call? They must have noticed that I didn't come back to work."

"Your cell was off," Teagan said. "I tried to call."

He pulled it out of his pocket and flipped it open. "It's on. Six missed calls. Finn?" He noticed the extra person standing with his children for the first time. "Is that you?"

"It is," Finn said.

"Mamieo sent him," Teagan explained.

"You're looking well," Mr. Wylltson said. "Come on over to the house. We'll fix some supper and talk."

Finn nodded. "I think I'd better."

Aiden grabbed his father's hand and pulled him ahead of Finn and Teagan.

"I thought"—Teagan glanced at her dad's back and lowered her voice—"you said you wouldn't come to the house?"

"Things have changed. Why are you whispering?"

"I don't want to upset Dad. What things?"

Mr. Wylltson turned around before he could answer. "What day is it, Tea?"

"Tuesday. Ms. Skinner is coming back tomorrow," Teagan said. "Are you sure you didn't fall or hit your head?"

"I'm sure," Mr. Wylltson replied.

"The Skinner came into our house without permission," Aiden said. "She found me in a closet."

Teagan explained as they walked, glancing at Finn now and then. Something must have changed. He wasn't a cautious wolf anymore. He was a hunting wolf, alert to everything around him.

"Son," Mr. Wylltson said when they reached the house, "what have I told you about staying at Mrs. Santini's?"

"Not to leave without permission," Aiden said.

"That's right. I expect you to mind me, even when I'm not there. I'll sort Ms. Skinner out tomorrow." Mr. Wylltson paused as they reached the front door. "And you owe Mrs. Santini an apology. Just think how worried she was."

"Tea made me apologize already," Aiden said.

"That's good." Mr. Wylltson unlocked the door.

Finn followed them through the house into the kitchen. He looked uncomfortable, and Teagan wasn't sure whether it was the walls around him or the changes in the room. Her mom's easel was gone, with nothing but a few spatters of green and yellow on the wall to show where it had been. There was a shelf above the random paint dots with a few knickknacks that reminded Teagan of her mother, and a green urn.

"John," Finn said, "I have some things to ask."

"Things?" Teagan repeated.

"Where . . . where did you bury Aunt Aileen?"

"Aileen never wanted to be buried," Mr. Wylltson said. "She said it was a waste of good land to put a coffin in it. She was cremated."

"Mamieo said she would be. This is a hard thing to ask, but I need to take that"—Finn pointed at the urn—"to Mamieo."

"She needs our mad money?" Aiden asked.

"Mad money?" Finn looked confused.

"Whenever we have pocket change, we put it in the jar," Teagan explained. "We're saving up for a rainy day."

Finn ran his hand through his hair. "I need Aunt Aileen's ashes. It's more important than I can say that I take them away from here."

"You can't," Aiden said. "Mommy wasn't in the ashes. They were just for remembering. We put them in the park so it could remember her, too."

"That would explain it, then," Finn said.

"Explain what?"

"That." Finn pointed out the window. Abby would have called the guy standing in the open gate to the alley "totally Abercrombie." He had the hair, the bod, and the attitude.

"What's he doing in our yard?" Mr. Wylltson asked.

"It," Finn corrected. "What is *it* doing in your yard. It 'poofed' into the park right behind you. I watched for it all the way here but didn't see it. It must have come the back way."

ABERCROMBIE boy walked across the yard to the back door and put his hand to the knob. Teagan knew the back door was locked; she'd checked it before they had started out to find their dad. But it opened, and he stepped inside.

"What's this?" He smiled at Teagan. His eyes were black from lid to lid, like pools of dirty motor oil. "Do I know you? Tell me your name."

"Don't tell it anything," Finn said. "Especially not your name. Names give them power over you."

The oil-slick eyes went to Finn, and narrowed. "Someone who knows the ways of the Sídhe?"

"The stink of goblinkind, you mean," Finn said.

"Goblin? Such foul language." Abercrombie boy tsk-tsked. "We are the Sídhe, and you were made to entertain us."

"Who are you?" Mr. Wylltson demanded. "And why did you just waltz into our house?"

"I waltz wherever I want . . . unless someone is strong enough to stop me." He made his fingers into a gun and pointed it at Mr. Wylltson. "You're not, old man."

"Get out of our house," Mr. Wylltson said.

"You were walking in Mag Mell," the *sídhe* said. "How did you do that? No human can walk there unless Mag Mell *remembers* them. But it can't remember you. I'd know if you'd been there before." He tipped his head and sniffed. "Something here smells like . . . old magic. Who are you people?" He turned to Teagan again. "You look so familiar. I think I'll take you with me. Fear likes to play with the pretty ones."

"Fear?" Teagan backed away.

"Fear Doirich, the Dark Man." Finn had a knife in his hand, and Teagan didn't know where it had come from. He didn't look a little scary anymore. He looked a lot scary.

"Finn!" Mr. Wylltson said sharply. "That's not necessary—"

"It is." Finn moved between Teagan and the goblin. "This thing isn't human. It doesn't follow your rules. You heard what the man said, goblin. Get out of this house. You're not welcome here."

"Finn?" the goblin spat. "The *Mac Cumhaill*? Keep the girl while you can. I'll take the little one first. He'll cry the longest." It spun toward Aiden.

"No!" Teagan shouted. Finn threw his knife as the goblin lunged. Mr. Wylltson shoved Aiden aside, and the *sídhe* caught his arm instead of Aiden. Tea saw Finn's knife sink hilt-deep into its back. And then it exploded. The force picked Teagan up and slammed her against the wall. She scrambled across the floor to Aiden, who was holding his ears.

"Where's Dad?" Aiden asked.

Finn's knife was lying in the middle of the floor. There was a misting of what might have been blood in a spatter pattern on the wall, but the goblin and Mr. Wylltson were gone.

Finn snatched up his knife and headed for the door.

"Where are you going?" Tea said.

"After them. Come on—it's not safe here."

Teagan grabbed Aiden's hand and followed Finn, barely keeping him in sight. He was waiting for them by the gate to the library park.

"Is this where the bad guy took Dad?" Aiden asked.

"I think so," Finn said. "But we can't follow them in. It will be dark soon." Even as he spoke, the air under the trees began to shimmer like a heat mirage.

"That don't look good," Finn said.

"What is it?"

"I've never seen anything like it, but something is happening, that's sure," Finn said. "We'd best get out of sight."

"My wild house!" Aiden dropped to his knees and scrambled into the overgrown trumpet vines. "We can hide in here."

"Get in quick, Tea. I'm right behind you." There was plenty of room in the wild house, but it was a little hard to see out.

"Good. It's good to have iron bars about us." Finn's knife was still in his hand. "The *cat-sídhe* don't like it, at least. Hush, now, not a sound."

Two shadows stepped out of the shimmering air. They were shaped almost like humans, but their heads were rounder, with ears like cats'.

Aiden sucked in his breath, and Teagan put her arms around him. He was trembling as he turned to hide his face in her shirt, but he didn't make a sound.

The shadow men grew darker as they walked toward the gate. They didn't move like humans. Their joints seemed to be in the wrong places, as if they were intended to walk on all fours rather than upright, and they had a strange bounce in their step. They passed within feet of Teagan, close enough for her to see that their hands were on backwards—the thumbs where a human's little finger would be—and that each long digit was tipped with a claw.

People walking down the sidewalk didn't seem to notice them. None of the drivers on the road turned their heads to look.

The taller shadow walked into the middle of the street, bent over, and stuck its head into the pavement as if it were looking for something beneath the surface of a pond.

A pothole the shape of the shadow man's shoulders appeared in the asphalt, and at least one driver saw it. He swerved to avoid the hole and narrowly missed a woman on a bike. She smashed into a parked car and fell sideways into the gutter.

The shadow man pulled his head out of the street, and the pothole disappeared. The smaller shadow man walked over to the cyclist, who was cleaning gravel out of her palms. It tipped its head one way, then another, as if it were studying her. It reached down, and for a moment Teagan thought it was going to help her up, but its hand didn't stop at her skin. It went right into her chest, all the way up to its wrist. It twisted something, then pulled its hand out.

The taller shadow watched, and when the short one was done, they both walked off down the street.

"Aiden?" Tea asked after the shadows had turned the corner. "Was that what touched Mom?"

"Yes." Aiden was crying. "It touched Mama . . . like that."

Teagan scrambled out of the wild house and ran to the woman.

She had finished with her palms and was examining her bike for damage.

"I saw what happened," Teagan said.

"Did you get his license plate?"

"No," Tea said. "Listen . . . I think you may be more badly hurt than you think. You need to go to the doctor."

"I've spilled my bike before," the woman said.

"This time . . . there might be internal injuries," Tea said.

"I'm sure I would feel it. Thanks for stopping, though. Bye." She swung her leg over the seat, climbed on, and started to ride away.

"You have your cell phone?" Finn was holding Aiden's hand and keeping one eye on the park. The shimmer had disappeared.

"Yes," Teagan said.

"Call 911."

The bicyclist made it halfway down the block before she wobbled, twisted violently, and fell over. They waited beside her until the ambulance arrived. Teagan saw them pulling a sheet up over the woman's head as Finn led her away.

"We can't go back to your house tonight," Finn said. "Those two, I think they're hunting."

"For us?"

"Most likely. And they won't be the only ones. The one that took your dad has set them looking."

"That goblin's not dead? But your knife . . ."

"The goblin just went back to where it came from and took your da with it."

"Where?"

"We'll have to follow to find out, won't we? But we can't go after them at night, if we can go at all." He looked around. "We need to get low fast. They'll go to your house, of course. The safest place might be the hole we were in, behind the gate. They wouldn't expect us to stay that close."

Teagan looked around at the dark openings to doorways and alleys. The shadows could be anywhere, dark against the dark, impossible to see.

They followed Finn back to the library and back into the wild house. Aiden was crying quietly, so Teagan pulled him onto her lap and wrapped her arms around him. Her cell phone vibrated.

"Tea." Abby's voice sounded insanely normal. "I'm on my way over—"

"No," Tea said too quickly. "Don't do that. I mean, I'm not home."

"That doesn't matter," Abby said. "Your dad can let me in. The shoes are in your closet, right?"

"No one is home," Teagan said. "We're spending the night somewhere . . . else."

"You're all having an overnight somewhere? What's going on, Tea?"

"Get off the phone," Finn said.

"Was that a guy's voice?" Abby asked. "It didn't sound like your dad. Why's he telling you what to do?"

"I'm . . ." Teagan looked around ". . . camping out. I'll tell you about it tomorrow. I can't talk now, Abby. But I'm okay. Really." Teagan flipped her phone shut and turned it off.

"Talk in daylight," Finn said without looking at her. He was definitely staying as far from her as possible. "Quiet, now."

Aiden tugged on Teagan's sleeve. He moved into a patch of light from the streetlamp. *Scared*, he signed in ASL.

Me, too, Teagan signed back.

Suddenly Aiden jerked and flailed. Teagan grabbed him, and Finn's knife flashed as he turned, looking for the danger.

What was it? Teagan signed.

A spider crawled on me.

We have to be quiet and still, Teagan signed emphatically. *Very still. Even if spiders crawl on us.*

She moved Aiden into the very center of the wild house, between her and Finn, and kept her arms around him. It was a good thing it had been unseasonably warm all week.

As the darkness deepened she focused on the patch of yellow light underneath the streetlamp. If shadows or *cat-sídhe* came up the street, they'd have to walk under the light. She'd see them. If something came from the park, though . . . There were long stretches of darkness there, like paths across the lawn to the trees. Had the shadows made any noise when they passed? Teagan tried to remember, but she couldn't. Sometime past midnight, she felt Aiden go slack with sleep.

She was still awake when the hunters came back, walking through the grayness before dawn. One of them was licking its claws like a child with honey on its hands. Teagan tried not to think about what could stick to a shadow to be licked off later. They walked straight to the trees, the dawn air shimmered, and they were gone. Still, she didn't move or say a word until the sun came up. Finn was sleeping with his head on his knees, and Aiden was curled up beside her. The park looked perfectly peaceful in the bright morning light. A robin searched for worms on the lawn.

"Finn," Teagan said softly. He lifted his head. "We need to talk before Aiden wakes up. You said the goblins serve Fear Doirich. Do you mean the man in the story Dad read to us when you came to our house?"

"The same. The goblin god who cursed Fionn for marrying Muirne."

"But that was prehistory. It's legend and myth."

"Tell that to the goblin who stole your da. He was probably around when that 'myth' was happening."

"What will they do to Dad?"

"I don't know." Finn rubbed his chin. "But the sooner we find him, the better."

"I think we should take Aiden to Mrs. Santini's house," Teagan said. "Before we go after them."

"If there were any safe place," Finn said, "I would send you both. You heard what the goblin said. It was telling the truth. They walk where they will. Mrs. Santini couldn't stop the thing if it came for your brother."

"Who could?"

"Mamieo." Finn waved a fly from Aiden's sleeping face. Finn seemed relaxed in the morning light, more settled. Almost the Finn she'd met four months ago. "She might be able to keep him safe."

Teagan fished her phone out of her pocket. "Call her."

"Call Mamieo?" Finn shook his head. "The woman doesn't own a phone. She borrows one when she has need. She expects me to meet her in Gary, Indiana, after I've collected . . . well, you know what I came for."

"You think all this has something to do with my mother's ashes?"

"I do," Finn said. "But don't ask me what." His stomach growled.

"Hey!" Aiden sat up quickly. "I heard something."

"Just my belly, boyo," Finn assured him. "It hasn't been near food for two days. We'll eat before we go on. My kit's back at the house anyway."

"Where are we going?" Aiden asked.

"To find your da, I hope." Finn crawled out of the wild house.

A little old lady walking her poodle gave Teagan a startled look when she crawled out of the bushes behind Finn.

"Shocking, isn't it?" Finn picked a twig out of Teagan's hair. "The way youth behave these days?"

The old lady pulled the dog to the other side of the street, looking straight ahead as if they didn't exist.

"Some people are not born friendly," Finn said.

When they got back to the Wylltson house, the front door was still unlocked and the back door still hanging open. The kitchen smelled slightly of rotten eggs, and flies buzzed around the blood spatter on the wall. Finn's kit was on the floor where he had left it. He checked through it while Teagan made peanut butter sandwiches for breakfast. Finn ate three and inhaled two glasses of milk. Aiden didn't want to eat at all, but finally managed a half a sandwich when Finn told him he couldn't come with them if he didn't eat.

Finn had his knife in his boot and his kit over his shoulder when they went back to the park. They stood together at the spot where the shadow men had appeared.

"Well," Finn said, "let's try it." There was no shimmering under the trees as they walked forward. Nothing looked out of place or odd. But as she passed under the trees, Teagan felt something brush her skin—and suddenly it felt as if a million tiny fingertips were touching her. She'd walked in this park a thousand times, and nothing like this had ever happened before.

"It's tickling me!" Aiden shouted.

Teagan gripped his hand and kept on walking. The tickling stopped as suddenly as it had begun, and Teagan blinked. The light around them changed. The sun was shining from a different direction; she was sure of it. The trees were still familiar, though. They were standing under the old willow. Behind it, the trees grew denser and darker.

"Where are we, Tea?" Aiden asked.

"I'm not sure." The air smelled wild and delicious, with none of the overtones of city exhaust or human refuse that always tinged the air of Chicago. There was no park fence in sight.

Teagan grabbed Aiden's arm and pulled him out of the way as a group of tiny, shaggy elephants walked out from under a bush.

They were the size of puppies, but they walked in a line like any respectable elephant herd, the smallest hurrying to keep up.

The bull paused, rooted through a pile of leaves with its proboscis, then blinked up at Teagan in nearsighted surprise. It lifted its trunk and made a squeaky trumpet sound. The whole herd bolted for the trees, but they didn't hide behind them as Teagan had expected. They walked straight up the rough bark of the trunks, apparently gripping it with their toes. Then they clung to the lower side of a branch far above her head and somehow folded themselves up until they looked like shaggy gray seedpods hanging from the tree.

"Did you see that, Finn?" Teagan asked. "Finn?" She was talking to thin air. Wherever they were, Finn hadn't come along.

"Look." Aiden pointed. A tree snake disturbed by the elephant herd launched itself into the air. It flattened its body, glided toward another tree, and wrapped itself safely around a branch.

"Where are we?" Teagan whispered.

"Someplace with elephant trees and flying snakes," Aiden said. "Where's Finn?"

The air shimmered even as he spoke, and Finn staggered into being, almost running into Teagan.

"There you are!" he said. "You had me worried, disappearing like that."

"What happened?" Teagan asked.

"It—whatever it is that let us in—wouldn't allow me to bring my knife," Finn explained. "I'd get halfway, and bounce back. Mamieo told me about this. No iron in Mag Mell. I had to hide the knife in the bushes before I could get through."

"Mag Mell?"

"The kingdom of Fear Doirich. Only one living soul has set foot here and come out to tell about it, and that's Mamieo herself." He didn't look happy.

"And?"

"We need to go quietly. Don't draw attention. Goblins walk here, and those that serve the wicked creatures."

NINE

I HEAR music," Aiden said. It was violin music, sweet and sad at the same time. They followed the sounds through a dark band of trees and into a clearing.

Teagan thought the fiddler was hidden behind a tree stump until she saw the stick-thin arms holding up the fiddle, and the rags hanging from what once must have been legs. The fiddler's hair, matted and full of twigs and bird droppings, hung almost to his knees. His ragged pants ended just below the hair. The soles of his bare feet were flat on the ground, but his toes were bent and dug into the dirt. They looked . . . *wrong*.

"Hello?" Teagan said. The fiddler started, the bow scraping across the strings like a scream. He turned his face to them. His skin was turning to bark. It already covered one eye and all of his mouth. He brushed the hair out of his remaining eye with the back of the hand that held the bow, and blinked at them. The eye closed, and a tear squeezed between the lashes.

"Can we help you?" Teagan knelt by his feet and brushed the dirt away from his toes. They curled, rootlike and too long, into the dirt. She tried pulling on one, and the fiddle screeched.

"You can't help him that way, Tea," Finn said. "It's a spell that's holding him. Unless it's broken, he's not going anywhere."

Teagan stood up and used her sleeve to wipe the tear from the fiddler's cheek. "I'll find a way to help you, I pr—"

Finn clapped his hand over her mouth. "You don't make promises in Mag Mell. Not until you understand what it means. Things work differently here—that's what Mamieo says. You've got to think before you speak. It could get you killed, you understand?"

Teagan nodded, and he let her go.

Finn turned to the fiddler. "Did Fear Doirich do this to you, then?"

The fiddle spoke a single note.

"He said yes." Aiden reached out and touched the filthy rope-like hair.

"We'll help you if we can," Finn said. "Come on, you two. Time to go."

"Finn," Teagan protested.

"There's nothing we can do for the man," Finn said. "We've got to find your da." He turned to walk into the dark woods.

The fiddler's eye grew wide when he saw Finn walking away. He turned to Teagan, and the bark where his mouth should have been stretched and caved in, as if that mouth had opened in a shout. Aiden's fingers were tangled in the rope hair, his own mouth open, tears on his cheeks.

"I'm sorry," Teagan said, pulling Aiden's hand away.

The fiddler shook his head wildly, pointing his bow back the way they had come.

"We can't," Teagan said. "We have to find my dad."

The fiddler put his fiddle to his chin and played savagely. He stopped and pointed back the way they had come once more.

Teagan shook her head.

Aiden put his hands over his ears as they walked away, and Teagan didn't blame him. The fiddle's warning had turned to sobs. They walked at least a mile before the sound of the music faded.

Aiden stopped. "It's wrong," he said.

"What's wrong?" Teagan asked.

"Our house is that way"—Aiden pointed over his shoulder—"but the fiddler is that way." He pointed ahead. "We'll be back to him soon."

"You're turned around, boyo," Finn said. "The sun's been at our back the whole time. We've been walking west." But they had gone only a few hundred more yards when they heard the sobbing of the fiddle again. It grew louder as they walked.

"I told you," Aiden said. "Everything's all twisty here."

"Let's turn around," Tea said. "We can follow our own tracks until we figure out where we went wrong. We won't find Dad walking in circles."

She took the lead, watching for footprints or broken vegetation where they had passed. The music faded behind them.

"We never came this way," Finn said.

"We did." Teagan pointed at a clear sneaker print and put her foot down beside it to make another. It was a perfect match, down to the gravel caught in the tread.

"All right," Finn said. "But none of this looks familiar."

They followed the tracks for ten more minutes, until they came to a sandy patch where the tracks clearly came up out of a deep green pool of water.

"That's not possible." Teagan pressed her foot in the sand. The print was still a perfect match. The tracks had to be hers.

"I told you it was all twisty here." Aiden pointed. "We should go that way."

"Then we'll follow you for a while, boyo," Finn said. "Everyone else has had a go." Aiden led them through bushes and marshy ground, but they never crossed their own tracks. When the trees thinned and grew taller, Teagan finally pulled him to a stop. "Where are we going?"

"Away from our house," Aiden said. "Because Dad isn't home."

"That actually makes sense," Finn said.

"Right." Teagan jumped and caught the lowest branch of the pine tree that towered above them. "I'm going to climb up and see if I can see the library. We have to have some idea which way we are really heading if we want to find our way back again." She scrambled onto the branch, then started to work her way higher.

"Do you see anything?" Aiden called.

"I'm not high enough yet," Teagan called back. A howl echoed through the woods. Teagan gripped the tree trunk as a chorus of howls answered. Something was moving through the brush on the far side of the clearing. It was coming too fast for her to get out of the tree and back to her brother.

"Aiden, Finn!" she called as loudly as she dared. "Hide. Hide now."

She didn't know if Finn heard her, or if the sounds themselves moved him, but he grabbed Aiden and dove for the thornbushes just as a doe burst into the clearing.

The young deer paused, her sides heaving, a bloody froth dripping from her nostrils. The doe's ears swiveled toward the baying.

She shuddered, then leaped forward again, past Finn's hiding place, under the tree, and out the other side of the clearing.

The doe had barely disappeared when her pursuers exploded into sight. The leader was a massive creature with a man's body and the head of a dog. There were two or three like him in the pack, and others with the legs of elk and torsos of men. Two looked as human as the goblin that had taken her father away. They ran naked and dirty at the back of the pack. Teagan wrapped her arms around the tree and prayed as they passed beneath her—for herself, for Finn and Aiden . . . for the monsters to go away.

One dog-headed man hesitated, his nose twitching as he turned toward Finn and Aiden's hiding place. He whined, licked his chops, then raced off after the pack. It took them only seconds to get through the clearing and disappear from sight, but Teagan had to force her hands to let go of the tree so she could scramble down.

"Who . . . what were they?" she asked as Finn came out of the bushes.

"Shape shifters," Finn said. "The goblins have strange powers. Some can fully take the form of beasts. Others can only partially transform."

"They were scary," Aiden said.

"You saw them?" Teagan asked.

"Not all of them. I covered my eyes so the monsters couldn't see me."

The air was ripped apart by a scream, almost human in its agony.

"They got her," Teagan said.

"Her?" Aiden asked. "You mean that deer?"

"She was a yearling doe. I think one of the man-dogs . . . smelled us."

"Let's get out of here," Finn said. "We need to talk to Mamieo."

"What about Dad?" Aiden whispered.

"We can't help him if we can't find him," Finn said. "Mamieo can help us do that."

"All right," Tea agreed. "Can you find the way out, Aiden?"

"I can find our house. It's that way." He pointed north—or what would have been north, if they had been walking west.

"You're sure?" Finn asked.

"I'm always sure."

Somewhere in the distance, a dog-headed man bayed. The sound sent shivers down Teagan's spine.

"They couldn't have finished their meal yet," she said. "A pack of hunting animals usually stays by the kill for a day or two. They wouldn't want to leave it."

"Maybe they don't hunt for the eating," Finn said. "Maybe they hunt for the killing."

The howl sounded again, and Finn glanced at her over Aiden's head. It was closer, and the pack answered with the same hungry sound it had when it was hunting the doe.

"You're sure we're headed toward home?" Teagan asked. Aiden nodded.

"Time for a piggyback, my man." Finn pulled Aiden up onto his back. "Tell me which way to go. Keep up, Tea." Finn set out at a steady trot, his long legs eating up the ground. He jumped logs and ducked under branches as if Aiden weighed nothing.

Teagan did her best to keep up. A dull ache started in her side, and she concentrated on breathing through it.

"How much farther do you think, Aiden?" Finn asked.

"I don't know how far," Aiden said. "I only know which way."

Tea glanced back over her shoulder. She couldn't see anything through the dense underbrush, but she could hear them coming.

"Don't look back, Tea," Finn said. "Just run. Keep up with me."

The pain in her side was stabbing, and Teagan thought her lungs would burst. She stumbled and looked back. She could see them. Human torsos and beast snouts alike were smeared with the blood of the doe they had just pulled down. They weren't running full out as they had been before. They were loping along, their tongues hanging out, enjoying the scent of fear.

"Teagan!" Finn shouted. "You have to keep up."

Teagan whirled and took off after him. Finn slowed, matching his pace to hers.

"Get Aiden out of here," she said, gasping.

"We're all getting out," he said. "Run faster." Aiden clung to Finn's back, his eyes closed. Teagan focused on her legs, willing her muscles to move faster, her steps to reach farther.

Suddenly, the air shimmered in front of her. She felt the tingle of a million tiny fingers on her skin, and she was fighting her way through honey-thick air. Something caught at her shirt . . . and she tripped and fell face-first onto the ground under the ancient willow.

Finn dropped Aiden and jumped for the knife he'd hidden in the bushes. He came up with it in his hand, but nothing came through after them.

"Keep moving," Finn said. "You carry Aiden now. There's no telling why they didn't come through, or if they're on their way."

Teagan took Aiden's hand. "I need to go home. Just for a little while. I'll figure it out there. I need to go home, Finn."

"All right," Finn said. "Just move." He relaxed a little when they made it to the street without anything poofing into the park behind them.

"Your shirt's ripped, Tea," Aiden said.

"Let's see." Finn stepped behind her. "It's half gone. You've got some scratches there, too. You can't walk around like that. It'll draw attention." He took a T-shirt out of his kit. Teagan pulled it on over her torn shirt. It hung almost to her knees.

Aiden held her hand as they walked down the streets. Teagan wasn't sure whether he was protecting her, or needed protection. Either way, he wouldn't let go.

"Not good," Finn said when they turned the corner onto their street. There were two police cruisers parked in front of the house, and a crowd gathered outside. The goblin that had taken their father was talking to a police officer. There was another one with him, older and taller. They both wore suits and wraparound sunglasses.

"There's the Skinner," Aiden said.

Teagan pulled out her cell phone to check the time. "It's three o'clock already. She came for her appointment with Dad." As they watched, the older *sidhe* pulled out a wallet and handed Ms. Skinner a card. He gave a card to the cop, too.

"Isn't that your friend Gabby?" Finn asked.

It was Abby all right. She was flirting with Abercrombie boy. The older man must have called him, because he gave Abby a dazzling smile, touched her arm, then stepped away to speak to the police. Abby started to follow him.

"No, no, no," Teagan said. "Those things are *not* messing with Abby." She pulled out her phone and punched a number on speed dial.

Abby pulled her phone out, glanced at the caller ID, then answered.

"Oh, my god," Abby said. "Everybody—"

"Shut up," Teagan said. "Don't say another word. Don't say my name. Who are those guys in front of my house?"

Abby turned and looked down the street.

"And don't look at me! Get away from them so they won't hear you talk."

"Not a good idea," Finn said. Teagan ignored him. Abby gave a flirty wave to the goblin when he looked at her, then walked farther away from them, the phone pressed to her ear.

"Come on." Finn took Teagan's elbow and started pulling her down the street in the opposite direction, away from the crowd. "Walk while you talk."

"What's going on?" Abby said. "I never knew you had so much family. You have a cousin Kyle and an uncle Leo?"

"I don't have a cousin Kyle or an uncle Leo," Teagan said.

"They're saying someone's after you. Someone named Finn Mac Cumhaill. Ring any bells? They showed the cops a photograph."

"Did you tell them anything?"

"I'm a Gagliano," Abby said. "What do you think?"

"I'm sure the cops are fine . . ."

"Yeah, right."

". . . but the other two are not. Finn's not the one who's after me, Abby. It's them, Kyle and that guy he has with him. It's really, really important that you don't tell them I'm here. Why are the cops even there?"

"Ms. Skinner thinks you've been murdered," Abby said. "The fascists won't even let me in to get the shoes. I mean, *I* didn't murder you, right? I need those shoes."

"Nobody kidnapped me," Teagan said.

"That's what Aunt Sophia told them. She said she saw Finn go in with you and your dad yesterday, and you and Aiden went out with Finn, and you all came back this morning."

"She told them it was Finn?"

Abby snorted. "Are you kidding me? The way she tells it, Finn's some kind of junior saint, and they are wasting their time. Is it him I just saw with you, Tea?"

"Meet me at your apartment, okay?" Teagan said. "And don't tell anyone I'm coming, especially not Kyle and Leo. I'll explain everything when I get there."

"Kyle and Leo?" Finn asked after she'd put her phone away.

"The goblins," Teagan said. "They're telling the police they're my relatives."

"Not a good idea," Finn said again. "Getting Gabby involved."

"She's already involved. Did you see the way that thing was looking at her? I'm not leaving without warning her."

TEN

"TAKE your shirt off."

Abby had gotten her apartment the day she turned eighteen. Teagan loved the place. It smelled of paint, turpentine, and fresh canvas; maddeningly comforting smells, and the walls were hung with canvases full of angels. The sketchpad on the table was also full of angels.

Abby never drew or painted anything now but angels. She said that all great artists went through phases, and when her angel phase was done, she would paint something else.

The tiny efficiency didn't even have a door on the bathroom, so Abby had thrown the guys out while she took care of Teagan's back.

Teagan peeled Finn's T-shirt off.

Abby gasped. "You said a *dog-headed man* did this?"

"I think it was the dog-headed man. I was too busy running to look."

Teagan leaned on the counter as Abby cleaned the scratches out.

"Abby?" Teagan said when the silence had gone on too long. "I know it's hard to believe—"

"You know what the problem is here?" Abby said. "Old books. They've damaged your brain, Tea."

"What?"

"Those books your family is always reading. You know why they call old books literature? Because they litter up your brain, that's why. I'm putting the peroxide on now. It might hurt. Focus on my babies. They're wiggling their little fins at you."

Teagan gripped the counter and focused on Abby's collection of Chinese fighting fish. They were the perfect babies for Abby. They could survive even when she forgot to feed them for days at a time.

"Ow, ow, ow!" The hydrogen peroxide trickled down Teagan's side.

"It hurts?"

"No," Teagan decided. "It's just cold."

"Don't be an infant." Abby wiped the trickles away. "You get yourself messed up, you take your medicine. I'm going to put some antibioticals on now."

"Ow! That *does* hurt. You don't have to grind it in!"

"I'm not grinding," Abby said. "Tell me about this cousin Kyle who took your dad."

"He's not my cousin; he's a goblin. Dad always said, 'There are more things in heaven and earth, Horatio, than are dreamt of in your philosophy.' I don't think he expected to be this right."

"That's from an old book, isn't it?" Abby said.

"*Hamlet.*" Teagan winced again. "It's a play, actually."

"See? That's what I'm talking about. It's messed up your brain. I saw this on one of those shows you have to watch when nothing good is on. Your brain's just inter . . . inter . . . I know this word. *Interpolating*," Abby said triumphantly. "That's it."

"What?" Teagan said.

"Seriously. Your eyes see stuff your brain don't understand, right? So it searches around for information, but all you got in there is litter from old books. Your brain is making all this up. You should watch some Maury or Dr. Phil. Get the real world into your head, you know?"

"The police at my house were not made up."

"That part's true. Your dad is missing." Abby finished with Teagan's back. "I'll loan you a shirt." She flipped through the shirts in her closet until she found one she could part with and tossed it to Teagan. "So what are you going to do, Tea?"

"I'm going to go to Mamieo's and try to figure out how to find Dad."

Abby pursed her lips. "I'm going to give you some advice, seeing as your mother isn't here to give it."

"You have a mother, and you never listen to her." Teagan pulled the shirt over her head. It was a little big, but it didn't hang to her knees the way Finn's had.

"Not when she tells me to give up my painting and marry a nice Italian boy. Other than that, I listen."

"So what are you going to tell me?"

"That"—Abby pointed out the window at Finn, who was sitting on the curb with Aiden—"is bad news, Tea."

"You thought he was cute when you first saw him," Teagan said.

"For, like, two minutes. Then I tried to melt him with holy water." Abby's eyes narrowed. "Does he still smell good?"

"Yes," Teagan admitted.

"And is he still *electric*?"

"Yes." *More electric.* He didn't even have to be near her. She could tell where he was, even with her back turned. "But he's different, Abby. He isn't making any moves."

"Just make sure he doesn't. The guy's eighteen and he doesn't have a car. He doesn't have a job. He has no future. And you're running away with him, because of some crazy stuff."

"If I were running away with a guy, would I take my little brother? I told you, we're going to see our grandmother." Teagan retrieved Finn's shirt and folded it up.

"The grandmother who never bothered to call after your mom died? Who you haven't seen in fifteen years? That grandmother? Have you thought this through? Have you thought about Aiden?"

"I *am* thinking about Aiden." Teagan put the shirt on the back of the couch and grabbed Abby's hands to keep her from pacing. "Finn is the only one who can help us right now. He's the only one who can keep Aiden safe. I understand why you think I'm crazy. I would have thought so myself, yesterday. Just do this one thing for me, okay?"

"What thing?"

"The guy who gave you his card. The one who's pretending to be my cousin?"

"Kyle."

"Stay away from him, okay? He's . . . evil. If he wants to hurt you, the police won't be able to stop him."

"Tea"—Abby shook her head—"I'm not just a pretty face. I got a brain, you know. I've met Kyle's kind before."

"Where?"

"At the kind of parties and clubs you don't go to. They wear those shades even at night. Girls who go with them sometimes don't come back. I'm not stupid."

"I know," Teagan said. "I know, Abby. There are worse things than Kyle out there, too. They might be with him."

Abby grimaced, then squeezed Tea's hands. "So, the cops are looking for you. The . . . goblins . . . are after you, and this Kyle kidnapped your father. Let me call my family, Tea. They'll give you a ride wherever you need to go. I don't care who these bastards are, I got uncles who can deal with them."

"No, they couldn't. But maybe Mamieo can. I need you to believe me."

"So, you quit your job?"

"What?"

"You would be working tomorrow if you weren't running away with that guy, right?"

Dr. Max. She'd worked all summer to regain his trust. There was no way she could leave without notice. Teagan pulled her hands away from Abby and took out her phone.

Agnes picked up at the clinic.

"I've got a . . . family emergency," Teagan began.

"Oh, my god," Agnes said. "Is everyone—"

"I'm really in a hurry, Agnes," Teagan said. "I'm going to be out of town at my grandma's for at least a week. Please let Dr. Max know. I'll explain more when I can. Gotta go."

Abby took a deep breath as Teagan put her phone away. "Okay. I believe that something really bad is happening now. There's no way you would risk losing that job for some jerk, right? So you've got to go to your grandma's. How 'bout money? You have money?"

"My purse is in the house," Teagan admitted. "I can't risk going back there."

"Tomorrow is payday." Abby pulled the cushions off of her couch. "All I got is the emergency fund." She shoved her hands down into the cracks and dug out a dollar and seventy-eight cents' worth of change.

"Thanks," Teagan said.

"You need water? I got bottled water for my fish." Abby took three bottles out of the cabinet. "And a chocolate bar."

"Your emergency ration? Are you sure?"

"Of course I'm sure." Abby pulled a super-size chocolate bar out of the back of her otherwise empty fridge. "Take the antibioticals, too. Somebody's got nasty claws."

"Some*thing* has nasty claws," Teagan said. "A dog-headed man."

Abby followed her outside. "Hey, Dumpster boy. I want you to know something. Tea is like a sister to me. I ever hear about you hurting her, I have people I can call. My uncles like Tea, you understand?"

"I'll keep it in mind, Crabby," Finn said.

"It's *Abby*, and you know it. You take care of them. Aiden's just a baby. And Tea's . . . if anything happens to her, I mean anything, I swear I'm coming after you."

"Imagine my terror," Finn said.

"We'd better get going." Teagan took Aiden's hand. "Thanks for everything, Abby. And remember what I said."

"I'll remember." Abby glared at Finn. "You remember what I said, Tea."

"I will. Abby . . . light a candle for us, okay? Light a candle."

Abby stood on the sidewalk, arms folded, glaring at them until they turned the corner.

"Told you she wouldn't believe you." Finn put the antibiotic cream and chocolate bar in his kit and fished out a length of clothesline.

"She believed enough. She believed me about Kyle."

He cut a length of cord and twisted it into a knot around the neck of a water bottle.

"Here you go." He tied it onto Aiden's belt. "Best to keep your hands free. You never know when you might need them. You want one, Tea?"

"Sure," Tea said. "Where'd you learn to do that?"

"From the Boy Scouts," Finn said.

"You were a Boy Scout?"

"Well, no. I knew two old Scouts. They'd have been Boy Scouts fifty years ago, I'd guess. They lived in a box, down by the expressway."

Teagan handed him her water bottle and watched as he tied another cord around the neck.

"You think we can walk all the way to Gary?"

"Walking will get us there eventually. Waiting won't. It's better to keep moving until we find Mamieo. But we'll keep our eyes open. Something usually turns up."

"What kind of something?"

"Hopefully something with wheels," Finn said.

"Yeah," Aiden agreed. "My toes hurt."

"Not surprising," Finn said as they stopped for the light. "You've walked a good way today, boyo. Do you want me to tell you the story of Mag Mell while we walk a little more?"

"Yes," Aiden said.

"This is the way Mamieo told it to me. All the worlds are born of song. Mag Mell was born of the Almighty's first song in the time before time. The people who lived there were the Fir Bolg. They had magic in their hands, magic for tending and mending all that the Almighty had made. Because, you see, Mag Mell was special. She was the world-between-worlds, always hidden, but with doorways here and there where they were needed into all the worlds of creation."

"Like our maid's stairs," Aiden said.

"A bit like that," Finn agreed. "After this green Earth was set in place, the Fir Bolg were given a door into Éireann, which we call Ireland today. They were to take care of it until the Milesians, the people who were to sing the Earth songs of Éireann, arrived.

"The Fir Bolg tended and mended and looked after Éireann, and grew to love it as well as they loved their own home, because it was a beautiful place.

"But before the Milesians arrived, Fear Doirich, the goblins' god, and Mab, the Queen of the Sídhe, came riding storm clouds and bringing their wicked servants with them; *cat-sídhe* and cobs, *bean-sídhe* and night hags, phookas and all of goblinkind, gifted in war and slaughter, polluting Éireann with their filthy touch."

Teagan caught a movement from the corner of her eye and jumped before she realized it was her own reflection pacing her in the window.

Finn laughed. "You've got to keep your eyes open. If that had been a goblin, now, it would have had you."

"Shut up." Teagan turned away from him just in time to see a carpet knife in the hand of a man walking toward them flick, cutting the purse strap of the woman ahead of her.

The thief had the purse, and was walking past Finn as the woman started to scream. Finn backhanded the purse snatcher hard with one hand and retrieved the purse with the other. His movements were almost too fast for Teagan to follow.

The thief seemed more confused than she was. He just kept walking, rubbing his jaw. Finn handed the woman her purse.

"Thank you," she said, clutching it to her chest. "I don't know what I would have done—"

"No problem." Finn flashed a smile so bright, Teagan was sure it contributed a full degree to global warming.

"Oh, my." The woman fanned herself, then dug into her purse and pulled out a five-dollar bill. "I don't carry much cash, but please . . . you deserve something for saving my purse."

"Oh, we could never—" Teagan began as Finn took the bill from the woman's hand.

"I could," he said. "It would be a great help. Thank you." Finn smiled again, with not quite so many megawatts.

Aiden gaped at Finn as the woman walked away. "Did the Boy Scouts teach you that?"

"Well"—Finn winked—"they did tell me to look out for the ladies."

"I can't believe you took her money," Teagan said.

"Beautiful, isn't it?" Finn held up the five. "You're looking at a bus ride across town. I told you something would turn up."

"You *hustled* her."

"Hustled?" Finn looked wounded. "I did nothing of the sort. I saved the lady's purse, and she was thankful for that. We've got a way to go before sunset, Tea. So are we riding the bus, or no?"

Aiden insisted on sitting by Finn, so Teagan took the seat across the aisle from them. She could even take two seats. The bus was empty except for a few commuters and a group in the back who looked like tourists from Japan.

"What happened to the Fir Bolg," Aiden asked when they were settled, "when the Dark Man and his bad guys showed up?"

"They fought against him," Finn said. "Fought with all their strength and all their courage. But Fear Doirich was not a man, or a Fir Bolg. He was a god, and an evil one at that."

"The good guys didn't win?" Aiden looked worried.

"No," Finn said. "The goblins were too strong. They ran the Fir Bolg out of Éireann and chased them back into Mag Mell. For hundreds of years, the goblins and their evil god ruled the land. And then the sons of men, the Milesians, came over the sea.

"Fear Doirich's magic was in his mouth, and he sang up a storm to smash their ships on the rocks and drown the Milesians before they could set foot on Éireann, but a bard named Amergin calmed the sea and the wind with a new song of his own.

"The Milesians were not fighters, not the way the savage Sídhe were. They were lovers of knowledge and poetry. They would have fallen if the Fir Bolg had not come out of Mag Mell to fight beside them."

The bus stopped, and the tourists all stood up. Finn waited until the crowd had passed before he continued.

"That day, though the Fir Bolg turned the tide of battle, Fear Doirich tricked them. When he knew at last that he couldn't win, he took his armies and fled into Mag Mell, locking the pathways behind them. The Milesians had won the home that had been created for them, and there was great rejoicing, but the Fir Bolg could not join in it. They had lost their home. They set out to wander the Earth forever, with no place to name their own."

"What happened to them?" Aiden asked.

"They became the Irish Travelers, of course," Finn said. "I thought you knew that."

"Wait." Teagan leaned across the aisle. "Are you saying Travelers aren't . . . human?"

Finn looked over the three other people left on the bus. "There's human and then there's human, isn't there? Some Fir Bolg married Milesians and became rooters. Some Milesians married Fir Bolg and became Travelers.

"It's the Fir Bolg blood that gives you second sight, and most Travelers have very little of it in their veins. They see otherworld creatures just as flickers in the corners of their vision."

"How about you?"

"I bleed like the next guy. I know that much is true."

"What happened to Amergin?" Aiden asked.

"Mab sent her sister, Maeve, to seduce the man," Finn said. "But the Sídhe princess heard him singing and fell in love instead. They ran away together."

"Did they live happily ever after?" Aiden asked.

"I doubt it," Finn said. "How could he be happy, married to a goblin?"

"It's an Irish story," Aiden said sadly. "We don't do happy endings."

"That's a fact," Finn agreed. He stretched out his long legs, leaned back, and closed his eyes. Teagan could see Aiden's face reflected in the tinted window above him. He didn't look like he would ever smile again.

"Are you sure this is where we want to get off the bus?" Teagan had driven though the South Side with her dad a couple of times, but she had never ridden the bus there, and certainly never walked through the neighborhoods.

The buildings were farther apart. Weeds grew up through cracks in the sidewalk, and graffiti shouted from fences and buildings. Aiden was half stumbling with fatigue. Teagan fingered the cell phone in her pocket. She'd decided to keep it turned off to save the battery for emergencies. Maybe she should have let Abby call someone to give them a ride. Aiden certainly couldn't walk all the way to Gary.

"Stop worrying," Finn said. "I've spent some time here. There's a place we will be safe tonight. We'll get there before sundown."

"A house?" Teagan put a hand on Aiden's shoulder when he started to wander into the street.

"Sort of." Finn gave Teagan a worried look. "Maybe not the sort of house you're used to, though. It's dry enough, unless it rains. Are you hungry, boyo?"

"No," Aiden said. "I'm thinking."

"Well, I'm thinking, too," Finn said. "I'm thinking we haven't eaten since breakfast."

They stopped at a convenience store, and Finn used the money Abby had given them to buy a foot-long hot dog. They squatted on the sunny side of the building against the red brick wall as Finn divided it into thirds. It must have been in the case all day, because the bun was wizened and crunchy.

A pigeon landed a few feet away, hopped once, wobbled, and almost fell over. It was dragging a string from one leg.

Teagan tore off a piece of the crusty bun and tossed it to the bird. The pigeon snatched it up. She tossed another piece and it came closer, close enough that Teagan could see the raw flesh where the string was attached. No wonder it was wobbling. If the string weren't cut off, the bird would lose its leg.

"Will you let me help you?" Teagan asked softly. The pigeon turned a beady eye toward her. She tossed it another breadcrumb. It gobbled it up, but fluttered a few feet away when she held the bread out with her hand.

"You want me to catch that creature for you?" Finn had finished his portion of the hot dog.

"Without hurting it?"

He rubbed his jaw. "I think so."

"You can't catch pigeons," Aiden said. "It's impossible. Lennie told me, and he tries all the time."

"Is that so?"

Finn peeled off his shirt and lay down in the dirt about six feet from Teagan. He spread the shirt over his chest, but held the edges. "Toss some bread on my shirt, boyo."

Aiden tossed a piece of bread, but it hit Finn in the face, then bounced toward the pigeon. The bird hopped toward the food, giving Finn the beady eye. It snatched it up, and Finn didn't move.

Teagan tossed a piece onto Finn's chest. The pigeon eyed it. Finn was so still, Teagan wasn't sure he was breathing. She tossed another piece, and it landed by the first. The pigeon spread its wings just enough to lift itself onto Finn's chest. As its feet touched the shirt, Finn sat up fast, wrapping the fabric around it.

"There you go." He bounced to his feet and held the bundled bird out to Teagan.

"Have you ever caught a pigeon like that before?" Aiden asked as Teagan unwrapped the pigeon, holding its wings together so it couldn't flap.

"I have." Finn shook out his shirt and pulled it back over his head. "The Boy Scouts taught me how it's done. They'd toss the crumbs and I'd catch the bird."

Teagan tucked the pigeon under her arm and pulled the leg out so she could examine it. It wasn't string at all. It was dental floss. No wonder it was biting into the flesh. "Do you have something I can cut this with?"

He took a small folding knife out of his pocket. "You want me to hold the bird for you?"

"That would be helpful."

Finn held the pigeon belly up while Teagan worked. It craned its neck, trying to see what she was doing. She managed to use the tip of the blade to cut the string, then pulled it out of the wound. "Aiden, I need the antibiotic out of Finn's kit."

Aiden dug through the kit, and when he had found it, Teagan smeared some on the bird's leg.

"That's the best I can do. You can let it go."

The pigeon flew up over the rooftop and disappeared.

"Why did the Boy Scouts want you to catch pigeons?" Aiden asked.

"Because they taste like chicken," Finn said. "A little, anyway."

"That's gross," Aiden said.

"Not as gross as starving, boyo. You should wash your hands, Tea." Finn found a piece of soap in his kit and poured water over her hands while she washed them, then washed his own.

"Finn," Aiden said suddenly, "did *anyone* ever beat a goblin?"

"Yes," Finn said. "Fionn Mac Cumhaill beat the son of Fear Doirich himself. I'll tell you about it while we walk."

"Why do we have to keep walking?" Aiden asked. "I'm tired of it."

"The *cat-sídhe* are less likely to find us if we keep moving."

"What's a *cat-sídhe*?" Aiden asked.

Teagan shivered, remembering the laughing cat face.

"Spies," Finn said. "They walk in the sunlight where shadows can't go, and send word back to their masters. Come on, I'll give you a ride, if you're tired. We've a ways to go still."

"Can I still hear the story?"

"You can." Finn squatted down and Teagan lifted Aiden onto his back.

Aiden wrapped his arms around Finn's neck. "Was Fionn the baby from the book Dad read?"

"You remember that?"

"I remember everything," Aiden said. "I just don't like to tell my teachers. How did he beat the bad guys?"

"Fear Doirich had one son, and Mab was his mother." Finn bounced to settle Aiden's weight, then started walking.

"Mab was Maeve's big sister?"

"The very one," Finn said. "Their son's name was Aillen, Aillen the Burner. The Dark Man would send him out to take a tithe of the bravest of the young warriors in Éireann.

"On Samhain's Eve, Aillen would come walking in the night, lulling the warriors to sleep with his music, stealing their minds with his words. When they were senseless, he would gather his tithe—the youngest and fairest, the boldest and bravest—heap them still sleeping into a pile, and then burn them to ash. No warrior was strong enough to stop him, though many tried."

Walking in the night . . . Teagan glanced at the sun. They still had some time before sunset. Before dark, when the shadows came hunting.

"When Fionn Mac Cumhaill had grown to a man, he came to join the warriors of Éireann," Finn continued. "On Samhain's Eve he sat with the tip of his stepmother's magic spear pressed against his own flesh, so that if he nodded off it would pierce him. When Aillen arrived, he found everyone asleep. Everyone but Fionn Mac Cumhaill. You're choking me, boyo."

"Sorry," Aiden said. "I was thinking about goblins."

"When morning came, they found Fionn stretched out on the ground fast asleep, the dead Sídhe prince beside him. Fionn had carried the goblin's curse from before he was born, but now there was war between the Mac Cumhaills and all goblinkind. In every generation since, there is one Mac Cumhaill who is born to fight the goblins."

"And that's you," Aiden said. "*The* Mac Cumhaill."

"A beast of burden, more like," Finn said. "You're choking me again, boyo."

I'M *thirsty*." Aiden slumped dramatically. "But my water's all gone."

"We'll fill all our bottles up," Finn said. "There's a shop a few blocks down that has a water fountain."

Teagan tried not to look as uncomfortable as she felt. The way people looked at her as they passed made her feel that her clothes were wrong, her hair was wrong, her *skin* was wrong. No one was unfriendly. They just stared, as if an alien creature were walking down their street.

An old lady shook her head and said, "What are you children doing here?" Finn smiled and winked at her, and she said, "Well, that's all right, then. Behave yourselves."

"Here it is." Finn stopped outside a corner store with bars on its windows and blinking neon signs advertising several kinds of beer. "I'll fill the bottles and be right back."

"Why can't we go in with you?" Aiden asked.

"Security cameras," Finn said. "The cops are looking for two missing kids and a Traveler. I don't want them seeing our pictures."

Finn went inside the shop with the water bottles.

Three teenagers were walking down the opposite side of the street. They wore their pants halfway down their butts, and the white boxer shorts beneath were dingy and so thin that skin showed through. Teagan leaned against the wall and tried to be invisible. It didn't work. One of them whistled, and they crossed the street.

"Hey, babe."

"Are you gang-bangers?" Aiden asked.

"Listen to the white boy talk! My name's Josiah, and we are friendly gentlemen. I've never seen you around here before. What are you doing in our neighborhood?"

"Walking," Aiden said.

"Like I said, I'm Josiah. This is Rondell, and Manuel." He flashed two gold teeth. "What are your names?"

"We're not supposed to tell anyone," Aiden said.

"Why would that be?" Josiah said. "Are you runaways? You need someplace to stay?"

"Maybe your sister wants to run away with me," Manuel said.

"Not interested," Teagan said.

"Oooo, listen to the bitch," Manuel said, leaning over her.

"That's an inappropriate word to use in the presence of a lady," Aiden said.

"Say what?" Rondell laughed.

"In-appropri-ate." Josiah shoved Rondell. "You heard him." He turned back to Aiden. "Where'd a little boy like you learn a big word like that?"

"My dad's a librarian," Aiden said. "And I'm not a little boy. I'm just small for my age."

"I been to a library once," Rondell said. Manny leaned close enough to Teagan that she could smell his sour breath.

"Are you small for your age, too? Lose the kid and come with me. I'll show you a good time, library girl."

"Get lost," Teagan said.

"They're just teasing," Josiah said. "Don't get unfriendly."

"You boys want something?" Finn had come out of the store. "I might have it for you, if you do."

"Finn," Josiah said. "Haven't seen you for a while."

"Don't want to see you now," Finn said.

"Yeah." Josiah grabbed Rondell's arm. "We're going."

"Why?" Manny asked. "This chica's sweet."

"That's Finn Mac Cumhaill."

Manny took a step back. "We're going."

"Later," Finn said.

"Why were they scared?" Aiden asked.

Finn shrugged. "Josiah's a friend of mine." He handed Aiden and Teagan their water bottles. "We go way back."

Teagan reached for Aiden's hand, but he ignored her and took Finn's instead.

"Could you beat a burner goblin?" Aiden asked.

"No, my man," Finn said softly. "I couldn't, and that's a fact. Fionn had a magic spear, remember? All I've got . . ." He shook his head. "I've got nothing. That's why we need to talk to Mamieo."

"Does Mamieo have magic?" Aiden asked.

"She has smarts," Finn said. "Right now, we need to be walking. We're three miles from our safe house. It'll take us an hour to get there, and the sun will be setting."

"Why can't we hitchhike to Gary?" Teagan asked as they started walking again.

"The goblins know we're traveling. They'll be looking along the roads with their tricks and traps. I wouldn't want to be picked up by one of Kyle's friends. We have to outsmart them long enough to get to Mamieo."

"And she'll know how to find Dad?"

"I hope so," Finn said.

They had walked for just over an hour, past warehouses and industrial complexes, when Finn led them across a weed-choked field and down the bank of a drainage ditch. It was almost sunset, and the air in the ditch was like moist, wet breath.

"Did we just walk through a ghost?" Aiden whispered.

"No ghosts," Teagan assured him. "It's just that cool air sinks, settling in the low spots." She should have borrowed a coat for Aiden when they stopped at Abby's. It was going to be colder than it had been the night before.

They followed the ditch until they reached a culvert that ran under the road. It had an iron grate with a rusted lock on it. Finn twisted the lock sideways and pulled it off.

"It's just for show," he said. "This is a hobo house. I found it when I was a kid." He pulled the grate open and ducked inside, then kicked his way through dried weeds and papers, curled and crisped by being soaked in rainwater, to the other side of the road. He tugged on the opposite grate, making sure it was fixed in place. "We'll be safe here for the night. Looks like we need to do a little house-keeping, though." He started kicking the piles of trash and weeds toward the entrance.

Teagan and Aiden helped out, pushing the debris out through the grate. When they had finished, the floor of the culvert was flat, dusty cement. Chunks had been ripped or hollowed out by floods of the past, leaving the rusty rebar inside exposed.

Thub-dub.

"What was that?" Aiden asked.

Finn pointed up. "A car on the road. You'll get used to it."

"Are the shadows coming here?" Aiden asked.

"The shadows and the likes of Kyle won't know where to find us tonight," Finn said. "The *cat-sídhe* are their spies, but you see those bars?" He pointed to the rebar ribs sticking out of the ancient cement. "Those have plenty of iron in them, and they are in the cement all around us. *Cat-sídhe* are lesser goblins, so they can't pass iron. We'll be safe enough here." He reached up to a shelf near the top of the wall and pulled out an old green ammo box. In it was a flashlight that didn't work when Teagan tried to click it on, a candle, and matches.

"It's closing time at the bagel place," Finn said. "I'll go get us some supper."

"It's almost dark," Teagan protested.

"If things get hairy I'll hole up someplace safe. You just stay here, and I'll show up at first light." He pulled a blanket from the shelf that had held the ammo box and spread it on the cement floor. "I'm not used to having company here, so this will have to do."

"Why do you have to wait until closing time?" Aiden asked.

"They don't throw away the leftover food until they close."

"You could steal food," Aiden said. "Like Aladdin—'Gotta eat to live, gotta steal to eat . . .'"

"Listen, my man," Finn said seriously, "killing, stealing . . . that's what goblins do. I'm not made of the same stuff goblins are. I'd starve before I'd be like them."

"To death?" Aiden asked.

"Yes, I've seen what they did to my family."

"And to Mommy," Aiden said.

"And to your ma. I'd rather eat dung than be like them." He grinned. "But don't worry. We won't be eating dung. Old Raymond puts all the food in a clean plastic bag before he throws it out. Could be he knows people will be looking for it." Finn opened the grate just enough to squeeze out, pushed it shut behind him, then scrambled up the bank.

Teagan folded the blanket in half, and they sat down on it.

"This is a nice house." Aiden yawned. He leaned against Tea, a dead weight. "We're going to have to go back to Mag Mell to find Dad, aren't we?"

"Yes." She put her arm around him.

"I didn't like that place. It didn't sound right."

"What do you mean?" Tea asked.

He shook his head. She could feel him relaxing into sleep, worn out from the fear and exhaustion of the day. She cradled him in her arms, watching the twilight deepen and trying to figure out whether or not she'd done the right thing by coming with Finn. She'd seen the shadows walk out of Mag Mell the night before. *Hunting.* That's what Finn had said.

But maybe he was wrong. Maybe the shadows weren't hunting for them at all, and Aiden would have been fine in his own bed, or at Abby's.

Something moved in the papers and leaves still piled along the far end of the culvert, making small scratchings and rustlings. It sounded like a mouse, or . . . a rat. Her eyes almost missed the movement when it came. A huge brown gutter roach crawled out of the leaves and headed straight for Aiden's pant leg.

Teagan waited until it was close enough, then leaned over and flicked it away with her fingers. The roach bounced against the cement wall, then scuttled away in the opposite direction, its legs moving twice as fast as they had before.

Something larger was moving in the ditch outside. Tea leaned closer to the grate, then jerked back. It was a *cat-sidhe*, like the one she had seen the day Tiny Tiddly died. Only this time it wasn't blurred by tears, and it didn't disappear when she blinked. *Second sight.* Finn had been right. If she'd never seen one before that day at the bus stop, it must have been because there were none around. Not until he came to visit.

This one's hair grew in patches. The bare flesh between the patches was gray-blue and dry. It walked upright, using its almost hairless tail for balance. Its face was flat and its mouth almost human, but the ears, whiskers, and eyes were all cat. It sniffed at the air, then turned toward the grate.

"What are you doing in there?" it asked in a baby-girl voice, and Teagan's scalp crawled. "Oyo!" The roach had made its way through the grate. The *cat-sidhe* pounced, grabbing it with little hands. It stuffed it into its mouth and chewed. Pale white roach guts leaked from its lips. It swallowed, then wiped its chops with the backs of its hands and focused on her once more.

"Ah, ah . . . what's your name?" it said. "Is it . . . Teagan? We want Teagan. We want Aiden."

"What for?"

"Are you Teagan? Ah, ah . . . you smell like Mag Mell. Were you there? Where are you going?"

Teagan didn't answer.

"Put your finger out here," the dead cat coaxed.

"Why?"

"Ah, ah . . . I want to taste it. Just one little lick."

Teagan's hand started to move toward the grate. Her muscles were moving in response to the *cat-sídhe*'s voice. She jerked her hand back. Finn hadn't mentioned this.

"Ah," said the cat. "Ah, ah . . . give me your little brother."

She could feel her arm around Aiden weakening, trying to let him go. "What do you want him for?"

"We want his blood," the cat explained. "His blood and his flesh. We're hungry."

"We?" She pinched her arm hard to wake it up.

"The brethren will be along soon," the cat said. "When there are enough of us, we can open the grate. Give him to me now, and I will only pop his eyes and suck the juice. You can keep the rest of him."

There was a scrambling sound outside, and suddenly Finn appeared. He kicked the goblin, and it sailed like a football down the ditch. He jerked the grate open and dove through, then pulled it closed behind him.

"How long has little ugly been here?" he asked.

"Just a few minutes," Teagan said. "He said they can open the grate if there are enough of them."

"They're liars."

"Could they use a stick?" Aiden whispered.

"I thought you were asleep," Teagan said.

"I could hear it talking." Aiden shivered. "It gave me a nightmare. Could they pull the door open with a stick?"

"I'll fix it so they can't." Finn dug around in his kit and pulled out his duct tape. He ripped off a section and wrapped it around the bars, holding the door shut. "There. Now they can't open it with a stick. And I'll stay right here inside, so you don't have to worry."

Aiden nodded.

"Look what I got." Finn pulled a tub of cream cheese out of his bag and glanced at Teagan. "Strawberry. Girls like strawberry, right?"

"Why did they throw it away?" she asked, taking the tub. It was still sealed.

"Expiration date was two days ago. They can't sell it. But it's still perfectly good." He pulled out a bag of bagels, fished his knife out of his boot, sliced one, and offered it to Teagan.

"Umm," she said. "Have you . . . cleaned that blade since it stuck in the goblin?"

Finn tossed the sliced bagel out through the grate and put the knife away. "We'll just rip and dip, then."

He tore off a piece of another bagel and scooped up a gob of cream cheese with it. "Dig in."

Teagan found Aiden a raisin bagel and showed him how to scoop up some cream cheese.

"Half tonight and half for breakfast," Finn said. "Make it last."

"Ah, ah . . . let us in." The *cat-sídhe* was back, and it had brought a friend.

"You couldn't come in even if we opened the grate," Finn said. "So go on with you." He took the candle from the ammo box, lit it, and set it up on a brick. He leaned close to Teagan's ear when she reached for more cream cheese.

"Did you tell them . . . anything?" he whispered.

"No," Teagan whispered back.

"We can hear you," the second cat said. "We already know everything. We can read your minds."

Finn snorted.

"Have you seen them all of your life?"

"I'll tell you in sunlight," Finn said. "Don't speak my name, or your own either. It's harder to resist them if they use your name."

Teagan nodded. They already knew her name. But they weren't sure, were they?

"Don't talk of where we've been or where we're going," Finn said. "And don't believe anything they say. They can't read minds."

"We'll find out." A third *cat-sídhe* had arrived. It was larger than the other two. Its bare flesh was pink and bloated, as if it had been decaying in the hot sun, and things moved under the taut skin. The cats started humming.

"Do you mind?" Finn said. "You're ruining our meal."

The bloated cat scratched at its hide, opening a wound. It pulled out something that wiggled on the end of its claw—a fat grub. It flicked it toward the bars of the grate. The grub flashed blue like a bug caught in a zapper as it passed through the bars and fell to the ground a burned black noodle.

"Goblin maggots." Finn shook his head. "Just when I think they can't possibly get any more disgusting, they find a way."

More goblins were appearing. They stood as close as they dared to the iron grates on both sides of the culvert, whispering. The candlelight reflected in their eyes, like dancing red embers.

"How many are there?" Tea asked.

"Don't worry about things like that," Finn said.

"The first one's voice . . . made me start to do things I didn't want to do."

"They can do that," Finn said grimly. "Especially if you're alone."

Teagan tried to ignore the *cat-sídhe*'s whispers while she ate. When they'd finished half of the cream cheese, she put the lid back on the tub, and Finn put it into his bag.

The *cat-sídhe* started to yowl.

Aiden put his hands over his ears. "That's not music!" he shouted over the chorus.

Finn studied him for a moment, then ripped a strip of fabric from the ragged tail of his shirt. He tore it into smaller pieces and ran them through the hot wax of the candle, then rolled them into little bullet shapes as they cooled.

"Earplugs," he said. "Here you go, my man." He fitted the earplugs into Aiden's ears. "Can you hear them now?"

"Just a little," Aiden whispered.

"Then you sing to yourself," Finn said loudly. Aiden nodded and started singing. The dead cats hissed and yowled, but Aiden smiled happily.

"I don't hear them when I sing."

"Good." Finn gave him a thumbs-up. He pulled a hoodie out of his bag. "This'll do to bundle the both of you." Teagan put it on and zipped Aiden in with her. It was warm enough to make her sleepy, even with the *cat-sídhe* only a few feet away.

"You're next, then." Finn made another set of earplugs and handed them to Teagan. She put them in her ears, and the yowling and hissing was almost gone. When she put her chin on top of Aiden's head, she was close enough that his song drowned them out completely.

She watched Finn roll his own earplugs, the flame of the candle bending and dancing in the drafts, making crazy shadows on the walls.

Before he put them in, he turned and said something to the cats. They bared their fangs and narrowed their eyes.

Teagan pulled one earplug out.

"What did you say to them?"

"Nothing I'd repeat in front of a lady. What would your da say?"

"You remember that?" Teagan laughed.

"I'm no human recorder, like your brother," Finn said. "But I remember the important things." The candlelight flickered on his face. "There were things I said to you the last time we met that never should have been said. I'm hoping they caused you no grief. I'm a wiser man now."

"Finn . . ." Teagan started, but stopped when the cats leaned closer to the bars.

"*Finn,*" Maggot Cat mimicked.

She'd given them his name.

"Did you say something to her once, Finn? Did you *do* something to her?"

"Do you *want* to do something?" a second cat asked. "Go ahead. Do it, Finn. We won't tell."

"Yessss," the cats hissed. "Do it!"

Finn backed away from her, all the way to the other side of the culvert.

"Good night." He twisted his earplugs in, turned his back to her, and stretched out on the cold cement.

Teagan blew out the candle.

Finn lay very still, but she could feel his presence in the darkness, an electric silhouette more distracting than the voices of the *cat-sídhe*, so bright she was sure there would be fireworks if she moved toward him.

Can I kiss you, girl? The memory was so clear she almost thought Finn had spoken from the darkness where he lay.

"We can make him do things," Maggot Cat said. "You know we can."

"I know you are liars."

"Give us your brother, Teagan," the cat said slyly. "Then you can have Finn. We really, really want Aiden."

Teagan put her earplug back in. Finn seemed sure the cats couldn't find a way into the culvert, but Teagan could see them in the moonlight, scratching as they dug at the dirt banks, trying to find a way past the bars. She pulled both arms inside the hoodie and wrapped them tight around Aiden. She was exhausted, but she couldn't let herself sleep. She wouldn't. Not until Aiden was safe.

TWELVE

FINN rolled over when the first light crept into the culvert. He sat up and pointed at Teagan's ears. Teagan started to reach for her earplugs and realized that both arms were still inside the hoodie. She fumbled, trying to find a sleeve, until Finn reached over and unzipped her cocoon for her. She took her earplugs out, waking Aiden as she moved.

"Good morning." Finn's breath made tiny clouds in the air.

The sun was up, if just barely. The *cat-sídhe* stood guard outside the grate on both sides of the culvert, their unblinking eyes fixed on Teagan.

"It's chilly!" Teagan said.

"It is," Finn agreed. His lips were blue from cold, and his bare arms had a bluish tinge as well.

He smoothed the dust on the cement floor and wrote, *Follow me.*

Teagan nodded, and signed to Aiden. He scowled. Aiden was usually grumpy in the mornings.

"Those ugly cats are still here?" He frowned as he took out his earplugs.

"Ah, ah . . . dibs!" the *cat-sidhe* that had seen them first the night before said. "The little one's mine. I called dibs on him last night."

"I thought they'd be gone in the morning, like the shadows."

"Shadows, shadows!" the cats yowled.

"We called the shadows." Maggot Cat scratched at the wounds on its belly again. "They're coming."

Aiden looked at Finn, but he just shrugged.

"They can't come out in daylight, boyo. The cats are talking trash."

"Highborn Sídhe are coming, too," a second cat said. "More than I can count."

"Would that be two or three of them, then?" Finn asked. The cat hissed. "They won't come around until noon at any rate. I've never known them to be early risers." He rolled up the hoodie and put it in his kit while Teagan folded the blanket and put it back in the hole in the wall. The candle, flashlight, and matches went back into the ammo box, and Finn slid it into its hiding place. He nodded at Teagan and started toward the grate.

"Ah, ah . . ." the *cat-sidhe* said as he came closer. "I'm going to bite you. I want to taste your blood."

Finn pulled his knife from his boot.

"Uh-oh," the *cat-sidhe* said, backing away, but Finn just slit the duct tape holding the door closed, then sheathed the knife.

"Keeee-yill, keeee-yill, keeee-yowll," Maggot Cat started yowling. The others picked up. "Keee-yill, keee-yill, keeee-yoherk." The one nearest the grate doubled over and coughed up a hairball.

"They're really pathetic in the daytime." Teagan moved closer to the grate to study them. "They look like they're diseased. It's not logical that any healthy living thing would look like that."

"It's their lifestyle, no doubt." Finn put the strap of his bag over his shoulder. "Don't feel sorry for goblinkind, Tea, not even the little ones like these. They will do us all the harm they can. Ready, Aiden?" Aiden nodded. Finn swung him up onto his back.

"They can't run fast," he said.

"Ye-hiss we can!" screeched the cats.

Finn shook his head.

"But they keep coming, and they never get tired. Don't listen to them, and don't stop, no matter what."

Teagan nodded, and Finn kicked the grate open. The *cat-sídhe* screamed as they tumbled out of the way. Finn ran right through the middle of them, kicking as he went. Teagan followed him. A small *cat-sídhe*, hardly bigger than a kitten, wrapped itself around her leg the moment she was outside. She kicked, but it dug its claws into her calf through the denim of her jeans and smiled up at her. She couldn't shake it, so she kept running.

"Keeee-yill!" it howled, digging its needle-like claws in deeper.

Finn glanced back once to make sure she was behind him as he scrambled out of the ditch. They ran across the weed field, the *cat-sídhe* pouring out of the ditch after them. The traffic was heavier this morning than it had been the night before. Finn turned and raced along the sidewalk, dodging pedestrians and watching for a break in the cars. People shouted at them as they passed. They made it to the corner just before the light changed.

"Keep going," Finn said. A car honked as they dashed across the street. The driver gunned his engine and plowed into the pack of *cat-sídhe* that tried to cross behind them.

"He can't see them," Finn explained.

The *cat-sídhe* hopped in place, not wanting to risk the tires and bumpers.

Teagan slowed, kicking to try to dislodge the *cat-sídhe* that still clung to her leg. She could feel the claws as it worked its way up the back of her thigh.

"Wait, Finn!" Teagan called. She twisted, trying to grab the creature.

A woman standing at the bus stop with her daughter said, "Are you all right, young lady?"

"No," Teagan said. "Get it off of me, please!"

"Get what off of you?"

"The cat, the cat!" She still couldn't reach it, so she sat down hard on the bus-stop bench, trying to smash it loose.

"What's wrong with that lady?" The little girl pressed up against her mother. "What cat is she talking about?"

"Don't look at her," her mother said.

Teagan bounced up and down until the *cat-sídhe* came loose. She grabbed it before it could sink its claws into her jeans again, and shook it at the woman. "This thing was clawing my butt."

The woman pulled her daughter away.

"Leave us alone," she said. "I . . . I'll call the police."

"Tea!" Finn had come back. He grabbed the *cat-sídhe* from her and flung it across the street. "Stop frightening the citizens. Let's go."

"What was wrong with that woman?" Teagan asked as she ran. "Couldn't she see I needed help?"

"No, she couldn't," Finn said. "She can't see the *cat-sídhe*. You were spinning and shouting at thin air. What was she supposed to think?"

Two sets of railroad tracks cut across the street, making a barrier of iron almost twelve feet wide. As soon as he was over it, Finn stopped running. The *cat-sídhe* had been gaining on them, but now they gathered, yowling and hissing along the tracks. None of them tried to cross.

"That's it, then." Finn let Aiden slide to the ground. "They can't follow us, at least not directly. We'll cut through the railyard, but they'll have to go the long way 'round. It's about thirty miles to Gary, along the tracks. The cats will come after us before we get there, of course, but we'll have a head start. When they catch up we can just walk between the rails."

The *cat-sídhe* had figured it out as well. They raced off down the street, looking for a bridge over the tracks.

"What will we do when a train comes?" Aiden asked.

"We'll figure something out. We're all right for the moment, though. Time for breakfast."

He took the bagels and remaining strawberry cream cheese from his bag, and they ate as they walked.

Turning and spinning and punching at thin air . . . That's what they had said her mom was doing when she'd had her breakdown. But if her mom had seen *cat-sídhe*, why hadn't she said so?

Hallucinations, delusional beliefs. Total break with reality. Maybe she had, and no one had believed her. They'd said she'd been babbling, too. Babbling like she had just before she collapsed?

"Aiden," Teagan said, "do you remember the words Mom said before she fell down?"

"The funny ones?" Aiden asked. "Like '*Tá me tuirseach*'?"

"It's the language of the old country," Finn said. "She said, 'I'm tired.'"

"After that," Aiden went on, "she said, 'Tá áthas fearg, Roisin, tá áthas fearg.'"

"'I'm sorry, Roisin, I'm sorry,'" Finn translated.

"Do you know anyone named Roisin?" Teagan asked. "A Traveler maybe?"

Finn shook his head. "Never heard the name before."

"If the cat-sídhe follow your family, wouldn't Mom have seen them?"

"Mamieo told me Aunt Aileen could never see them, even in the old country. She didn't have the second sight. I didn't know, or I'd never have come. When I had to leave you—" Finn glanced at Teagan and then quickly looked away.

Teagan felt the heat creep through her.

"—I mean, leave your family . . . it was the first time I knew what it really meant to be the Mac Cumhaill."

"What does it mean?" Aiden asked.

"That I can never have anybody of my own." Finn looked straight ahead.

"You mean like a girlfriend?" Aiden asked.

"I do," Finn said.

"You could get a big scary one," Aiden suggested. "Lennie said his dad married his mom because she was scary. Even the Mob was scared of her."

"Aiden!" Teagan said, but Finn was laughing.

"I could. But if she was so terrible the goblins themselves fled at the sight of her, don't you think I'd be afraid, too? How could I kiss the girl?"

"Maybe you wouldn't have to kiss her," Aiden said.

"It's expected, though."

"You could always shut your eyes." Aiden demonstrated, scrunching his face. "That's what I do when I see monsters."

"That might work, then," Finn said, his voice suddenly more serious. "But I'd never ask a girl to walk the roads I walk. The Mac Cumhaill never dies old and gray, my man. Not one ever has. I'll not be leaving broken hearts behind me when I go."

"Like that pretty lady with the purse?" Aiden asked.

"A smile or two never broke a woman's heart, boyo. It just warms their cockles is all. You'll find that most ladies appreciate—"

"There's something I've been wondering about," Teagan interrupted.

"Cockles?" Aiden asked. "Because that's what I'm wondering about."

"Not cockles," Teagan said. "We've got to figure out—"

"But what *are* cockles?"

"Mollusks," Teagan explained. "But in this case, it probably refers to *cochleae cordis*, which is Latin for the ventricles of the heart."

"I never knew that," Finn said. "You must inherit that brain from your da. It's impressive."

Teagan stopped. "Why are we talking about heart ventricles? We need to figure out what's going on. It doesn't add up."

"She didn't like the purse lady," Aiden said in a stage whisper.

"This has nothing to do with the purse lady," Teagan said. "Think about it. Both Aiden and I can see the *cat-sídhe* and the shadow men. I think my mom saw them at least once, no matter what Mamieo says. And Kyle said you could only get into Mag Mell if it 'remembered you,' but Dad walked in Mag Mell, and we did, too. How could Mag Mell remember any of us?"

159

"I've been puzzling over it myself," Finn said. "The only one I know with any answers is Mamieo."

"Why did Mamieo want Mom's ashes?"

"She didn't say why she wanted them. Just to go and fetch them, and fast."

"Here come those cats," Aiden said. The *cat-sidhe* had gone the long way around, but they were running full out along the outside of the railyard to catch up.

"We'll talk about it later, then," Finn said. "When the cats aren't about. Let's go." They walked on the ties between the rails.

"Yee-eww can't lose us," Maggot Cat yowled when it caught up. "We called others."

"I thought you might," Finn said.

More and more cats arrived, on both sides of the tracks.

"Walk right in the middle, Aiden. Don't be afraid. They can't reach us."

"But what if—"

"Shhh," Finn said. "Let's not give them ideas."

They walked single file, Teagan first, Aiden in the middle, and Finn bringing up the rear as the *cat-sidhe* paced them, snarling and cursing, and speaking in a guttural, hissing language of their own.

Aiden started humming to himself. Teagan ignored him and focused on the voices of the *cat-sidhe*. They were saying something important. She walked closer to the rail, trying to make out the words in their yowling.

"Tea!" Finn shouted. "Don't listen to them. They're calling you over where they can touch you. If they do, it gets much harder not to obey them. Goblins steal your will away, or try to. It's worse if you're tired. You didn't sleep much, did you?"

"Um," Teagan said. It was happening again, the same way it had the night before, when the *cat-sídhe* had tried to get her to give them Aiden. Her arms had felt so weak then, but now it was her legs . . .

"Tea!" Finn pushed past Aiden and grabbed her shoulder. "You're drifting. Look, there's a bridge ahead of us." A steel railway bridge arched over the tracks. "Keep your eyes on it. That's where we're going. Can you do it?"

"Yes." Teagan fixed her eyes on the bridge and started walking again, straight down the middle of the tracks.

"Good." Finn dropped back behind Aiden again. "You'll learn to ignore them. It takes practice."

The bridge spanned a small river. Teagan stopped to listen for trains before she started across. The cats yowled, hissed, and spat behind them, but couldn't follow them over the bridge.

"You think we've lost them?" Teagan asked when they reached the other side.

"Nee-oooowww!" Maggot Cat launched himself into the air, dropping and splashing into the river, then flailing wildly to keep his head up, fighting against the current that dragged him downstream. The other cats followed, leaping off of the bank like lemmings, churning through the water.

"It will slow them down a bit," Finn said. "Some of them might drown if we're lucky."

They walked for a half an hour in peace before Teagan heard the yowling start again. The cats were coming. What were the chances they would walk thirty miles without ever having to get off the tracks to let a train pass? And when they did—

She heard a clacking behind them and glanced over her shoulder. A railway maintenance truck was coming down the tracks. It passed the cats without slowing down. Of course, the driver couldn't see the goblins.

"Finn," Teagan said, "we have company."

"Step off and let him pass before the cats get here," Finn said.

They stepped off of the tracks, but the truck didn't pass. It stopped. The driver opened the door. His red-blond hair was pulled back in a ponytail, and pale blue eyes peered out through round glasses.

"What are you kids doing on the tracks?"

"Walking." Finn studied him. "We're in a bit of a hurry."

The cats were running now, covering the distance quickly—too quickly.

"They're coming, Tea!" Aiden grabbed a stick and held it like a bat.

The driver turned and looked back down the tracks. He scratched his head.

"You want a lift?"

"Yeah," Finn said. "Thanks."

"Lose the stick, kid," the driver said. "You guys can ride with me in the cab." Teagan climbed in quickly. Finn lifted Aiden in, and she pulled him onto her lap. Finn took the window seat.

"Name's Raynor," the driver said as Teagan watched the *cat-sídhe* disappear in the rearview mirror. "Raynor Schein."

Aiden squinted at him.

"'Rain or shine'?"

"That's the way it sounds." Raynor nodded. "But not the way it's spelled." He showed Aiden his badge.

Aiden studied the letters, and then the man's face. "I can't read. What did you eat for dinner last night?"

"Me?" Raynor said. "Pizza."

"Did you find it in a Dumpster?"

Teagan pinched him, and he whirled to look at her.

Don't talk about that, she signed. All they needed was for Aiden to tell this guy they'd slept in a ditch and eaten from a Dumpster. He'd have cops waiting for them in Gary.

Why not? Aiden signed.

Teagan tipped her chin down and tried the Look. She'd been practicing for months but it still wasn't as good as her mother's had been.

Aiden glared back at her, but he sat still.

"So, Mr. Schein . . ." Teagan started.

"Raynor." He smiled at her. "I'm not anybody's mister. Just a fellow doing his job."

"What is your job?" Aiden asked. Teagan nodded. That seemed innocuous enough.

"Keeping folks safe. Today I'm making sure the tracks are free of obstacles. Where are you kids going?"

"My grandma's house," Aiden said. Teagan glanced at Finn, but he only shrugged. Aiden grilled Raynor about how the truck ran on the tracks, and whether or not they could outrun a train.

When they arrived at the station in Gary, Raynor said, "You kids have an address for that granny? This is the end of my run. Just let me turn in my keys, and I'll give you a ride."

"That would be great," Finn said. "Thanks."

"You really think it's okay?" Teagan asked Finn as they waited.

"I think so," Aiden said.

"I agree with the boyo. There's something odd about that one, but he's no goblin. And I'm all for getting to Mamieo's faster."

Raynor came bounding back across the railyard.

"Now"—he rubbed his hands together—"you get to meet Brynhild." He led them across the parking lot to an antique truck. It looked like it could star in a car show, bright red and polished until it almost glowed. The slightly flattened top of the headlights and the chrome grille grimace gave it a decidedly determined look.

"She's a 'fifty-seven Chevy," Raynor said. "They just don't make them like this anymore." He wiped a speck of dust from the hood with his shirtsleeve. "Three fifty engine, upsized high-draft four barrel . . . Want a peek under the hood?"

"We're in a bit of a hurry," Teagan said. Raynor looked so disappointed that she added, "Did you restore it yourself?"

"Every inch," Raynor said, pulling the door open. "Finished the upholstery and the paint job this summer." The beige and black interior had a distinctly new-car smell.

"The only thing that's not original is the sound system," Raynor said. "Some things have improved in the last sixty years. Play artist The Doors, Brynhild." "Riders on the Storm" sang through hidden speakers.

"I know that song," Aiden said. "I don't like the part about the killer on the road."

"Neither do I." Raynor laughed. "Morrison was seeing things that nobody else could see, I guess."

"He was?" Aiden looked worried.

Raynor nodded. "That's what the 'killer on the road . . . brain squirming like a toad' bit is about. It happened when he was a little kid, on a road trip across New Mexico with his folks. He saw a family of Indians on the road, dead from a terrible bloody accident. No one else remembered seeing it. Not his mom or dad or sister, and there was no record of the incident with the police."

"Or maybe they gave the bad guy a ride," Aiden said, "and he stuck his hands in their head and made them forget."

"It messed the kid up for life, whatever happened," Raynor said. "The rest of the song is good, though. 'Gotta love your man.'" He winked at Teagan. "Love is what it's all about."

Aiden and Raynor sang along with the sound system, and Finn shouted directions over the choruses.

They pulled into a dilapidated drive-in theater. The screen was sagging and no longer white. Some of the speaker poles were bent, and others broken off. Finn pointed toward the back of the lot.

"There it is," he said. "The Tank."

It was the oldest motor home Teagan had ever seen. The bumper was dented and it seemed to be held on by baling wire. Rust stains flowed from the corners of the barred windows.

"Thanks for the lift." Finn opened his door and slid out.

"Any time," Raynor said as Finn lifted Aiden out.

"Bye, freegan!" Aiden waved as Teagan hopped out and carefully shut Brynhild's polished door.

"Bye, Aiden." Raynor waved back. "It was good seeing you again." The truck pulled away.

"Again?" Teagan said. "You knew him?"

"I was going to tell you," Aiden said. "But you *looked* at me. He was the freegan from the alley."

"Who?" Finn asked.

"The day you got beat up," Aiden said. "He drove up the alley, remember? He's fixed up his truck now."

"But—"

"Finn!"

Teagan turned to find a tiny old woman in the motor home door.

She was wearing bright pink lipstick, and her hair was a perfect puff of white, pulled into a thin bun on top of her head and capped with lace. Her eyes were green glass beads, sharp and young despite her wrinkled face.

"Finn Mac Cumhaill," she said, "what have you done this time?"

"Mamieo"—Finn pulled off his bandanna respectfully—"I've brought Tea and Aiden."

MAMIEO looked Finn over, head to foot. She shook her head. "Which part of 'bring Aileen's mortal remains' did you not understand?"

Finn folded his arms. "The part where they were scattered in the park," he said. "Making them difficult to gather."

The old woman turned to Teagan and Aiden, and her expression softened.

"It's sorry I was to hear about your dear *máthair*." She came down the steps and took Teagan's hand. Up close she was even tinier than Teagan had thought, but her grip was strong. "I loved Aileen like my own child. Though why my grandson is dragging you across the countryside . . . shank's mare, by the look of it, I don't know."

"There's reason, Mamieo," Finn said. "The Highborn Sídhe are walking."

"May the Almighty be with us"—the old woman crossed herself—"and smite dead those who stand against us! Do you know this for certain?"

"One came into the Wylltsons' house," Finn said. "He carried John Wylltson away. We followed him to Mag Mell—"

"You did *what*?" Mamieo pressed her hand to her heart.

"We went to Mag Mell," Aiden said. "But we couldn't find Dad."

Mamieo swayed, and gripped Teagan's shoulder. "I need my nitro." Finn took the old woman's elbow and helped her up the steps.

"Come on, then," he said, and Teagan and Aiden followed them into the motor home. Inside, it looked like an Irish cottage, with lace curtains on the windows and a crisp doily on a small table. There was a bookcase that held every book Aileen Wylltson had ever written, and an ancient Bible under a crucifix on the wall.

Finn helped Mamieo to a seat at the table. She fumbled with a basket of pills, picked up a bottle, and held it at arm's length.

"Lord, would it be too difficult to make my arms longer, or my eyes sharper?"

"You could just wear your reading glasses on a loop about your neck," Finn said, "and let the Almighty worry about more important things."

"More important? Pha." Mamieo snorted.

"Let me help you." Teagan picked out the nitroglycerin bottle and opened it for the old woman.

"Thank you, dearie." Mamieo shook out a pill, put it under her tongue, and leaned back, eyes closed.

"That'll give her heart a jump." Finn sounded a little worried. "She'll be fine in a minute or two."

"And why wouldn't my heart need a jump?" She sat up, green eyes flashing. "Those that go to Mag Mell don't come back again, Finn Mac Cumhaill! And me that frail, that I couldn't come after you if I was needed!"

"Tea, Mamieo?" Finn asked.

"Of course we need tea!"

Finn took the kettle from the stovetop, filled it, and put it on the burner.

"Sit down, Aiden," Mamieo said, "and stop fidgeting."

Teagan lifted Aiden onto the bench seat. He scooted over to make room for her, then fixed his eyes on Mamieo.

"You're really wrinkled," he said.

"And you're a wee green pratie," Mamieo shot back. "Now—tell me everything."

Teagan started with the shadow touching her mother.

"And you saw this shadow, pratie?"

Aiden nodded.

"My poor Aileen," Mamieo said. "After all that time, the damn things came for her."

"There's a *cat-sídhe* out there." Aiden had scooted over to the window. "It's jumping up and down and looking in." A face appeared in the window, disappeared, then appeared again, like a fuzzy bouncing ball with ears.

"Draw the lace and ignore the beastie." Mamieo reached over, pulled the curtain shut, and adjusted the ruffle. "They're always about, keeping an eye on me."

"Why can we see them?" Teagan asked.

"It's the second sight, of course. And doesn't it mean your own *máthair* was of the blood?"

"You mean Traveler blood?"

"Of course I do, dearie." Mamieo looked very pleased about it. "Considering how she was found, it's not too surprising. How much have you told them, Finn?"

"I told them about the Fir Bolg and the coming of the Sídhe to Éireann and Mag Mell." Finn put a bowl of sugar on the table. "And how the Milesians came at last."

"They'll need to know more than that," Mamieo said. "Fetch some biscuits. The pratie looks hungry."

"Yes, Mamieo." Finn pulled a tin of shortbread from the cabinet. Mamieo moved the salt- and peppershakers to the pill basket and pushed it to the back of the table to make room for the tin. Finn sat down beside her.

"In the time before time," Mamieo began, "when the Almighty sang many worlds into being, he laid them side-by-side, all unaware of one another—"

"The multiverse?" Teagan took a shortbread cookie.

"The what?" Mamieo asked.

"The multiverse," Teagan said. "A hypothetical set of all possible universes. It includes everything that physically exists. Space, time, all forms of matter, energy"—they were all looking at her blankly—"parallel worlds, alternate realities?"

Mamieo glanced at Finn.

"You should hear her go on about mollusks," he said. "It's impressive."

Mamieo patted Teagan's hand. "We'll just call it 'creation,' dearie, and get on with the story.

"In the time before time, as I was saying, when all the worlds were new, the Almighty made three peoples more powerful than any others. These three could walk in any world: the Aingeal, first of creation, were messengers and guards; the Highborn, made for leadership and war; and the Fir Bolg, made to mend and tend, and given Mag Mell as their own."

The kettle started whistling, and Finn got up to make the tea.

"Then the Sídhe took Mag Mell away," Aiden said.

Mamieo snorted. "They call themselves the Sídhe, as if they were one people and one flesh, but they are not. They are a chimera of peoples, cobbled together by the Dark Man's will.

"The Highborn—those that served the Almighty but do so no longer—are unearthly beautiful but wicked to their very core. They've lowborn cousins that creep and crawl, afraid of the light because they are too hideous to look at, but they're closely related to the Highborn just the same. Then there are Fear's own servants, the shadows, and many lesser creatures such as the *cat-sídhe*. All of them gathered from worlds here and there, and brought to Éireann long ago."

"Why Ireland?"

"To kill the Irish, I expect, before they could save this world."

Finn set the teapot, cups, and a small pitcher of milk on the table, and settled in again.

"The Irish saved the world?" Teagan asked as Mamieo poured the tea.

"It was the Milesian blood in their veins that did it," Mamieo explained.

Aiden reached for the sugar cubes, but Teagan caught his hand. "Just one," she said, scooping it up with a spoon and dropping it in his cup. "Finn said the Milesians were 'sons of men.' They were just humans, right?"

"Weren't they some of the Almighty's favorites, though? He made them lovers of knowledge, monks and scribes, minstrels and mages. As time passed, they mixed with all the peoples of the isles, and the Fir Bolg as well. By the time history began, they had become the Irish."

171

"But *how* did they save the world?" Aiden asked as Teagan poured milk in his tea.

"When the world fell into the Dark Ages, who was it that hid the books and kept the learning alive? Who kept the old stories and songs?" Mamieo slapped her hand down on the table. "It was the Irish, and weren't they called to the task by the Almighty himself?"

Teagan took another cookie. Multiverses and magical people were hard to believe. It would have been a lot harder, though, before she saw the shadows and *cat-sídhe*. But even if she accepted it all as true, it felt like pieces of the puzzle were missing.

"Why did the goblins come for my mom?" Teagan asked. "Even if she was part Fir Bolg, why her, and not another Traveler?"

"If I knew that," Mamieo said sadly, "I might have been able to help the girl more. She didn't know herself. I'll tell you what I can. Isn't that night burned into my mind?

"The Travelers had gathered at Selsey, near Chichester and Bosham, on Samhain's Eve. It was the year after my own dear man had passed, and didn't I have trouble sleeping on such a stormy night, with lightning tearing the clouds and punishing the marsh?" She shook her head. "I was just thanking the good Lord that all of mine were safe at home when I heard it—the howling of terrible hounds. It was the Hunt, as sure as there's mold on Pádraig's bones. The sound of it can send grown men cowering under their beds. And those who know—" She shook her head and pressed her lips together.

"Know what?" Aiden asked.

"That evil is hunting some poor child through the night, a girl child stolen from her home with no one to help her, no place to run—the very thought can drive men mad."

Teagan shivered, remembering the blood stained muzzles.

"What did you do?" Aiden asked.

"I'm a *máthair*, aren't I?" Mamieo drew herself up. "I made sure my own were tucked safe in bed, put on my shawl, and went to see what could be done. And by the end of the road, in front of St. Wilfred's chapel, I met the Green Man."

"Weren't you afraid?" Aiden asked.

"Not of himself," Mamieo said. "He's true enough. 'Let me through,' I told him. 'Let me into Mag Mell.'

"'What would you do there, Ida?' he asked.

"'I'm a Christian woman,' I says. 'I'll do what I can. You should be doing something yourself, you leafy ox of a man. Can't you hear the baying?'

"'I'm not strong enough to stop them,' he says, 'but I can do this.' He grabbed the corner of the night and ripped a hole into Mag Mell.

"'I'll leave a light on for you,' he says as I step through. 'You'll never be coming home without it.'

"The storm was worse in Mag Mell, black as Hell itself, and laced up with lightings. I ran towards the sound of the *sídhe* hounds and the *bean-sídhes* . . ."

Teagan glanced at Finn. She couldn't imagine anyone running *toward* that pack, but he was nodding as if he believed every word.

". . . and I saw her—a girl stumbling through the woods in a thin dress and bare feet. She was all of twelve, and small for her age. She was terrified out of her wits, and tried to get away from me at first, thinking I was one of those that hunted her, but I'd had plenty of practice herding children. I gathered her up and held on until she stopped fighting and sobbed in my arms. Didn't the Almighty give me the strength to run then? With her in my arms and their hot breath behind us! I ran for the light the Green Man was holding.

"He laid his hand on the child's head and blessed her when we went out, and she stopped shaking. 'Take the child west if you want to keep her,' he says. 'Tomorrow will be soon enough.'

"I took her into St. Wilfred's first. We crawled under the altar, and I prayed for them all—my own babies at home and the one shivering beside me. The *bean-sidhes* and the hounds screamed and howled around the eaves of that church, but they couldn't come onto sacred ground, could they? And with the dawn they were gone.

"We started working our way west towards America the very next day, and when we boarded the ship we left the goblins behind us for a time. Aileen never spoke a word—not one word but her name for a whole year. When she did speak, she didn't say a word about that place. She could remember none of it. She had no second sight, but there was *draíocht* about her, that's certain. Her mind was easier in the West.

"It took the cats some time to find us in the New World. Your mother was happily married by then, with babes of her own."

"*Draíocht?*" Teagan asked.

"Magic," Finn said.

"Did you know all this?" Teagan asked Finn.

"Of course he didn't," Mamieo said. "The goblins watch and listen, don't they? We keep things quiet. When the cats caught up with us at last, I told the family to stay away from Aileen, alone like she was. The goblins had come with a vengeance, they had. I lost my son and his wife to them. Lost track of my grandson as well for a few years, because he didn't have the sense to come and find me. Not until after . . ."

Finn was studying his hands. Mamieo sniffed.

"Been on the road some days have you, Finn?"

"A few," Finn said.

"I can tell it." She pointed toward the back of the motor home. "You could use a shower, boy."

Finn turned pink, but he looked from Teagan to Aiden.

"You got them here," Mamieo said. "I can keep them safe while you clean up. There's enough water if you're careful."

Finn nodded. He took his bag and went back to the bathroom.

"It's not much of a shower," Mamieo said as the water started, "but it will do. Why don't you go look at your *máthair*'s books, pratie? They're on the shelf there."

Aiden wiggled under the table, crawled out, and went to the bookshelf. Mamieo leaned close to Teagan.

"I don't know how much time we have." Mamieo nodded toward the shower door and lowered her voice. "The boyo can't hear a thing, not with the water running. He'll not tell you, not after what happened to your *máthair*."

"Tell me what?" Teagan said.

Mamieo poured herself a little more tea, took a sip, and dabbed at her bright pink lipstick with a napkin.

"Forty-five years ago," she said, "I walked into a room and there stood Rory Mac Cumhaill, big as life. Took one look at him, I did, and my heart stopped beating."

"You've had heart trouble that long?"

"Heart trouble!" Mamieo laughed, and her eyes almost disappeared into her wrinkles. "Heart trouble it was, girl, but not the kind you're imagining. It wasn't something those wee explosives could ease. When my heart started pumping again, it had changed forever." She sighed. "And his had too, of course. That's the way of it. Ah, Rory. A *ghrá mo chroí*, love of my heart. You were a deadly fine man." She sighed, then leaned forward and took Teagan's hands. "My lover's been gone these twenty-nine years, but there never was another for me. That's the way the Almighty made us. The way he made the Fir Bolg."

"I'm . . . sorry for your loss." Teagan was not quite sure what else to say.

"I'm not done with my tale yet, am I? I was just trying to give you some understanding. After he had been at your house, Finn came to see me. He was that troubled." Mamieo studied Teagan's face intently. "You understand what I'm saying?"

"Not . . . really," Teagan admitted.

"Good Lord, girl, do I have to spell it out for you? There's been just one name pounding in that boy's heart ever since he first saw you, hasn't there? Your name, Teagan Wylltson. I'm thinking his name is in your heart, too, girl."

Teagan blinked.

"Finn's the last of Fionn's line. He'd go to Hell for you. He went into Mag Mell, didn't he? So—so don't you go getting my boy killed. I'm depending on you to keep him safe."

"Me? Keep *Finn* safe?"

Mamieo nodded seriously. "That's what I'm asking. You are your *máthair's* daughter, and Aileen could always . . ." Mamieo tipped her head. "Will you look at that, now?"

Teagan turned. Aiden was sitting cross-legged on the floor in the middle of a sunbeam, singing "Down on the Corner" softly as he looked at his mother's book.

"People come from miles around to watch the magic boy . . ."

His hair shone like a golden halo. Even the dust motes around him were glowing.

"Don't let his looks fool you," Teagan said. "He's no angel."

"Of course he's not an *aingeal*!" Mamieo said. "But did you see—"

Something heavy landed on the roof, and Aiden looked up. Footsteps walked the length of the motor home and stopped above the driver's seat.

The roof squeaked as weight shifted, and Kyle's face appeared upside down outside the windshield. He grinned and disappeared.

"Aiden, come here," Teagan said, but before he could move, Kyle flipped into the motor home. The windshield rippled as if it were water as he passed through it, rearranging itself as he landed graceful as a gymnast. Teagan grabbed Aiden and pulled him back against her.

"Get out, goblin." Mamieo was standing up, her fists clenched.

"Not that again. Why do you Travelers insist on using such foul language? I am *Highborn Sídhe*. Sit down, old woman, and I might let you live."

Mamieo turned around and sank back into her seat, groping for her pills at the back of the table.

Kyle laughed and looked at Teagan.

"What did you tell Abby, Tea? She doesn't want to see me anymore. She wouldn't give me her address."

"We won't tell you what it is, either, bad guy," Aiden said.

Teagan glanced at the shower. The water was still on. Finn couldn't know the *sidhe* was here.

"You won't tell me?" Kyle said. "Oh, well. I'll have to use the Internet, then. I have her phone number. Reverse lookup is easy, isn't it?" He sighed. "Too bad you can't use technology to find your dad. He needs you so badly."

Mamieo had missed her nitro bottle and picked up the pepper-shaker. She peered at it, holding it at arm's length, then put it back. Teagan didn't dare offer to help her. If Kyle knew she had a bad heart . . .

"Where is my dad?" Teagan said when Kyle started to turn toward the old woman.

"With Fear Doirich, of course." Kyle turned back to her. "Fear isn't treating him well, I can tell you that. He's stealing the poor man's mind bit . . . by . . . bit. I don't know how much is left. But I do know that Fear's curious about you two. Very curious. He's set everyone to looking for you." He took a step closer. "Come with me." Kyle offered his hand. "I'll take you right to your father."

The urge to reach out and touch him was so strong Teagan had to grip Aiden's shoulders hard.

"Or not." Kyle smiled again. "How about you, Aiden? You want to come with me, don't you?"

Mamieo stood up again and turned to face Kyle. "I said, 'Get out, goblin.' I don't like repeating myself."

Kyle bared his teeth. "Who do you think you are, hag?"

"Your worst nightmare, boyo," Mamieo said, and tossed a handful of white crystals into his eyes.

Kyle screamed. His eyes bubbled and melted like slugs. As Teagan pulled Aiden away, she caught just a glimpse of Finn coming out of the shower, naked and dripping wet, with his knife in his hand.

"Mamieo, get back!" Finn shouted. "Let me have him!"

Mamieo wasn't listening.

"Help me, girl!" the old lady barked, and then she was after Kyle like a fox after a mouse, pushing him backwards as he howled.

Teagan shoved Aiden aside and jumped to help Mamieo.

"His legs, his legs!" Mamieo shouted when they had him against the dashboard.

Teagan grabbed them and lifted as Mamieo pushed, tipping Kyle backwards. The glass rippled again as he went out, and sealed behind him. He landed on the gravel of the drive, still screaming and clawing at his melted eyes.

"*Go n-ithe an cats thú is go n-ithe an diabhal an cats!*" Mamieo shouted after him, shaking her fist. Whatever it meant, Teagan hoped it was just as nasty as it sounded.

Teagan turned around to check on Aiden and realized Finn was still standing naked in the middle of the motor home, knife in hand. She put her hands over her eyes and turned back quickly.

"Are you all right, Aiden?" she called.

"Yes," Aiden said.

"Find a seat." Mamieo slid behind the wheel. "We're moving." She glanced in the rearview mirror. "Put the knife away and find your pants, Finn. He's not coming back in, and you're embarrassing us all."

Teagan waited until she heard the bathroom door close before she grabbed Aiden, shoved him onto the bench seat by the table, and sat down beside him. Mamieo's empty saltshaker was rolling across the tabletop. Teagan grabbed it and put it back in the pill basket.

Finn came out of the bathroom again, clothes on this time. He looked straight ahead as he stalked past the table and sat down in the passenger's seat beside Mamieo.

"I told you I'd take care of things, boyo," Mamieo said. "There was no need to make a spectacle of yourself."

"You turned red all over, Finn," Aiden said helpfully. "So did Teagan. As red as Kool-Aid."

The back of Finn's neck went from pink lemonade to Blastin' Berry Cherry.

"Yeah," Aiden said. "Like that."

"I don't want to talk about it," Finn said.

FOURTEEN

"WHERE are we off to, Mamieo?" Finn asked.

"It's a goose chase," Mamieo said. "With us being the goose. When the goblins go a-hunting, they expect you to run. I want that spying *cat-sídhe* to see that we're going south before I turn the Tank around. I can shake the cats for a night, until we've figured out what's to be done."

"I know what's to be done," Finn said. "I'm going back to Mag Mell to bring Mr. Wylltson out, and you are keeping Tea and Aiden safe."

"All by yourself, is it?" Mamieo snorted. "Those taken by Fear Doirich don't come out."

"What about Aunt Aileen? You brought her out, didn't you?"

The Tank swayed and leaned as they curled around the ramp onto the freeway. Teagan grabbed Aiden as he slid across the bench seat, and Finn gripped the armrest.

"We don't know that the Dark Man took her," Mamieo said when they were on the freeway.

"But we know she came out," Finn said. "And Saint Pádraig, too. What about him?"

"Saint Patrick went to Mag Mell?" Teagan asked.

Mamieo glanced at her in the rearview mirror. "He made it out by the skin of his teeth, and him with two holy *aingeals* walking by his side. How did you find your way out? You had no Green Man holding a light for you, nor *aingeals* holding your hands."

"I knew the way," Aiden said.

"Did you, now?" Mamieo glanced in the mirror again.

"Kyle goes in and out, too," Aiden said.

"Kyle?"

"The goblin that came in the windshield," Teagan said. "He said his name was Kyle."

"You should have run over him," Finn said.

"And send him straight back to Mag Mell, full of news? He'll find his way back eventually, but it will take him some time without his eyes. Let him stumble about a bit while we figure out what to do."

"Oh, my god." Teagan pulled out her cell phone and pressed a number on speed dial. "I've got to talk to Abby before he finds her."

"It's about time," Abby said when she finally picked up. "Where are you?"

"I'm with my grandma. Listen, Abby, you need to get out of your apartment. Kyle followed us, and . . . he's looking for you. He said he was going to use the Internet to find you."

"Let him look. I'll deal with him."

"No, Abby, he's got some . . . really bad friends."

"Goblins?" Abby asked.

"Yes," Teagan said. "They are going to hurt you to get to me."

There was a long silence. "Tea . . . Finn doesn't have you dealing drugs or something, does he?"

"No. You need to find someplace to stay—someplace other than your apartment."

"I love my apartment. I'm not leaving it because of some boogeymen."

"This is life and death, Abby, I swear."

"How long?" Abby asked, and Teagan almost wept with relief.

"A couple of days," Teagan guessed. "Until I call you, okay?"

"Okay, I'll find a place. But just for a couple of days. I've got a life, you know."

"Good," Teagan said. "I'll call you, I promise." She hung up and turned back to Mamieo. "Why is it that goblins can kill us, but all we can do is send them back to Mag Mell?"

"They can't kill your immortal spirit," Mamieo said. "It takes more than a goblin to do that. You can't kill theirs, either. And isn't it the spirit of that foul thing that we see walking here wrapped in skin and bones of his own making? You can send *that* flesh back to its maker."

"Where are his real skin and bones?" Aiden asked.

"His mortal bits are sleeping in Mag Mell." This time she turned half around, not bothering with the mirror. "Speaking of sleep, you look done in, girl."

"She hasn't slept for two nights," Finn said. "Not used to the life."

"I thought as much." Mamieo nodded. "You and the wee pratie lie down on the bed back there and shut your eyes. There's nothing but driving going on. No excitement, and you're as safe as we can make you."

Tea looked back at the bed. If she didn't get some sleep soon, she was going to fall over.

"Promise you won't leave without me, Finn."

"He'll not leave you behind," Mamieo said. "I'll see to it."

Finn glared at the old woman. "Mamieo!"

"What?" Mamieo glared back.

"I brought them to you so you could keep them safe until I get things straightened out. It's my fault, isn't it? And my responsibility to set things right."

"Teagan," Mamieo said, "take your brother back to the bed and get some rest."

"I'm not sleepy," Aiden began. "I want to hear what you're saying, and . . ." He met Mamieo's eyes in the mirror.

"Get in that bed and go to sleep."

"Yes, ma'am." He grabbed Teagan's hand and pulled her to the back of the motor home. Mom had clearly learned the Look from Mamieo.

Teagan boosted Aiden up on the bed, then crawled in after him.

Mamieo and Finn were arguing, their voices too low against the rumble of the Tank for her to make out the words, but not low enough to conceal the tension.

It's my fault, isn't it? That's what Finn had said, and he was right. *If he had never come to the Wylltsons', house* . . .

Teagan closed her eyes, but she couldn't stop the tears. She was glad when Aiden started snoring and the voices were completely drowned out. She was stinky and dirty and more tired than she had ever been in her life, and she didn't know what to do next.

Teagan woke once to find that Finn was sleeping on the floor, his arm over his eyes, and Mamieo was still driving. When she woke again, the Tank was standing still, and it smelled like . . . Chinese food. The light was fading outside.

Teagan eased away from Aiden and stepped carefully over Finn on her way to the front. It took her mind a moment to register what she was looking at through the windshield: tall piles of sand, and past them wild, white-capped water. There was a wooden sign announcing that they were at Warren Dunes State Park. She'd come here with her parents once. They'd slid down the sand mountains on cardboard, and picked Michigan blueberries the next day. Aiden had eaten so many that he'd had a stomachache on the way home.

The park was autumn empty. All the summer vacationers had gone home, and even the day visitors had left for the evening. Mamieo stood on the wet sand, staring out at the wild lake with a blanket wrapped around her. Her white hair had come out of its bun and was dancing around her in the wind.

Teagan eased the door open, slipped out, closing it quietly behind her, and immediately wished she had a coat, or at least Finn's hoodie. She could feel winter behind the north wind.

"Awake, are you?" Mamieo asked when Teagan walked up. "I was hoping to speak to you alone again, girl." The old woman took the blanket from her own shoulders and wrapped it around Teagan.

"Don't you need it?" Teagan asked.

"I like the bite in the wind," Mamieo said. "It reminds me that I'm alive. Walk with me." They started down the sand, keeping just out of reach of lapping waves. "I want you to know I consider you and Aiden my own grandchildren, just as much as that knuckle-headed Finn. I'll do everything I can to help you, but I'm afraid it won't be much. I'd never have gotten into Mag Mell myself if the Green Man hadn't torn a hole for me."

"There was no Green Man when we went in," Teagan said. "Kyle said that you could only walk in Mag Mell if it 'remembered' you."

Mamieo nodded. "Even goblins speak the truth upon occasion. I've been discussing the situation with the Almighty. Trying to get my mind around the meaning of it."

"Did the Almighty say anything?" Teagan asked.

"Isn't the Almighty always saying something, girl? Speaking through everything created, whispering in your hopes and dreams. Urging you to get on with business?"

Teagan glanced at the wrinkled face in surprise, and Mamieo laughed.

"You thought listening to dreams was only for the young? I hear that voice more clearly now than ever before. 'There's still work to be done, Ida,' the Almighty was just saying. 'Be about your tending and mending. Creation needs to be put to rights.' That's the business I will be about until I lay these old bones down. Finn tells me you are a mender as well. Taking care of creatures great and small."

"I'm trying."

"It'll come clearer as you go, and take some unexpected turns, no doubt. It always does. Finn said Aileen's ashes were scattered in the park. Why was that?"

"Mom loved the park. She loved the trees."

"It is the trees, then." Mamieo nodded. "I thought it might be. Aileen's ashes woke them, and they've been talking about you amongst themselves."

Teagan considered this, and decided that talking trees were not any stranger than being chased by goblins.

"What does that have to do with Mag Mell?"

"'Tis Yggdrasil," Mamieo said, "the first tree, of course. Don't his roots bind all the trees of all the worlds of creation? When the trees spoke of your *máthair*, Mag Mell heard through Yggdrasil. She heard of you from the trees your *máthair* loved."

"She?" Teagan said. "Mag Mell is a she?"

"She's not like this world. You'll see when you go back."

"I'm afraid." Teagan was shivering. "It was like a nightmare. But my dad's trapped in that nightmare. I won't leave him there. Mamieo . . . will you watch over Aiden for me? I don't want to take him back into that place."

"Wasn't that the very thing that Finn was asking?" Mamieo said. "Only he wanted to leave the both of you. But I couldn't give him my answer until I had time to walk and listen."

"And?"

"You got into Mag Mell through the memories of the trees," Mamieo said. "How did you get out again?"

"Aiden knew the way." Teagan's heart sank. How could they get out without him?

"There's something else," Mamieo said. "If what I suspect is true . . ."

"What?"

"We'll see after supper. I'm not sure of it myself yet. But for now there are some things you'll need to know. There are stories of those who walked in Mag Mell and never came back normal. If you hadn't had the ancient blood in your veins, it would have driven you mad."

"What about Dad?"

Mamieo walked silently for a few steps.

"There's nothing broken that can't be mended," she said at last. "If the man is broken when you find him, remember that."

"Why do things like Kyle even exist?" Teagan asked. "Did God create them evil?"

"Of course not." Mamieo stopped to pick up a piece of blue beach glass. "Why would the Almighty do such a wicked thing? All creatures," she said when they walked on, "from the moment they exist, set about *becoming* through their own free will. Some are becoming more of what they were meant to be, and some becoming less. The Dark Man . . . he's had half of eternity to become less than he was meant to be."

"Devolution," Teagan said. "Like George MacDonald wrote about in his fairy tales. Mom read them to us."

"A MacDonald, was he?" Mamieo sniffed. "Scottish, then. I've known some of the Glen Coe clan, and they were never better than they had to be."

"I've heard the same about Irish Travelers," Teagan said.

Mamieo laughed. "And truer words were never spoken. The Fir Bolg have the charm on them for certain. Sure and it makes them political heroes and great leaders of men!"

It *makes flustered women give them five bucks just for a smile; that's what it does,* Teagan thought.

"The charm doesn't leave the Fir Bolg," Mamieo said. "Even them that abuse it. They speak lies, and people believe them. People want to believe them." She glanced sideways at Teagan. "Finn's not like that. He's listened to the wee voice every day of his life. He 'feels the Almighty close by his side.'"

"Like in my mother's prayer."

Mamieo nodded. "It's made a gentleman of him."

"I thought he acted that way because he was *the Mac Cumhaill*," Teagan said.

Mamieo sighed. "And wouldn't he be happier if he wasn't? He's asked too many questions about me and my Rory. About how I've lived alone all these years."

A light was on in the motor home when they turned around, and Teagan realized how dark it had become.

"Someone's awake," Mamieo said. "You like Chinese food, girl?"

"No," Teagan said honestly. "But I'm hungry enough to be glad to have it today."

The old woman laughed. "You're an honest one, at least. It's the fortune cookies I like."

"Mamieo," Teagan said as they walked back along the shore, "what was it you said to Kyle after we tipped him out the window? Was it in Irish?"

"Good Irish Gaelic, but not good Christian words, I'm afraid. 'May the cat eat you, and may the cat be eaten by the devil.' It's a curse, and I shouldn't be using it. You don't have any of the blessed language, of course. Your dear *máthair* could never learn it."

Both Finn and Aiden were sitting at the table when Teagan came through the door. They'd gotten out the plates and silverware for supper, and there was a small pile of fortune cookies between them.

"I'm being held prisoner," Aiden said. "Finn wouldn't let me go out, even though I could *see* Teagan!"

"Well, let's have some prison food, then, pratie," Mamieo said. "Since we're all in the lockup together now. I've just one thing to do before we eat. Where's your phone, girl?"

Teagan pulled it out of her pocket and turned it on. Surprisingly, she had three bars of service. She handed Mamieo the phone. The old woman held it at arm's length and squinted.

"Why do they make the numbers so small? Here." She handed it back. "You dial." Teagan punched in the numbers as Mamieo recited them, then gave the phone back to her.

"Jackie?" Mamieo said. "This is Ida. I need you to pick up three packages at the Dunes Park tomorrow morning. Yes, in Michigan." She listened for a moment. "Of course I know you're in Chicago. Where else would you be, man? I'll need you here by six a.m. You'll want to travel in sunlight on the way back to town, just to be safe."

She handed the phone back to Teagan. Someone was swearing loudly into the receiver on the other end.

"Just hang it up." Mamieo waved her hand. "He'll be here."

Teagan hung it up and took Aiden to the sink. She scrubbed his hands and then her own, promising herself she would ask about a shower as soon as they had eaten.

When they were all seated at the table, Mamieo bowed her head over the noodles. "Go *dtaga do ríocht*," she said. "'May Thy kingdom come,' for those of you without the gift of tongues."

Mamieo did most of the talking during supper, covering many of the same things she'd told Teagan as they walked, about Mag Mell, Yggdrasil, and the memories of trees. Now and then Finn would ask a question, but Aiden was still playing at being a prisoner, so he ate slumped over his plate.

"Now for the most important part," Mamieo said after Teagan had cleared away the plates. She reached for a fortune cookie, hesitated, then took another instead.

"Go on, choose one, pratie," she said. "People can have a little fun, even in prison."

Aiden took a cookie, then Finn. Teagan picked up the last one.

Mamieo broke hers open and pulled the small paper out. "'Your rare talents will bring successes.' Well, that's good to know, isn't it? What does yours say, Finn?"

"'Your life is a daring and bold adventure,'" Finn read.

Mamieo clapped.

"Aiden?"

He handed his fortune to Teagan. "'You will make a new friend,'" she read.

She cracked her own cookie open and pulled out the ribbon of paper.

"'You love Chinese food.'"

Mamieo laughed. "Three out of four isn't bad. I'll need my makeup kit." She pushed herself to her feet, went to the bathroom, and came back with a little purple bag.

"This is the part I don't want any spying *cat-sídhe* to see." She emptied it onto the table, then sorted through old lipstick tubes—all of which seemed to be the same shade of pink—and almost-empty pill bottles.

"I wouldn't want them to see that, either," Aiden said. "Finn's purse has lots better stuff in it."

"Ha!" Mamieo held up an old-fashioned face powder compact. "Here it is." She popped it open, and goose bumps rose on Teagan's arms.

"It smells like . . . Mag Mell," Teagan said.

"Mag Mell and dirty feet. I was a poorer woman when I fetched

Aileen out of the place. The boots I wore had holes in them. When I took them off, I found that I'd brought a bit of Mag Mell with me. A bit of *draíocht*. This world is made of stardust and gases, you see, but Mag Mell . . . she's made of glamour."

Mamieo powdered up the small puff and dabbed it on her face and nose. Teagan knew her mouth was hanging open, but she couldn't help it. Mamieo was . . . beautiful. It wasn't that her wrinkles had disappeared. It was just that they didn't matter anymore.

The old woman laughed at the looks on their faces.

"I use it now and then, when I need to make a good impression, or negotiate a deal. So a bit of it floats around the place." She scooped up a tiny pinch of the dust. "Now, if I saw what I think I saw in the sunbeam this morning . . . Come here, pratie."

"You're not putting makeup on me." Aiden backed away. "I don't want to be pretty."

"Of course you don't," Mamieo said. "And I'd do no such thing. I'm going to dribble a bit of it over your head while you sing. Come over here beneath my lamp."

Teagan nodded, and Aiden moved over under the light.

"Now, sing the song you sang when you read your *máthair*'s book. No—don't look up. Just sing."

Aiden frowned, but he started singing "Down on the Corner."

Mamieo rolled the dust between her fingers, and a fine line of it fell into Aiden's hair.

"Sing it like you mean it," Mamieo said. "Like you did this morning."

"I *felt* like it this morning." Aiden folded his arms. "But I don't feel like it now."

Mamieo's eyebrows went up. "What do you feel like, then, pratie?"

"'Jailhouse Rock,'" Aiden said.

"Sing that, then, if you must!"

Aiden started rocking like Elvis, pelvis wiggle and all. Mamieo trickled another pinch of dust over his head. It fell from her fingers, then slowed, spinning in the air and gathering light until it shone like gold.

He started the second verse and the dust spun harder, forming a tiny spiral galaxy that hovered above him like a crown. When he finished the song, the golden dust rained down around him like tiny falling stars.

"That's it," Mamieo breathed. "That's what I saw when he was reading his mother's books."

"But . . . how can he do such a thing?" Finn asked. "I've never heard of such a gift amongst the Travelers. Is it from Aunt Aileen?"

"It must be," Mamieo said. "And if it does this to glamour dust, what will it do to Mag Mell herself?"

"Would Teagan have the gift, too, then?" Finn asked.

"Tea can't sing," Aiden said. "She'll hurt your ears."

"Try it," Finn insisted.

Teagan sang while Mamieo trickled dust over her head. She could tell by the hands over Aiden's ears that the singing wasn't any good, and by the look on Finn's face that the dust wasn't spinning.

She sneezed. "It wasn't shining, was it?"

Finn grimaced. "Maybe it's the wrong song."

"Nope," Aiden said. "It's just bad singing. And it didn't make you any prettier, either."

Mamieo snapped her compact shut and stood up. "You two be deciding what you need to take with you. I'm going to teach the pratie a song."

"Socks," Finn said. "We'll need socks."

"Take them out of my drawer, then." Mamieo dragged Aiden toward the front of the motor home.

"Socks?"

"Never travel without clean socks," Finn said. "Your feet are that important."

"We need to fill the water bottles, too." Teagan took them to the sink.

Mamieo was singing to Aiden in the cab of the motor home. Her thin voice quavered, but Aiden wasn't shouting the way he did when Teagan sang.

"What is she teaching him?" Teagan asked when she took the water bottles back to Finn. He tipped his head and listened.

> "Atomriug indiu
> niurt tríun
> togairm Tríndóite
> cretim treodatad
> foísitin oendatad
> i nDúilemon Dáil . . ."

"It's 'Pádraig's Shield,'" Finn said. "It goes something like this:

> 'I arise today
> with a mighty strength,

invoking the Trinity,
believing in the threeness,
confessing the oneness
of the Creator of Creation . . .'"

Teagan leaned closer to hear his words. Electric arcs jumped between them, and her stomach went tight. Finn swallowed hard and backed away from her.

"Why don't you check Mamieo's medicine cabinet for anything that might be useful while I find the socks?" he said. "She won't mind."

"Salt," Teagan suggested, pretending she hadn't noticed that he was trying to get away. "Can we take salt?"

"It's only useful when they've left their true body behind." He was avoiding looking at her. "If we meet Kyle in Mag Mell, his body will be like ours."

"Got it." Teagan had to edge past him to get to the bathroom door. She slipped inside and shut it behind her.

There's been just one name pounding in that boy's heart ever since he first saw you, hasn't there? Your name, Teagan Wylltson. If Mamieo was right, Finn loved her. Which was ridiculous. Attraction can happen at first sight, sure. Electricity. But not love.

Unless you were a Traveler like the Mac Cumhaill. *He's asked too many questions about me and my Rory. About how I've lived alone all these years.* That's why Finn was avoiding her. He'd tried to explain it to her in the railyards.

I'd never ask a girl to walk the roads I walk. The Mac Cumhaill never dies old and gray. . . . Not one ever has. I'll not be leaving broken hearts behind me when I go.

But it was supposed to happen to you both at the same time, like it had to Ida and Rory. *What had happened when she first met Finn?* She wasn't sure throwing up was a sign of love. *Was his name in her heart?* Teagan frowned. She'd wondered about him while he was gone, sure. But he hadn't been constantly on her mind or anything. *Does he think I'm in love with him?*

"It will take more than a few sparks and a stomachache, buster," Teagan said to herself as she jerked open the medicine cabinet. "This is about finding Dad."

She chose some sterile gauze, a plastic box of Band-Aids, and one Ace bandage. She couldn't decide what else might be useful. What do you pack when you're planning a rescue mission to hell?

PART III: MAG MELL

FIFTEEN

JACKIE turned out to be a fat but punctual cabby, who wasn't pleased to be driving half a day without a fare. He'd nodded grimly at Mamieo as they crawled into the cab, then slammed the door and headed back to Chicago without saying a word.

If Teagan hadn't had time to clean up—though it had been a sponge bath rather than a shower, because there wasn't much water left in the Tank's reservoir—she'd have thought the look on the cabby's face was because they smelled bad.

As it was, she was sure it was just his personality, and the fact that he would be making two round trips today. He'd be headed back to Gary as soon as he dropped them off. Mamieo had decided to take the Tank and leave it at the old drive-in as a decoy, then have Jackie come back and take her to the Wylltsons' house to wait. She wanted to be nearby when they came out of Mag Mell.

Teagan had sent a text to Abby explaining as much as she could and asking her to get Mrs. Santini to let Mamieo in when she arrived.

"This is it." They were the first words Jackie'd spoken in the two hours since they'd climbed into his cab.

"It is," Finn said, eyeing the gates to the park behind the library. "Thank you."

The cabby grunted, and waited until they were almost out of the cab before he started away. Finn grabbed his kit and managed to swing the door shut, even though the cab was already moving.

"Okay." Teagan tried to ignore the tight, sick feeling in her stomach. "Let's go."

"Wait." Finn took his knife out of his boot and hid it in the bushes again. "Now we go."

Teagan couldn't make her feet move. Going into Mag Mell the first time had been easy because she hadn't known what was waiting for them beyond the trees. This time, she knew.

"Come on." Aiden took her hand. "Dad needs us." Teagan let him pull her along.

She felt the million tiny fingers rippling over her skin. *The memory of trees.*

Then the touching stopped, and they were standing in Mag Mell. If it hadn't smelled like magic, Teagan would have been sure it was a different place entirely. They had stepped into a stand of tall conifer trees. There was no sound of a hunting pack, no fiddler's tune, just the buzz and hum of insects, and a whoosh of wind high in the trees.

"What do we do now?" Teagan asked.

Finn shrugged. "Mamieo said to try singing to Mag Mell. Why don't you try that song she taught you, my man?"

"She said that song's for if we meet bad guys." Aiden tipped his head, listening. He started humming, then singing softly.

"What song is that, then?" Finn whispered.

"Jim Croce's 'I Got a Name,'" Teagan whispered back.

"And *I carry it with me like my daddy did.*" Aiden was really belting it out now. "*I'm living the dream that he kept hid . . .*"

Suddenly, something *changed*. Even the wind in the treetops stopped. It was as if Mag Mell herself had paused to listen. And then the birds chimed in. They were singing with Aiden. When he reached the line about going down a highway, the trees and bushes moved, opening a path where there had been none before.

Aiden stopped singing and sucked in his breath. "I'm awesome!"

"Very, my man," Finn agreed. "Keep singing."

And he did. The forest thinned, and bees buzzed through honeysuckle-sweet air. It was . . . beautiful. Teagan wondered where the fiddler was, and if he could hear Aiden's song. It was hard to imagine him in *this* Mag Mell. It was hard to imagine any goblin in this place.

They walked for an hour without seeing one frightening thing. Aiden would walk silently for a long time, listening, then burst into song, singing bits and pieces of several in a row, as if Mag Mell herself were changing the station when she grew tired of the lyrics.

Teagan giggled, and Aiden glanced at her.

"Tea, are you all right?"

"I'm fine."

More than fine. Was it Mag Mell, or walking near Finn? She didn't have to look at him to know where he was. Two steps behind her, to the left. She could feel him there like a warm glow. *There's been just one name pounding in that boy's heart ever since he first saw you, hasn't there?*

"You're smiling," Aiden said. "You haven't done that in a long time."

Tiny bubbles were bursting inside her, as if her bones were

effervescing with joy. *I'm smiling. How can I be smiling when Dad needs me? When I'm in this place?* Teagan forced herself to concentrate, to remember the dog-headed men and the pack. The bubbles almost went away. Almost.

Teagan focused on following Aiden and keeping her head. The path wound down out of the piney woods, and farther down still, through meadows, and then under spreading sycamore-like trees, with broad leaves and camouflage-patterned bark. The growths on their huge trunks looked almost like gnomes trying to work their way out of the bark and step out into the fern fronds around them. A hummingbird-size creature with huge eyes flashed past Aiden's head and disappeared into a fern.

A few moments later Teagan saw it again, a blur of motion against the green. It was clearly following Aiden, zipping from hiding place to hiding place, peeking at him as he sang. It didn't look large enough to be dangerous, but she kept an eye on it anyway.

The ground grew spongy, and here and there they passed ponds where bubble-eyed creatures peered out at them. When Aiden stopped singing, they disappeared under the surface of the pond, leaving nothing but ripples behind.

If they came out, it would be like the scene from *Sleeping Beauty* where Briar Rose sang to all the little animals as they danced. . . . Teagan clapped her hand over her mouth to keep from erupting in giggles. Aiden was singing some kind of marching song. That wouldn't do. She wanted to see the little pond creatures come out. Well, Mag Mell wasn't the only one who knew how to change Aiden's station. She started to hum softly.

"*I know you. I walked with you once upon a dream . . .*"

Aiden picked it up, his voice as sweet as any Disney princess's.

The bubble-eyed creatures' heads popped out of the water. They were frogs. Dozens of them hopped, wiggled, and scrambled up out of the ponds. Teagan's mouth fell open.

They weren't just frogs. They were frog *people*. They wore little vests and carried long walking sticks.

A shrewlike creature darted out of the undergrowth, and a frog-man threw his walking stick at it like a javelin, pinning it to a tree trunk. It squeaked and kicked for a second, then went still. The frogman retrieved his spear, then took the carcass by the tail and dragged it toward the pond.

"A lot of them, aren't there?" Finn whispered. "I don't like this."

"They don't look dangerous," Teagan said.

Aiden didn't seem to think so, either. The frog folk started to croak a chorus for Aiden's song, their throats expanding and deflating as they sang, their wide feet slapping out the rhythm. Their chorus almost drowned out Aiden's voice.

"We're drawing too much attention," Finn shouted over the racket. "What are you singing, boyo? Change the song!"

Aiden stopped and shook his head.

"Hey"—he glared at Teagan—"I'm not a princess! You made me sing—"

Something launched itself off of a limb and landed in Aiden's hair, screaming like Mamieo's teakettle. Aiden screamed as well, and Finn snatched it out of his hair and held it up by its wings.

"Is it a bug?" Aiden slapped at his head. "Does it have a stinger?"

"It looks like a girl," Finn said.

"A sprite," Teagan said. "I think it's a sprite, like the ones in Mom's books."

The sprite was barely four inches tall, with tattered brown

wings and a hard exoskeleton patterned like sycamore bark. Her pale hair stood out like dandelion down, and her eyes were amazing. They seemed to glow with internal light like a cicada's tiny ocelli, but the sprite's eyes weren't tiny. They were large, clearly compound, and constantly changing.

A kaleidoscope of colors whirled across them when she looked at Aiden. She chirped, then grabbed at the only thing she was wearing—a scabbard strapped to her thigh—and pulled out a white sliver that looked like it was made of shell.

Teagan blinked. "Look out, Finn, she's got a—"

"Shit!" Finn flung the sprite into the bushes.

"—knife," she said, half a second too late. The shell blade was less than half an inch long, but judging from the blood dripping from Finn's finger, it was razor sharp.

"Where did it go?" Aiden started toward the bush. Finn grabbed him and pulled him away with one hand while he flung blood from the other.

"Stay back," Finn said as the sprite came out of the leaves, buzzing like an angry hummingbird. It was the creature that had been following Aiden, peeking at him from behind tree trunks—Teagan was sure of it.

The sprite climbed into the sun like a tiny fighter jet, then turned and dove, slashing at Finn as she came. He slapped her again, and she tumbled head over heels in the air, righted herself, and attacked once more.

"Back away from Aiden," Teagan said. "I don't think she's going to hurt him. I think she likes him."

"Are you sure?" Finn asked.

"She's not mad at me," Aiden said. "She's mad at you."

Finn backed away. The sprite put her knife away and hovered in front of Aiden, chirping like a canary.

"She's happier now," Aiden said.

"She may be"—Finn squeezed his bleeding finger—"but Mag Mell is not." Dark vines were creeping across the path that had been clear in front of them. "Sing, Aiden. Ignore the damn . . . darn bug, or sing something to make it behave."

Aiden started singing "Lucy in the Sky with Diamonds." The sprite did a somersault in the air, squealed like a groupie, and dove into Aiden's hair.

Aiden froze. The sprite settled in, whirring her wings and spinning her kaleidoscope eyes as she searched through Aiden's curls.

"What's she looking for?" Finn asked. "Fleas?"

"Maybe," Teagan said. "Social grooming is usually a sign of affection."

"What does that mean?" Aiden asked, still not moving.

"It means she likes you."

"I'm not grooming her back. No way."

"Just ignore her and sing," Teagan said, digging in Finn's kit for the antibiotic and a Band-Aid. "Maybe she'll go away." She put the Band-Aid on Finn's finger when the blood stopped dripping.

Mag Mell settled down as Aiden sang, even though he was stomping along the path with his arms crossed. The vines retreated but still moved restlessly.

Finn and Teagan walked behind him, watching the sprite in his hair. She wasn't grooming him, Teagan decided. She was setting up house. The sprite was weaving his hair into a nest, her hands working the curly locks together with great skill.

A bottle fly buzzed around Aiden's head, and the sprite's hand shot out and snatched it from the air. She stripped the wings off, dropped them in her nest, and started munching on the fly's head while its legs waved wildly.

"Looks like Aiden won't have a mosquito problem," Finn said. "Not with that bug around."

"Her name is Lucy, like in the song," Aiden said. "I've decided to keep her."

"That will be easier than trying to get rid of her, I expect," Finn said.

"She's fascinating." Teagan leaned over to get a closer look. Lucy finished the fly and started grooming herself, licking her hands and rubbing them over her face and along the strands of her dandelion mane.

Aiden changed his song, and the path wound in between deep ponds of green water. Dragonflies hovered over lily pads, and the frog people crept out again, marching along beside them as they walked.

The underbrush cleared around Aiden as he went. Tree branches arched over clear pools of water, and Teagan saw golden fish flash just beneath the surface. Finn walked close to a pool and leaned over.

"It has no bottom," he said. "You can see down . . . forever." The frog people huddled together in groups, rather than in long marching lines as they had before.

"They don't like this place," Finn said. "Let me walk ahead of you, Aiden. Watch the trees, and stay away from the pools." He stepped past Aiden and took the lead.

Aiden let him get a few yards ahead, then glanced sideways at Teagan. "That was mean, Tea."

"What was?"

"Making me sing a princess song."

"The prince sang it, too."

"When I sing, things do what I say in the songs, don't they?"

"Yes." Teagan didn't like the look in his eye. "Aiden Quinn, what are you—"

"*Sha-la-la-la-la-la*," Aiden sang. "*Music play . . .*"

Teagan's brain spun trying to remember the lyrics. It was from *The Little Mermaid* . . . but she hadn't heard it in years, not since she'd watched the DVD with Abby.

The frog folk around Aiden's feet started croaking loudly and off-key, waving their spear sticks as if they were trying to warn Aiden. *Something was wrong.* Teagan tried to process two images— the frog people waving frantically, and Finn walking toward her, a dazed look on his face.

"*Do what the music say,*" Aiden crooned. "*You wanna ki—*"

"Aiden!" Teagan grabbed him and clapped her hand over his mouth. *You wanna kiss the girl.* That was the line.

Finn stopped, looking even more confused. He put a hand to his head.

Teagan took her hand off Aiden's mouth, grabbed his shoulders, and shook him hard. "Don't you dare use your songs on Finn!"

"Stop it, Tea," Aiden said. "I was just playing!"

The sprite hissed, jumped from Aiden's head, and grabbed Teagan's nose.

Teagan let go of Aiden and tried to pull the sprite away, but it was holding on tight and reaching up inside her nostril.

"Ow!" The sprite was plucking nose hair. The pain was incredible. "Make her stop!"

Aiden laughed, dancing backwards.

"Aiden," Finn shouted, "watch where you're going!"

Aiden's heel caught on a root, and he landed on his backside at the edge of a deep pool. A scaly green arm flashed out of the water, and long fingers twined in Aiden's curls. He screamed, and the sprite let go of Teagan's nose.

Aiden flipped onto his stomach and tried to scramble away from whatever had him by the hair. The sprite streaked for the hand, knife out, just as an almost-bald head appeared.

Teagan knew her instantly. *Ginny Greenteeth. She drowns travelers in bogs.* Teagan lunged forward and grabbed Aiden's foot.

"I want to be part of your world," Ginny Greenteeth said. Her mouth opened wide, showing knobs of teeth and a thick black tongue.

Aiden screamed again.

"Don't let her get me, Tea!" he shrieked. Lucy slashed at the goblin's fingers with her blade, but it bounced off the scales. The sprite squealed in anger and flew at the water goblin's eyes. Ginny snatched the tiny girl from the air with the hand that wasn't tangled in Aiden's hair and tossed her into the pond. Golden fish rose around the sprite, and suddenly Lucy was fighting for her own life.

"Tea!" Aiden begged. "Don't let her get m—"

The goblin gave a giant heave and Aiden's head and shoulders went underwater.

SIXTEEN

TEAGAN dug her heels into the slippery moss, scrabbling for traction, and pulled on Aiden's foot with all her might. His shoe came off and she lost her grip just as Finn grabbed his other leg. Inch by inch, Ginny Greenteeth was dragging Aiden under. He was kicking wildly, but Teagan caught his leg again.

"Can he hold his breath for long?" Finn asked.

"Not very." Teagan could feel Aiden's kicks weakening. "We've got to think."

"No time for that. Hold on tight." Finn let go of Aiden's leg, tossed his kit aside, and dove into the pool. The splash threw Lucy up onto the bank, where she gasped and shook. Finn's head bobbed above the water—he took a breath and disappeared.

Aiden stopped kicking.

"No!" Teagan shouted, and pulled with all her strength. Suddenly Aiden popped out of the water and Teagan fell backwards. She scrambled to her knees, grabbed Aiden's leg again, and dragged him farther from the pool. His face looked pale in the green forest light, and his eyes weren't open.

That's what a drowned person looks like. A dead person. Lucy had shaken herself dry enough to fly. She landed on Aiden's chest, ran up to his face, and started slapping it and crying, trying to make him wake up.

"Stop it." Teagan pushed the sprite away. She could see the life draining out of Aiden, as it had drained out of her mom, but his body hadn't gone all *wrong* to the touch yet. There was still time to fight for him.

You have to think your way through things, even in the midst of it. Use your brain, girl.

It was no different from animal rescue. She'd given mouth-to-mouth to newborn puppies before. Aiden was just larger. Teagan turned him on his side, and water oozed out of his gaping mouth.

She stuck her finger in, making sure he hadn't sucked in anything that would block his breathing, then turned him onto his back again, pinched his nose shut, and gave him a puff of air. His chest rose, then fell. She did it again. And again.

Suddenly water gushed up from inside Aiden, spraying all over her and soaking Lucy. Tea turned him quickly onto his side and held on to him as he emptied his guts. When he finished, he looked around wildly.

"What—" He had a coughing fit and leaned against Teagan. "Where'd she go?" The surface of the pond was smooth. No Ginny. No Finn! She'd forgotten about Finn!

A clammy hand grabbed Teagan's shoulder, and she spun around.

"Is he okay?" Finn was dripping wet, and there were green weeds stuck in his hair. He looked almost as pale as Aiden had.

"How did you . . ." Tea began.

Finn pointed at the pool behind them.

"They're all connected underneath," he said. "It's not like our world. The dirt layer is thin, and the roots of the trees go down twisting and tangling into the water. It's another world. Lots of shiny fish."

"Thank God you're a good swimmer!"

"Can't swim a stroke," Finn said, clutching his stomach. "I just pulled myself along by the roots until I saw light, then came up. Uhhh." He fell to his knees, his face twisted in pain.

"What's wrong?"

Finn stuck his finger down his own throat, gagged, then bent over as he retched up a puddle of water and something that looked like a long green grub. It had a hooklike claw on the end.

"Is that . . ."

"Her toe," Finn said.

"You *bit off her toe?*" Aiden's voice was hoarse.

"Seemed like the thing to do at the time," Finn replied. "I couldn't think of any other way to make her let go of you. I didn't mean to swallow it, though. It just went down with a mouthful of water."

The toe was long and thin and had too many joints.

"It looks more like a finger." Teagan poked at it.

"Acts like one, too," Finn said. "She was holding on to Aiden with her hands and clinging onto the roots with ten of those. She'll make do with nine now."

The toe twitched and rolled over. It started to pull itself inchworm-like toward the pool. Aiden moved his feet to let it pass, but Teagan snatched it up.

"What are you doing?" Finn asked. "Let the nasty thing go."

"No," Teagan said. "I'm keeping it."

"Why?"

"In case we need it." That was the way it worked in fairy tales. You never knew what strange thing you would need. She tore off a piece of her T-shirt, wrapped the wriggling toe up tightly, and put it in her pocket.

Finn pulled Aiden to his feet. Lucy landed on his head, keening about the state of her wet nest.

"All the pools are connected?" Aiden moved closer to Finn. "That goblin lady could be in any of them?"

"That was no lady," Finn said. "It's not a word I'd use for goblinkind."

Tea found Aiden's shoe and helped him put it on. The frog people were back, croaking solemnly among themselves and pointing at Aiden.

"We'll just stay away from ponds. Can you sing, Aiden?"

"No." He rubbed his throat. "I think that water scratched me up."

"We can find our way out of this bog." Finn picked up his kit. "Come on."

Teagan held Aiden's hand, being careful to stay as far as possible from the water. The frog folk hadn't abandoned Aiden, even though he couldn't sing. They hopped along at his feet.

Avoiding the ponds grew more difficult as the path led deeper into the swampy area, where the trees looked like mangroves and the water was the color of strong tea, stained by the leaves that had fallen into it. Some of the pools were completely covered with leaves, making them impossible to distinguish from the flat, damp ground. Dark shadows, long and lithe as sea eels, moved in the depths.

At times they walked ankle deep in water when the path disappeared. Then the frog folk took the lead, splashing single file ahead of Finn, their big eyes goggling at the trees as well as the pools.

Teagan was sure that something in this swamp hunted frogs, and she had a feeling she knew what it was. They were on a relatively dry patch between two flat, leaf-covered patches when the frog folk started croaking an alarm again.

"She's back." Teagan pulled Aiden close just as Ginny Greenteeth's head rose from the leaves beside them. Aiden clung to Teagan, the frog folk huddled at their feet.

"Sing her away," Finn said. Aiden tried, but his voice was just a hoarse whisper.

Ginny Greenteeth laughed. "Your words can't touch me. I'm *sidhe*, ain't I? Stormrider, a nightmare crawler, born to reign and rule. Your puny tune can't hurt me."

Teagan could smell the goblin woman's breath. If Ginny Greenteeth was a female *sidhe*, it was no wonder Kyle went clubbing in Chicago.

"And born to lie," Finn said. "I expect the boyo's tune would work just fine if he could sing it out." Ginny bared her square teeth.

"It's all right." Finn took Aiden's other hand. "I won't let her get you. She'd be like a salamander outside the water. You're not afraid of salamanders, are you?"

"Maybe," Aiden said.

"Shut your mouth, toe eater," Ginny Greenteeth hissed. "I'll hunt you forever. I'll find you."

"Come get it, salamander. I'll deal with more than your nasty little toe."

"What have you done with it?" Ginny squinted at him. "It was burning, burning . . . but now it's not. I called, but it didn't come back to me. What have you done?"

Teagan took the wrapped-up toe out of her pocket. It was twitching frantically.

"Is this what you're looking for?"

"Give it to me!" Ginny blurted. "I ache for it!" The toe in Teagan's hand writhed, as if it longed for its owner as much as she ached for it. Ginny's eyes fixed on Teagan.

"When I call the Dark Man, he will make you give it back. We're supposed to tell him if anyone strange comes in. He will make you suffer. He will send the pack, and they will hunt you through the woods."

Aiden trembled. Teagan couldn't shut the goblin up, not by force. But there were other ways.

"No," Teagan said. She held up the toe. "You are going to *promise* not to call the Dark Man, or tell him anything about us."

"Why would I do something so stupid?" the goblin asked.

"Because if you don't, I will swallow your toe."

"That's disturbing," Finn said.

Teagan ignored him. "Do you remember the burning? That was the gastric acid in Finn's stomach, dissolving your flesh. I'll swallow your toe and stay away from your pools and ponds until it's digested, flesh, bone, and nail."

"They'll catch you," Ginny said. "They'll rip it from your belly. They always catch the ones they hunt. There's no way out of Mag Mell for you."

"Really?" Teagan said. "I knew someone who got away. A girl."

"*That* girl?" She had the goblin's attention now. "What do you know about her?"

"I know how she got out." That was true. "I know how I am going to get out, too, with your toe inside me . . . unless you promise not to tell the Dark Man we're here."

"You have to promise, too," Ginny said slyly. "Promise to give me back my toe."

"Careful, Tea," Finn said. "Promises always work in favor of the *sidhe*."

Teagan took a deep breath. Ginny Greenteeth was from one of her mom's books. Characters in those books used promises like magic. It was like a chess game, each word a piece with certain possibilities, certain risks. You had to win by thinking, by strategy.

"I promise," Teagan said carefully, "to give your toe back *if* you promise not to tell anyone we are here"—the goblin woman would think of a way around that, Teagan was certain—"*and* with your flesh and with your bones, to keep us safe, whatever comes." That last bit sounded like a promise her mom would have written into a fairy tale. Teagan was quite pleased with it.

"Two promises? No!"

Ginny started to sink into the water, and Teagan was afraid she had lost her. She pulled the cloth off of the squirming goblin toe and held it over her open mouth.

"Don't!" Ginny bobbed back up, thrashing like a fish fighting a line. "Don't." She slapped the leaves on the water, then went still.

"I promise," Ginny said, "I will not tell anyone you are here, and with my flesh and with my bones, I'll keep you safe whatever comes—except from the Dark Man himself. No one can stand against *him*. Now give me my toe."

Teagan bit her lip. Had her words been tight enough? Could the goblin find a way around them? Promises always had loopholes. It would be best to keep the toe a little longer.

Ginny started sobbing as Teagan wrapped it back up. "Please, *please* give me my toe. I didn't mean to hurt your brother. I only wanted to look at him."

"For Pete's sake, don't cry," Teagan said. "I'll give it back before we leave Mag Mell."

"Stupid girl!" the goblin said. "You're the Dark Man's meat!"

"Toss her the nasty toe," Finn said, "and be done with the game. You have her promise."

"Yes!" Ginny said. "Toss it to me!"

What would her mom have done?

"No," Teagan said slowly. "This isn't a game. It's about finding Dad and getting him out of here. I have her promise and she has mine. But I'll keep the toe until I'm sure it isn't useful anymore."

SEVENTEEN

YOU treat my promise that way?" The goblin woman spat water at them. "If you don't keep yours, I'll take your brother. Fear will let me have him. I never wanted to look at him. I wanted to pull him down and squeeze him until all his bubbles came out!"

The goblin disappeared beneath the leafy surface of the water. Teagan turned to find Aiden and Lucy staring at her in horror.

"Come on," Finn said. "Let's get out of here."

"But what about what that goblin said?" Aiden asked. "Tea did promise."

"We'll deal with it when the time comes," Finn said. "That pond woman is lowborn. Reality will twist to a Highborn's advantage if they've tricked a promise out of you. But I don't think the salamander has it in her. She was spawned in mud and slime. That was disgusting, by the way."

"What?" Teagan flushed. "Threatening to swallow her toe? You swallowed it the first time."

"I barfed it up again, didn't I?"

"Teagan ate bugs once," Aiden said. "In science class."

"Worms are not bugs. And they were fried."

Both Finn and Aiden grimaced.

"For Pete's sake. I had to buy time somehow. If I hadn't made her promise, she'd have called Fear Doirich by now, and the pack would be after us."

"True enough." Finn took the lead again.

Teagan was relieved to find the ground growing firmer as they walked. They left the frog folk behind as the land rose into a sycamore wood, but without Aiden's song, they had no clear path.

Aiden tried to sing, but his voice was so hoarse that it hurt Tea to listen to it. He stopped and put his hand to his throat, his eyes tearing up. "What if bad guys come and I can't sing?"

Lucy fluttered around his head, her eyes flashing red, then took off into the trees.

"Save that voice, my man." Finn picked up a fallen branch the length and thickness of his arm. "I'll take care of the bad guys a little while."

"All right." Aiden wiped his nose on his sleeve.

Lucy appeared again, fighting her way through the air, struggling to control a beetle almost as big as her head. It was buzzing madly, trying to get away. She flew right at Aiden's face and tried to push it into his mouth. Aiden clapped his hand over his lips.

"No," he shouted through his fingers. "I don't eat gross things! Give it to Teagan!"

Lucy let the beetle go, and it buzzed away like a heavy cargo plane, dropping down low over the mossy ground. The sprite studied Aiden, her arms folded, her eyes spinning, then zipped away again.

"What's she doing?" Aiden asked.

"I think she's trying to cheer you up," Teagan said.

Lucy was back very quickly this time. She was carrying a fat, knobby berry.

"Looks like a blackberry," Teagan said. "Don't eat it, though, we don't know—" The sprite had already popped the berry into Aiden's mouth.

"Tastes like a blackberry, too," he said, smacking his lips. "Thank you, bug." Lucy did a somersault and zoomed away again.

"Let's be moving." Finn swung his club. "The farther from that swamp, the better."

Teagan took Aiden's hand. "I'm sorry I made you sing the princess song. That was wrong. It's not nice to trick people into doing things you want them to do."

"I'm sorry I . . ." Aiden glanced at Finn. "You know." Teagan squeezed his fingers.

Lucy came back with another berry. Aiden opened his mouth, and she popped it in, then zoomed away again.

"You could bring the rest of us some of those," Finn said when she appeared with yet another. The sprite hissed at him and went back to feeding Aiden, a tiny mother bird trying to fill up her impossibly large chick.

Eventually they left the berry bushes behind, and Lucy gave up and settled in to re-weave her nest.

"You're not going to leave me with the Dark Man, are you?" Aiden asked when the swamp was well behind them.

"Of course not," Teagan said. "Why would you even ask such a thing?"

"I heard his song while I was under the water. He said he was keeping me forever."

"Don't be silly. He doesn't even know we're here."

Aiden shivered. "His song said I was going to be . . . dead here."

Finn stopped and turned around. "That's not going to happen. I won't let him keep you, boyo. We'll leave this place together."

Aiden studied him. "You promise?"

"I promise," Finn said without hesitating.

Aiden nodded.

"Besides, how would he keep someone like you? I thought you said you were awesome."

Aiden's lips curved up. "I am," he said. "Just a little."

Lucy had apparently finished weaving to her satisfaction. She took a short flight and pulled a flower off a branch, brought it back, and set it triumphantly on Aiden's head. Aiden reached up and grabbed the sprite in one hand and the flower in the other.

"No flowers." He threw the blossom away. "I'm a boy. I don't want flowers in my hair." Lucy's eyes turned dark blue.

"You're okay." Aiden set her back on top of his head. "Just no bugs and no flowers." The sprite chirped happily and spun her kaleidoscope eyes.

The landscape had changed again. Giant ferns grew beside the path.

Finn touched Teagan's arm and pointed. The trees ahead of them were different from any they had seen in Mag Mell. They twisted and twined together into the form of a . . . cathedral.

Aerial prop roots, like those of ancient cypress trees, anchored each thick, woody trunk to the forest floor, twisting into fantastic flying buttresses before they plunged into the ground. The trunks that formed the walls stood so close together that if they hadn't separated twenty feet above the ground, bending and intertwining to form an arched roof, Teagan might have thought it was a single massive tree.

There was a doorway, and a well-used path leading up to it.

"You think Fear Doirich lives here?" Finn whispered.

"I don't know," Teagan said.

Up close, the trees looked even more like a solid, moss-covered wall.

"Mom painted this," Aiden said.

He was right. Their mom had painted sprites and Ginny Greenteeth, too, but this was different. This had been her favorite painting, a scene she loved.

"Fear Doirich doesn't live here." Teagan was certain of it. "But I really need to know who does. Come on." Her stomach knotted as she walked up to the open doorway.

There was no door and no way to knock against the mossy walls, so Teagan stepped inside, Aiden and Finn right behind her. It felt like stepping into a chapel, a house of worship made from living plants. Ivy cascaded down the walls.

She heard Aiden draw in his breath. The carved wooden table, the candlesticks, the sunlight through the branches . . . it was another of her mother's paintings.

There was a pale girl sitting in a chair just inside the door, an embroidery hoop in her lap. Ivy twined through her long blond hair and flowers hemmed her dress. She was intent on her needlework. Next to Aileen Wylltson, she was the most beautiful person Teagan had ever seen.

"Excuse me," Teagan said.

The girl looked up in surprise. Her embroidery hoop fell to the ground as she stood.

"Aileen!" she said, and started rattling in a language that sounded like Mamieo's Gaelic. Her words trickled off when she saw Teagan's brown eyes. She looked at Finn and Aiden, then stopped speaking entirely, uncertain.

"I can understand most of it," Finn said. "She's been waiting for your mother."

"Has she seen Dad?" Aiden asked.

Finn spoke again, but the girl shook her head.

"Aileen?" Her voice was pleading.

Finn touched Teagan's arm. "Aileen's *deirfiúr*, Teagan." He pointed to Aiden. "Aileen's *mac*, Aiden."

The girl put her hand over her mouth and shook her head. She came closer and studied Teagan's face. Tears filled her aqua-blue eyes, and then she was speaking so fast that the words seemed to be tripping over one another. When she stopped, Finn nodded at her.

"I didn't get all that," Finn said. "But I got enough. Teagan, Aiden, I'd like you to meet your aunt Roisin. Your mother's younger sister."

"Aunt?" Aiden said. "I have an aunt?"

Teagan was doing the math in her head, and it didn't add up. This girl couldn't be more than fifteen. If Aileen had left Mag Mell when she was twelve, that was . . . twenty-seven years ago. But her mother *had* known a Roisin . . . and made her a promise.

Roisin looked warily at the sprite peeking out of Aiden's hair. She said something, and Finn replied with a nod.

"She says sprites are nasty creatures," he translated. "They pull nose hair."

"Don't I know it." Teagan rubbed her nose. "Ask her what Aileen promised her."

When Finn finished the question, Roisin turned luminous eyes on Teagan and started speaking, gesturing to the hall around them.

"She promised she'd make a way for Roisin to get out of Mag Mell. The Dark Man was keeping them both, but Aunt Aileen brought her here"—he waved his hand at the hall—"to Yggdrasil's hands, to keep her safe. This is the one place in Mag Mell that Fear Doirich cannot walk."

"Tell her that something happened to Mom, but she remembered her promise before she died."

Finn had hardly started when Roisin swayed. He caught her arm to keep her from falling.

"What's wrong?" Teagan moved to her other side to help.

"She didn't know her sister was dead," Finn said. "I could have done a better job of breaking it to her."

Teagan took Roisin's other arm, and they helped her to a chair. Finn knelt beside it and started talking very softly.

"What's he telling her?" Aiden asked.

"About Mom, I think," Teagan said as Roisin's eyes lifted to her. "And about us."

As Finn went on, Roisin's face grew white and still, and then her head bowed. By the time he was finished, the girl's long blond hair was a curtain in front of her face, but Teagan could tell she was crying.

"She's been waiting for her sister," Finn explained, "a very long time."

Teagan heard a thump and turned to see something hopping down the stairs. It was fluffy, orange, and had a Cheshire grin on its face. It bounced down two steps at a time, then walked upright, its catlike head held high and its long tail twitching.

"*Dia duit*," it said in a little-girl voice, and bowed.

"Is that *cat-sídhe* talking Gaelic, too?" Aiden asked.

"It is." Finn reached for his club. "It said, 'God to you,' which means hello."

Teagan touched his arm. "Wait," she said. "It's not like the ones at home. It doesn't look sick."

The creature jumped up on Roisin's lap, and the girl wrapped her arms around it. It put its paws on each side of her head and tipped its face up to look into her eyes, then made a sympathetic mewling sound, for all the world like a mother cat comforting a kitten. Roisin wiped her tears away with the heels of her hands, and hugged it harder.

"She's got a *cat-sídhe* for a friend?" Aiden asked.

"I told you there was something wrong with the ones we've seen," Teagan said. "Healthy creatures don't grow maggots in their bellies." The *cat-sídhe* wiggled out of Roisin's arms and jumped to the floor.

"What's its name?" Teagan asked, pointing and hoping her inflection was enough to convey her meaning.

"Grendal," Roisin said.

"Grendal," the *cat-sídhe* agreed cheerfully.

Lucy peered over the top of her nest and hissed. Grendal flattened his ears and hissed back.

"Grendal!" Roisin said. The *cat-sídhe* spat and stalked into the corner. He folded himself up and watched Lucy through narrowed eyes.

Roisin spoke to Finn, and he nodded.

"She says *cat-sídhe* eat sprites," he said.

"Not my sprite." Aiden backed away from Grendal. "No cat's eating my Lucy!"

"You don't let her come out of her nest, then," Finn said. "I'll keep an eye on the cat."

Teagan stepped closer to Finn. "Ask her about my mom. Why was she here? Where are they from?"

Roisin listened intently as Finn asked the questions, then nodded and started talking again. Teagan couldn't understand the words, but she did recognize some names. Amergin . . . Éireann . . . Doirich. They were from the stories Finn and Mamieo had told.

Roisin had managed only a few sentences when Finn stopped her and pointed at Teagan.

"*Seanathair?*" Finn said. "*Seanathair?*"

"*Cinnte!*" Roisin nodded.

"What?" Teagan said.

Finn's face had drained of color.

"What's wrong?" Aiden asked.

He glanced at Teagan, shook his head, then stood and started pacing as Roisin went on. When Roisin was done, he stopped and ran his hand through his hair.

"Finn," Teagan said, "what's going on?"

He took a breath. "There was one man Fear Doirich hated more than Fionn Mac Cumhaill and all his line together: Amergin, the Milesian bard who locked him in this place. The Dark Man swore to enslave or destroy every living drop of Amergin's blood. He captured the family and brought them here. He tortured and killed Amergin's wife, then stole the man's life one bit at a time, until he died."

"So?" Teagan said.

"So, he was your grandfather, Tea," Finn said. "Amergin the bard was your own grandfather. Aileen and Roisin are his daughters."

"Wait," Teagan said. "You said Amergin married a . . . who was my grandmother, Finn?"

"Maeve, the sister of Queen Mab."

Teagan could hear the strain in his voice.

"Maeve was your *máthair*'s *máthair*. That's why Aunt Aileen's ashes opened the memory of the trees. She promised to make a way for her sister to leave. There is power in the promise of a Highborn goblin, and she knew it when she wove her words."

"Our mom was part . . . goblin?" Aiden's voice squeaked on the word.

EIGHTEEN

N O." Teagan wrapped her arms around Aiden. "That can't be right. It's not . . . logical. Amergin and Maeve lived in the time before time, if they lived at all. They lived so long ago they have become legend."

"Look around you, girl," Finn said. "We're in the heart of Mag Mell, cupped in the hands of a tree that's been praying since before man's time began. You're carrying a goblin toe in your pocket, and your brother's got a human bug living in his hair. What part of this is logical?"

"None of it," Teagan admitted. "But . . . why isn't Roisin older? If it were true, she would be thousands of years old."

"Time doesn't move fast here," Finn said. "She said it's stilled by Yggdrasil's prayers. There's more, Tea. There's the reason the Dark Man kept the girls alive. They had none of their father's gift themselves, but they carried the promise of Amergin's song in their bodies." Finn flushed red. "Fear Doirich expected them to bear him children. He planned to breed a new race—part Sídhe, part Milesians, and part god—completely bent to his foul will. Your mother ran away while she was still a child."

"But Roisin isn't old enough to . . ." Teagan blushed herself. She'd known three girls who'd had babies in their sophomore year, but it still seemed wrong.

"She hasn't left Yggdrasil's hands since she . . . since she became a woman," Finn said. "The Dark Man and his wicked shadows are too foul to step on this holy ground. The Highborn can come here, and those that follow them, but they can't drag her from this place against her will. The girls claimed sanctuary."

"And Mom?"

"She knew what the Dark Man wanted. She couldn't stand being trapped. The goblin blood was strongest in Aileen, so she made her baby sister a *promise* and went out. She promised that even her death would make a chance for Roisin to be free. Aileen never expected Mamieo to come walking in the night. Roisin waited for your mom, and while she waited, she grew up."

"She's not grown up yet," Teagan said.

Finn shrugged. "One of the Highborn who visited here to convince Roisin to leave would disagree with that. He fell in love with the girl. His name is Thomas. There is not much power in Roisin's promises—the goblin blood is not as strong in her—but she promised to marry the fellow. He promised to love her as long as his heart beat. I expect Fear Doirich has taken care of that. She hasn't seen Thomas in a long time."

"Ask her if Thomas plays the fiddle," Aiden said.

"Good thought." Finn asked the question, and Roisin shook her head, and there was another conversation with Finn questioning and the girl explaining.

"Thomas doesn't play the fiddle, but his slave-pet Eógan does."

"Slave-pet?"

"A human he stole from Éireann," Finn explained. "The goblins steal beautiful children to be their slaves, and keep them as long as their beauty lasts and they are entertaining. Thomas was quite proud of Eógan's talent. He'd had the man since he was a six-year-old child. But when Eógan tried to run away, Thomas asked Fear Doirich to . . . *plant* him so he couldn't leave."

"Goblins steal little kids?" Aiden frowned. "Mom wouldn't do that."

"Because she wasn't a goblin," Teagan said. "She must have been one of the children they stole. They must have lied to Roisin since she was a baby."

Roisin jumped up. She pointed to the door, rattled a sentence to Finn, and motioned urgently for them to follow her.

Finn snatched up his kit. "We need to get out of sight right now. She says company's coming."

Roisin led them to the wall, pulled aside the hanging ivy, and pointed up.

"She wants us to climb," Finn said. "She says there's a hiding place up there. She used to hide in it with Aileen."

Teagan pushed Aiden up over her head. He grabbed onto the bark of the tree-wall like a monkey and started climbing. Finn boosted Teagan up, and she grabbed the rough bark with her hands, kicked the toes of her sneakers into the cracks, and pulled herself up after Aiden.

About eight feet above the ground, there was a place where a branch had fallen, leaving a hollow in the trunk like a niche where you'd keep the statue of a saint.

Aiden scrambled in and pressed against the back. Teagan crawled in after him and pressed against him. The ivy curtain hung green and heavy in front of them, but not too heavy for them to catch glimpses of the hall through the leaves and vines. It was a perfect hiding place—for two small girls.

When Finn reached the niche, he handed his kit to Teagan, then swung around so his back was to the tree, his feet braced against the bark rim and his arms gripping bark on both sides, holding Teagan and Aiden in place like a human cargo net. An electric net. The sparkle was back in Teagan's bones.

"You're squishing me," Aiden said.

"Shhh," Teagan whispered. The toe in her pocket was twitching like mad. "She's coming."

Who? Aiden signed.

Teagan pointed as Ginny Greenteeth walked through the door. She held up a large bowl for Roisin to see, then limped to the table and set it down. Aiden shrank back as far as he could. Lucy's eyes flashed like green fire, and she pulled on Aiden's hair until he winced.

Roisin pointed to Ginny's foot and asked a question. Ginny grimaced, showing her peg teeth, and shook her head.

Aiden pinched Teagan to get her attention.

Are we goblins? he signed.

No.

A dog-headed man walked through the doorway, a dripping haunch of something that might once have been an ape on his shoulder. He dropped it on the table.

A flight of sprites came in after him, but they bore as much resemblance to Lucy as the *cat-sídhe* did to Grendal. Her wings might be tattered, but theirs were greasy, batlike, and foul. They landed on the fresh meat and started ripping it with their teeth.

Grendal, outnumbered twenty to one, had retreated to the top of the mantel, his ears flat against his head, while Roisin helped herself to a bowl of whatever Ginny Greenteeth had brought to the party. She was eating it with a wooden spoon while she talked to the dog-headed man. Teagan watched the girl lick the spoon, then dip it back into the bowl. She was sure anything brought by the water goblin had to be disgusting, but Roisin seemed to be enjoying it. It looked like whatever was on the spoon *wiggled* as she lifted it to her mouth. She laughed and held the spoon out to the dog-headed man, who licked it clean with his long pink tongue.

The hall filled with creatures from her mother's books—the servants that Mab and Fear Doirich had brought with them on the storm clouds—so near Teagan could see every whisker and wart. Each one bowed to Roisin and Ginny as they came in as if they were royalty.

Aiden pinched her again.

Are goblins good fighters? he signed.

We're not goblins.

Finn shifted his weight, leaning back against them. She was closer to him than she had ever been before, close enough that she could feel his heartbeat. *There's been just one name pounding in that boy's heart ever since he first saw you, hasn't there?* How could her name be in the Mac Cumhaill's heart if she had even a drop of goblin blood? It couldn't.

Finn says goblins are evil, Aiden signed.

We need to be really, really still. No more finger talk.

But what if—

Teagan used the Look. She was getting better. Aiden gulped and stuck his hands in his pockets.

Finn must have misunderstood what Roisin had said. Teagan had seen goblins, and her mother was not like them. Roisin wasn't like them.

The toe spasmed in Teagan's pocket, and Ginny Greenteeth looked up as if she'd heard her name called. She left the table and prowled around the hall, then came back, stopping and sniffing the air just beneath them. A dark sprite flitted about her head. Ginny slapped it away and continued her search. The water goblin's eyes examined the floor, then lifted to the ivy curtain.

Teagan pulled the toe out. It was struggling desperately, fighting against the cloth it was wrapped in. Ginny's eyes met Teagan's through the leafy vines. Teagan lifted the toe and shook her head. The water goblin grimaced, then lowered her eyes and took a seat just beneath them.

Something fluttered in front of Teagan's face. The dark sprite had come to see what Ginny Greenteeth was looking at. Its eyes flashed black and red when it saw them. It opened its mouth, but before it could make a sound, Lucy hit it, moving like an air-to-air missile.

They tumbled above the heads of the crowd, legs and arms and wings tangled, dropping behind Roisin's couch. The only one who noticed was Grendal from his place on the mantel. Aiden squirmed, and Teagan thought he was going to try to go after Lucy, but Finn shifted his weight again, squishing Aiden in place.

Grendal left his perch and went to investigate, but Lucy appeared again before the *cat-sídhe* got there, cradling something in her arms.

She rose into the air, flew down the hall, and disappeared into a hiding place of her own, high up and out of sight. Grendal came out from behind the couch a few minutes later, jumped back onto the mantel, and started licking his paws and cleaning his whiskers.

Something new came through the door, and Teagan felt Finn's heartbeat quicken. It was Kyle, in the flesh.

He took a seat at the table and helped himself to a bowl of whatever Ginny Greenteeth had brought. There was a sense of foulness about him, as if something unclean had entered the room, and it changed the very air of the great hall.

Kyle glanced across the table at Ginny Greenteeth, and Teagan's flesh crawled. His eyes weren't pools of oil. They were amber, ringed with green.

Finn had made no mistake. *The goblin blood was strongest in Aileen. . . .* Cousin Kyle had her mother's eyes.

It felt like something nasty was spreading through Teagan's body, something filthy pumping in her veins. Suddenly lots of things made sense, things she hadn't wanted to think about.

Like Aiden's ability to make Finn do what he wanted when he sang.

Goblins steal your will away . . .

And her mom's uncanny skill at any game of strategy.

Mab, the Queen of the vile Sidhe, gifted in war and slaughter . . .

What would Mamieo have done if she had known the sort of creature she was tucking in with her own children? But she couldn't have known. Aileen hadn't known herself. Had the Green Man blessed Aileen on her way out of Mag Mell like Mamieo had thought? Or taken her memories and her second sight? Maybe that *was* his blessing. It allowed her to live a normal life. Until the shadows found her, and brought everything back.

Teagan's body felt so heavy that she was surprised Finn could hold her in place.

She squeezed her eyes shut and tried to mouth the words of the prayer her mother had taught her. The prayer Aileen had learned from Mamieo. Would the Travelers' Almighty even hear a goblin's prayer?

NINETEEN

TEAGAN woke to find a large wet spot on Finn's shoulder. She wished that she could say it was all tears, but she knew it wasn't. At least part of it was drool. She'd slept with her mouth open and slobbered all over him just as she did on her pillow. Female goblins probably all drooled when they slept.

She lifted her head, and a string of mucus stretched from her face to his shoulder. Great. Tears and drool and snot that had dripped from her nose as she cried silently for half of the night. Her head felt like it was full of cotton, and her eyes felt puffy and wouldn't quite focus.

Aiden's arm was laced through her own, his curly head slumped against Finn as well. Something glittered in his hair.

Her brother, the goblin. Somehow, she didn't think his teacher would be surprised by the news.

She took a deep breath. Nothing Roisin had told them changed the reason they had come to Mag Mell. She had to find her dad, and get both him and Aiden out of here alive, and she had no time to think about the rest of it just yet.

Teagan blinked hard and managed to focus her eyes. The glitters in Aiden's hair were bug wings Lucy had used to decorate her nest. How long would it take Finn to process everything Roisin had said?

"Teagan," Finn asked, "you awake?"

"Yes." He'd called her Teagan, not Tea. He was processing already. Teagan wiped her face with her hand. She didn't have anything to dry his shirt off with.

"Good. I need you to hold on to Aiden."

"Are you climbing down?" Teagan asked, grabbing Aiden's collar.

"Not . . . exactly." Finn toppled forward into the ivy. It broke his fall, twisting him around so that he landed on his back.

Teagan made sure Aiden was fully awake and helped him turn around and start down, then followed him. Finn was still lying flat on his back when they reached the ground, his lips drawn back in a grimace.

"Are you in pain?" Teagan asked.

"Yes," he squeaked.

She knelt beside him. "Don't move. Is it your back or neck?"

"Arms"—he flopped over—"and legs. Asleep." His face twisted in pain. "Go away. Don't just stand there looking at me."

"You sure you don't need help?" Teagan asked.

"I'm sure."

Roisin was sleeping on the couch where she'd curled up while the nightmare party raged around her. After the chaos of the night, the sound of one Fir Bolg body hitting the floor didn't stand a chance of waking her.

Teagan walked over to the table, trying not to look at Finn, who was doing an excellent imitation of Jim Carrey being attacked by a swarm of invisible bees. He stood up and staggered in a circle, waving his arms and making horrible faces.

236

"What's wrong with him?" Aiden asked.

"Circulation returning." Teagan hoped that was all it was. "It feels like pins and needles sticking you."

She scooped up a spoonful of slime from the bowl Ginny Greenteeth had brought. It was dead tadpoles in thick jelly. No wonder the frog folk hated Ginny. She made their children into pudding.

"I'm hungry," Aiden said.

"Not for that you aren't." Teagan took the super-size candy bar Abby had given her out of Finn's kit, broke it into two pieces, and gave Aiden the smaller one.

"I like this breakfast," Aiden said, sucking up the chocolate spit that started to leak out of his mouth.

Finn managed to make it to the table, walking as if he were only a little drunk. Teagan handed him the other half of the candy bar.

"Don't you want any?" Finn glanced at her and glanced quickly away. He was processing, all right.

"No." Teagan motioned toward the bowl on the table, then realized he couldn't see the motion if he wasn't looking at her. "I lost my appetite when I saw the tadpole pudding."

Lucy appeared, flying loop-the-loops above them, a bag made of leaves in her arms. She pretended to slide down a sunbeam, landing in front of Aiden. When her feet were on the table, she opened the bag and pulled out the head of the dark sprite, presenting it to Aiden with a flourish and a bow.

"Good girl!" Aiden said. "Here." He broke off a piece of chocolate and held it out to her. The sprite nibbled it cautiously. Her eyes went kaleidoscopic and she tossed the severed head aside, grabbed the chocolate, and started stuffing it in her mouth.

Teagan leaned closer to examine the dead sprite's head, fascinated and disgusted at the same time. The lights in its eyes had gone dark, like the simple eyes in the head of a cicada do when it dies. She reached for it, but before she could touch the thing, Finn flicked it as if it were a finger football. It arced into the ivy.

"Hey, that was mine!" Aiden said.

Lucy dropped her chocolate and pulled her tiny knife.

"If you were any bigger, bug"—Finn shook his finger at her—"you'd be scary. You threaten me with that sticker, and I'll squish you."

"Let Lucy alone." Aiden pushed Finn's finger away. "That other sprite was going to tell the monsters where we were. She saved us."

Aiden glared at Finn, his hands curled into fists and every line of his body a challenge to fight, like a Chihuahua daring a Great Dane to make one false move.

"Aiden!" Teagan put her hand on his shoulder. He ignored her, completely focused on Finn.

They studied each other for a moment, then Finn nodded. Aiden relaxed, as if some hugely important thing had been decided between them.

"I apologize, bug," Finn told the sprite. "You can have a piece of my chocolate, too." Lucy turned her back on him. She hadn't forgiven him, even if Aiden had.

"We'll find Dad today," Aiden said. "So let's hurry. I have show-and-tell at school on Monday, and I want to take Lucy."

"This is a big place, boyo," Finn said. "A whole world."

"Mag Mell's helping me," Aiden said confidently. "We just had to come visit Aunt Roisin first."

Grendal jumped up onto the table and narrowed his eyes at the sight of the sprite sitting cross-legged in the sunbeam, licking her fingers. He muttered something Teagan was sure was a curse, then stalked over to the bowl of tadpole pudding and started lapping it up.

"Are we going to say goodbye to Aunt Roisin?" Aiden asked.

"Before we leave," Teagan said.

"First, clean socks." Finn tossed Teagan a pair of neatly folded old-lady socks for her and one for Aiden. "We should have done this yesterday."

"Our shoes were still wet, so it wouldn't have mattered," Teagan said.

"It'll matter today. We'll raise blisters walking in crusty socks."

Teagan kicked off her shoes and started to pull her socks down. They were crusty, all right—hardened with dried mud.

"Roll the dirty ones," Finn said. "It'll help keep the mud from messing up my kit. I'm going to look around outside."

Aiden pulled his shoe off, and Teagan nearly gagged. Something foul had started to grow between his toes, fed by the damp and warmth of his feet. It smelled like a stinky cheese factory.

"When was the last time you changed your socks?"

"The last time you made me," Aiden said.

"Which was?"

"Last week. I didn't mean to get stinky, Tea. I couldn't *find* any clean socks."

"It's all right." *When was the last time she had checked his laundry hamper?* "We'll just wash your feet off, and you can dry them with your shirt."

That would give her time to work out what to say to Finn.

Gee, Finn, sorry you've been risking your life for a couple of goblin spawn . . .

She finished rinsing Aiden's feet off with her bottled water and helped him dry them before she gave him his fresh socks.

"That's it," Teagan said. "We'll need some more water, and we've got to get going." She walked over and sat down on the corner of the couch where Roisin was curled up, a slight frown on her face. She'd held herself like a queen as she sat at the head of the table the night before, mouth firm and head high, but the hand that hung off the edge of the couch, palm up, fingers curled, was the hand of a child.

Teagan pressed her lips together. Engaged at fifteen. Was that normal in this crazy place? Roisin needed one of Abby's lectures about men.

"Roisin." Teagan touched the girl's shoulder. Roisin sat up and looked around wildly.

"It's all right," Teagan said. "It's just me. Do you have water?" Teagan held up her almost-empty water bottle and pretended to drink.

Roisin nodded, and led her to a basin carved into a tree. Water filled it as if it were a spring, spilling over the rim and trickling down to sink into the dirt of the floor.

Roisin took a wooden dipper from the wall, filled it, and held it out to Teagan.

It was wonderful, though not cold. Finn came back in while Teagan was filling the water bottles.

"That's good thinking," Finn said.

Roisin looked from Finn to the bottles, then grabbed Teagan's arm and started babbling.

"She's figured out we're leaving," Finn said. "And she's afraid of being left here. She wants us to wait here for Thomas. She says it's safe here."

"Dad's not safe," Teagan said. "We have to go find him." Finn translated, and Roisin's eyes welled with tears. She shook her head.

"Why doesn't she come with us?" Aiden asked. "We'll take care of her."

"She's afraid," Finn said. "She's lived here a long time, boyo. Maybe she's seen enough to take the courage out of her."

"Do you know the way to Fear Doirich's house . . . or castle . . . or whatever he lives in?" Teagan asked.

Roisin covered her ears and shook her head.

Finn repeated Teagan's question, but Roisin just shook her head harder and started to cry in earnest.

"I'm sorry," Teagan said. "We really have to go. Aiden, you try to cheer her up, okay? I need to talk to Finn."

"We need to talk about something?" Finn followed her back to the table.

"Yes." Teagan glanced at Aiden. "Things have changed. You don't have to go any farther with us. I think you should stay here with Roisin."

"Stay here?"

Teagan nodded. "My mom's promise was to Roisin, and it will make a way for her to get out, because Mom was Highborn Sídhe, right? And their promises have power. If you are with her, you can get out, too. Go back to Mamieo."

"And leave you and your baby brother to face Fear Doirich alone? What kind of a man do you think I am?"

"The Mac Cumhaill," Teagan said flatly. "Born enemy of goblin-kind. You know Roisin was telling the truth about who we are."

"I knew it the moment she spoke the words," Finn said. "But I've a promise to keep."

That's right. He'd promised Aiden that he wouldn't let Fear Doirich keep him . . . and that they'd leave together. *Finn was trapped by a promise to her brother . . . who just happened to be a Highborn goblin like their mom. He had even less choice than he'd had before.* Teagan felt a great hollowness starting to grow inside her. Finn was trapped, bound tight by goblin webs and wiles.

"You have to do this, don't you?" she said softly. "Is there any way we can release you?"

Finn glared at her, then shook his head. "Aiden! Come on. Time to go get your da." He stalked toward the doorway.

Roisin followed them to the door, and stood weeping in the arch as they walked away.

"*Slán leat,*" she called, waving.

"*Slán agat,*" Finn called back.

"What does that mean?" Aiden asked.

"'Goodbye,'" Finn said. "Goodbye from the one who stays, good-bye from the one who leaves."

Aiden started singing "I Got a Name." His voice wasn't strong, but it was much better than it had been the day before. The trees and bushes shifted, and the path appeared. Mag Mell seemed as happy this morning as she had been the day before, when Aiden first arrived with his songs.

Bright sprites and spriggans darted through the trees, warned off by Lucy's hisses or knife if they came too close to her boy. When she wasn't busy chasing away other sprites, she danced in the air above Aiden as he sang, a fan at her own private concert.

Finn was grimly silent, lost in his own thoughts or watching the woods.

Teagan tried to focus on Aiden rather than trying to figure out what was going on in Finn's head and heart.

"You don't need to sing for a bit," she said when Aiden's voice started to rasp. "You can start again if the path fades."

It not only didn't fade, but Mag Mell led them through more berry bushes, where they ate their fill. Lucy chased a beetle down for her own brunch, then played with Aiden, catching flowers he tossed into the air.

They'd walked through the morning when the path abruptly doubled back on itself and Teagan lost all sense of direction. Their water bottles were almost empty again, and they hadn't seen a spring for hours. Teagan wasn't sure they could trust any water they did find in this place.

The landscape had become bleak. There were many dying trees and very little undergrowth, as if there was something poisonous in the soil. Fungus and mold grew from bark-bare limbs and trunks in an unhealthy bloom. There were no creatures at all that Teagan could see.

Lucy settled into Aiden's hair and worked on her weaving, peeking out now and then and chirping unhappily. The still woods seemed to suck up the sounds, as if they were absorbed into the slime molds and curtains of fungus.

Teagan caught a movement from the corner of her eye, but when she turned to look, there was nothing but the pale, bare trunks of dying trees. When she looked at the trail ahead of her, she saw the movement again. This time she didn't turn her head but tried to process what she was seeing in her peripheral vision.

Shadow men. Shadow men who were hardly more than mist were pulling themselves up out of the moldy ground, then settling into the darkness under the trees. Teagan glanced at Finn. He nodded. He'd seen the dark mists rising, too.

"Aiden." Teagan cleared her throat. "I think it's time to sing again."

"No," Aiden said. "I don't want to sing. This place is too sad."

"I know." Teagan took Aiden's hand. "But I want you to close your eyes and sing Mamieo's song anyway."

"You mean there are monsters here?" Aiden looked around, and Teagan saw him stiffen.

"It's *them*," he whispered.

"You can send them away." Teagan tried to sound positive. "Sing the song Mamieo taught you." The shadow men were growing more solid, more visible.

Aiden started to hum, and they turned their blank faces toward him.

A tall shadow, closer than the rest, leaned over Aiden. Teagan pulled her brother back as it reached out. The shadow spread its long fingers and pressed its hand against her face. It felt like feathers touching her, brushing *through* her skin and into her mind, starting to *twist*. Vomit rose in her throat. The light started to fade . . . and then Aiden's voice cut through the darkness.

> "Atomriug indiu
> niurt tríun
> togairm Tríndóite."

The light came rushing back, and Teagan swallowed down the bile. The shadow man slunk back, dissolving, drifting over to join the other dark vapors in the deeper shadows.

Lichens spread across bare rock as Aiden sang, their tiny flowers the only color in the landscape. Toadstools sprang up around the path as he walked, adding their red caps to the lichens' celebration. Even here, Mag Mell was trying to rejoice when Aiden sang.

> "... *cretim treodatad*
> *foísitin oendatad*
> *i nDúilemon dáil* ..."

Suddenly, the lichen bloom rusted, and the toadstools melted into rot. Life was losing whatever battle it fought here. A wail of terrible grief filled the air around them.

"What was *that?*" Aiden whispered. Shadows that had been drifting away turned toward them again.

"Sing," Teagan said. "You have to keep singing, Aiden." The shadow men were moving faster now.

Aiden squeaked, then put his hands over his eyes. "Monsters can't see me, monsters can't see me," he chanted, then started to sing again.

"It's working, boyo," Finn said, putting his hand on Aiden's shoulder and guiding him down the path. "You're doing it. Keep walking."

The weeping continued around them, and the shadows lined the path, but none reached out to touch them.

Aiden sang them through the dead forest, until the shadow men sank back into the ground, but the sobbing increased as

Aiden's last note faded. He took his hands off his eyes and spun around.

"Who's crying?" he shouted. "I wasn't singing a sad song!"

"It's Mag Mell herself," Finn said. "Weeping for her children."

"It's making my heart hurt."

"Mine, too," Finn said. "But you've got to keep singing, boyo. You're the only one who can get us through."

"I know," Aiden said wearily.

Mag Mell's sobs turned to sighs as the trees ended at the foot of a tall hill. The ruins of a castle sat atop it like a crumbling crown.

"I can't sing anymore," Aiden said. "My voice is too dry."

"That's okay," Teagan said. "You did a good job."

"I know," Aiden said, clearly feeling more cocky. "I can beat any bad guy here. That's how awesome I am."

They climbed up to the base of the old castle wall.

"Listen!" Teagan said. It was her dad's voice. He was telling a story, as if he had a room full of preschoolers listening to him.

They ran, following the voice until they found an opening where a gate had rotted away. They scrambled through into what had once been a garden.

"Dad!" Aiden shouted.

Mr. Wylltson was sitting on a rock. His eyes were red, and his lips were dry and cracked. Aiden threw his arms around his father's neck, but Mr. Wylltson didn't seem to see or hear him.

"Dad?" Aiden shook him, but Mr. Wylltson just went on telling his story, to nobody at all.

TWENTY

W HAT'S wrong with him, Tea?" Aiden asked.

"I don't know." Teagan waved her hand in front of her father's face. He didn't respond. His clothes were filthy, but she couldn't see any blood or signs of injury . . . at least, no physical injury.

She took his hand. He let her lift it, offering no resistance at all. His skin was papery and dry. She pinched up a fold on the back of his hand. It stood up in a ridge even after she had let go.

"He's dehydrated, for one thing."

"What do we do?" Aiden asked.

Teagan rubbed her temples. She had no idea. She had no idea how to fight spells or magic. . . .

"Try singing, Aiden."

Aiden took the hand Teagan had been holding and sang very softly, first the lullabies that his father had sung to him as a baby, and then the songs that Mag Mell loved. Mr. Wylltson never even shifted his eyes toward Aiden. He just spilled his story words into the air.

Teagan leaned down. "DAD!" she shouted. "It's time to go home!" His face turned ever so slightly toward her.

"*Tyger,*" he whispered.

"Dad?"

His eyes focused on . . . no, not on her. He wasn't looking *at* her, he was looking *into* her. His voice grew stronger.

> *"Tyger! Tyger! burning bright,*
> *In the forests of the night,*
> *What immortal hand or eye*
> *Could frame thy fearful symmetry?"*

"I don't like that one, Dad!" Aiden covered his ears. "It's about a scary thing!" Mr. Wylltson never looked away from Teagan.

> *"In what distant deeps or skies*
> *Burnt the fire in thine eyes?*
> *On what wings dare he aspire?*
> *What the hand dare seize the fire?"*

It was mesmerizing, as if the words were resonating in the marrow of her bones. Teagan forced herself to breathe, to move away from his gaze. His words trailed off, then wandered into nonsense poems and nursery rhymes.

"He's warning us." Finn looked around the barren garden.

"I . . . I'm not sure. Maybe." She wasn't sure what had just happened, but she knew she didn't have time to figure it out right now. She'd sort it out when everyone was safe. "We need to get some water into him. Does anybody have any left?"

Finn had a little. He tipped Mr. Wylltson's head back while Teagan poured the water in, a trickle at a time. Mr. Wylltson made a gargling sound as the water going down met the words coming up, but he swallowed.

"He needs more than that," Finn said.

"There's good water through that gate."

Teagan spun, looking for the speaker. It was a raven chained in a thorn tree. Its wings were stretched wide.

"I said"—the raven stopped, beak open to pant, then went on—"there's water through that gate. But take it for yourselves and leave this place. It would be kinder to let your father die." The raven's head drooped. "Please, God, let us both die soon."

"It's a shape shifter," Finn said, walking closer to the thorn tree. "I've heard of shifting into dogs, elk, wolves, or something in between, but a ratty black bird? Sucks to be you, my man."

"I know," the raven gasped.

"It's hurt." Teagan moved close enough to see that the thorns were not just holding the raven in place—they stabbed through its feathers, clearly piercing the flesh beneath. A fly buzzed around one of the sticky wounds, and Teagan brushed it away.

"What's wrong with my dad? Why would it be kinder to let him die?"

"Fear Doirich tore a hole in him. He is emptying your father out, stealing his soul, everything he holds dear, one word at a time. I'm afraid he will last a few days longer." The raven paused, panting again. "But I am almost done. Almost done."

"You need water, too, don't you?" Teagan asked.

"I drink when it rains," the raven said.

Finn kicked at the dusty soil. "Been a while, then, hasn't it?"

"Yes," the bird said simply.

"The water's through that gate, then?" Finn studied the garden again. Aiden was holding his father's hand, and aside from Mr. Wylltson's words, everything was still. "Is it far?"

"Not far. There's a spring-fed fountain in the old courtyard." The raven's head flopped down, and its beady eyes closed.

"We've got to fill our water bottles anyway," Finn said to Teagan. "Don't go anywhere until I get back."

He gathered up the bottles while Teagan worked her way between the thorny branches until she could reach the raven. It was still breathing, even if its head did flop limply to one side.

The golden chain looked thinner than a light necklace. She took it in both hands, trying not to move the bird, and pulled. The raven's head shot up, and it gasped in pain.

"Please," it said. "Please, no. I'm the only one who can break it."

Teagan stepped back. "If you can break the chain, why don't you?"

"It's a promise," the raven said. "Fear pulled it out of my body link by link, and wrapped it around me so that I would feel the pain of it every day. The longest thorn bites my heart now. I can feel its tooth with every beat, but the promise is unbroken. At last, at last it is finished." The raven's body spasmed as it gasped for air again, then it turned a beady eye to Teagan.

"Your father spoke of your mother at first, of how he loved her, how she died. Fear Doirich liked that. He sat on that stone bench and listened, licking up the words, loving the pain. But your father figured it out. He stopped spilling his life and started telling stories. When those are done, when they run out, his memories will pour out. And when the last one leaves . . . he will be nothing."

"*Tea.*" The fear in Aiden's voice made Teagan look up.

"God help us," the raven said. "It's him."

A man was walking toward her across the garden. He looked like a wizard, a prince, a movie star. A god. He was the most beautiful creature Teagan had ever seen, every movement, every feature perfect, and perfectly cruel. He had a scepter in his hand with a golden globe on the end that matched the thin golden circlet on his brow.

Kyle was beside him. He tossed back his hair and flashed his Abercrombie smile.

"Welcome to the nightmare, little cousin," Kyle said. "Where's your filthy Fir Bolg boyfriend?"

Teagan resisted the urge to glance toward the arch where Finn had gone. Fear Doirich stopped in front of her, taking his time as he looked her up and down.

"Stop looking at my sister like that, bad guy." Aiden had run over to stand beside Teagan. "And let my dad go."

Fear Doirich ignored Aiden. He stepped closer and ran his fingertips down Teagan's cheek. There was no life in his hand, no warmth. It was like being caressed by death.

"I know you, Aileen's child." His chill breath smelled of the grave, as if he had been feasting on rotted flesh. "I called you here."

Kyle was foul, but this was something different. This was the essence of the shadow men multiplied, made flesh. This was evil.

"You didn't call me anywhere." Teagan hoped she didn't sound as frightened as she felt. "I came after my father, and I'm taking him home."

She started to pull Aiden toward her father, away from the goblin god.

Fear Doirich sang a single note. The air around her vibrated, and she felt something whip around her ankles. Roots had sprung from the ground, lacing themselves around her feet. She struggled to take another step, but couldn't.

"I called you here to take Roisin's place." Fear Doirich spread his arms. "Amergin's blood, and it's all mine. I will kill Roisin the moment she steps out of Yggdrasil's hands, Thomas. I have all I want right here."

"No!" the raven rasped.

Fear Doirich slashed with his golden scepter, ripping the raven from the thorn tree. It flopped like a wounded pigeon beneath the bush, tangled in its still-unbroken chains.

"Stop it!" Aiden shouted. "Leave that bird alone!" Kyle caught Aiden's arm and twisted it behind him.

Fear Doirich examined the smear of blood and single black feather stuck to the globe of his scepter.

"I said, stop it!" Aiden bellowed. Kyle jerked him up off the ground, but Aiden kicked at him and started to sing "Pádraig's Shield." Kyle froze. Ginny Greenteeth had clearly lied about whether or not Aiden's song would work on the Sídhe. Kyle was as stiff as a mannequin.

Aiden twisted away from him and dropped to the ground. The roots holding Teagan's feet writhed.

"Keep singing, Aiden." One foot was almost free. "Keep singing!"

Fear Doirich laughed. He opened his mouth and sucked in Aiden's words as if he were ripping them from the boy's throat, then roared them out again, twisted and discordant. Mag Mell screamed in agony, and the roots tightened around Teagan's ankle. Kyle reached for Aiden again.

"He's mine," Fear Doirich said, and Kyle backed away. "I am your god, goblin child." The Dark Man stepped toward Aiden. "You will never be strong enough to play my game. I know the Song of Creation. I am your god, and this is my will: I'm going to kill you, and feed you to the dirt of Mag Mell. But you already know that. You heard my song when you were underwater, remember? I was singing it just for you."

Teagan felt goose bumps rise on her arms. Fear Doirich *had* known they were in Mag Mell. All her word games with Ginny Greenteeth had been wasted.

"I let you hear it because I wanted you to know. I wanted you to be afraid for as long as possible before I killed you." He licked his lips. "I like it when little things are afraid. When they cry. I knew when your mother died, Aiden. Did you know that? I'm the one who sent the shadows hunting her. Hunting for all those years."

"I hate you," Aiden said.

"Good." Fear smiled. "Before this creation, your ancestors hated and feared me so much that they made a covenant with me to save their own pitiful lives. They swore by the blood of their own children split open before me that goblinkind would serve me forever."

"I don't believe you," Teagan said. "How could any sane creature make a covenant like that?"

"It was easy," Fear Doirich said. "I made it so easy for them." At least he wasn't looking at Aiden anymore. "I will make it easy for you, Teagan." He stepped closer to her.

"Dad!" Aiden called.

"He can't hear you," Kyle said. "The man thinks he's sitting in his nice, safe library telling stories to kiddies."

"Get away from us, bad guy!" Aiden spat at Fear Doirich. "Go n-ithe an cats thú is go n-ithe an diabhal an cats."

The Dark Man laughed. "Any cat that could eat me would choke brother Satan on the way down. Watch, Teagan." His voice was eager. "I want you to *see*."

He lifted his scepter. Teagan knew what he was going to do, as if he had spoken pictures right into her mind; pictures of blood in Aiden's curls, and white bone shards.

"Run, Aiden!" she shouted, straining to move her feet, to reach anything she could throw at Fear. "Run!" She saw a flash of motion as Finn came through the archway, but he was too far away to stop Fear.

The scepter rose and had started to fall when Lucy launched herself out of Aiden's hair, a streak of hissing rage. Fear Doirich twisted, swatting the sprite like she was a baseball, sending her tumbling into the thornbush.

Aiden screamed as the Dark Man swung again, but this time Finn was between them. He caught the golden ball in his left hand.

"You'll not be touching Aiden," Finn said. "Nor Teagan, either." Finn's hand sizzled, and the smell of scorched flesh filled the air.

"The Mac Cumhaill himself!" The Dark Man tipped his head. "Come to me at last. All locked up in Mag Mell as I have been, I was afraid I would never have any visitors."

"Mmmmm-mmm." Kyle took a deep breath of burned-flesh smell. "Burned hero. Smells goooood."

Finn was shaking, but he didn't let go of the golden ball.

"Do you know who this girl is, Mac Cumhaill?" Fear asked. "She's a goblin. Born to be your enemy and my chattel. Her brother is mine; her people are mine. I am going to do anything I want with them. Bend them, break them, use them. Kill them for pleasure when I am done."

"Get out of here, Tea," Finn said through clenched teeth. "Take Aiden and get out of here."

"Can't," Teagan said. "I'm tied down."

"Your little goblin girl's grown *attached* to Mag Mell," Kyle said, putting his arm around Teagan's shoulders.

"Leave Tea alone!" Aiden shouted. "Leave everybody alone!" He put his hands over his eyes and started belting out "Pádraig's Shield" again.

Kyle froze, his arm still around Teagan. Fear Doirich opened his mouth, sucking Aiden's voice in.

"Give up," he said after he'd swallowed Aiden's last word. "None of you are going anywhere."

"Crap," Finn said, and hit him.

FEAR Doirich's head snapped back, and Finn hit him
again.

The roots that held Teagan's feet in place twisted, and she
wrenched one foot free, leaning away from Kyle's frozen form.

*You have to think your way through things, even in the midst of it. Use
your brain, girl.* She could almost hear her mother's voice. There had
to be something she could do.

Fear Doirich dropped his scepter and twisted away from Finn,
singing as he turned. Roots exploded out of the ground around
them, showering them with dirt and reaching for Finn, but the
Dark Man's words were garbled by blood and smashed lips. Some of
the roots whipped at Finn, while others seemed to dance in time to
Aiden's song.

Fear's magic was in his mouth. Teagan pulled her other foot free as
the roots holding her started to dance.

"Keep singing, Aiden! You're doing it!" She scrambled to Finn's
bag and ripped it open, throwing things aside until she found his
duct tape and a rolled-up sock.

"Take him down, Finn," she shouted. "I need him on the
ground."

Finn lunged for Fear Doirich, knocking him to the ground and throwing himself on top of him. Fear turned his head and bayed like an animal. The sound made Teagan's hair stand on end. He opened his mouth to bay again, and Teagan shoved the sock in it. He spat it out while she was ripping off a piece of duct tape, then clamped his lips shut, using his tongue to form words behind his teeth like a ventriloquist. The rocks around them started to melt and transform into troll-like creatures.

"Shut him up," Finn said as the rock wall behind him stood up.

"I'm working on it." Teagan leaned hard on Fear's temple with her elbow to keep his head still, and pinched his nose shut. He gasped, and she stuffed the sock in his mouth and slapped the tape across his lips. The rock creatures froze.

Fear was fighting desperately now, but Finn managed to wrench his arms behind him so Teagan could tape his wrists together. Teagan took a good kick to the head before she managed to get his ankles taped together. Fear wiggled like an angry worm.

"You won't be messing with Teagan," Finn told him. "I won't have it, god or no."

"*You* won't have it?" Teagan nudged the worm with her toe. "I'm the one who shut him up."

"All by yourself," Finn said. "It was impressive. No help from me or the boyo."

Teagan blushed. "I mean—"

"Think nothing of it," Finn said. "I make a habit of rescuing ladies. Saving purses, things like that. It's part of the job."

"Help." Aiden gasped between the words of his song. His voice sounded like he'd had too much whiskey—husky and rough—but his words were still holding Kyle frozen in place.

Teagan grabbed the tape and scrambled to where the *sídhe* stood. She was worried that she wouldn't be able to move Kyle, but his arms twisted back like one of Aiden's action figures. She taped his wrists. Finn kicked his ankles together, and held him upright while Teagan taped them.

"Good job, boyo," Finn said as Aiden stopped singing. Kyle toppled like a tree, landing face-first beside Fear Doirich's foot.

"Hold his head." Teagan tore off a small piece of tape.

"What are you up to?" Finn asked as Teagan pried one of Kyle's eyes open.

"He's a bilocate." Teagan taped his eyelashes to his eyebrow, holding the eye open. "Mamieo said that the flesh part of him was 'sleeping in Mag Mell' when his spirit went walking. I don't want him dozing off so that he can be waiting for us when we get out of here."

"You think taping his eyes open will work?"

"I have no idea." Teagan taped the other eyelid up. "But it's worth a try. Are you all right, Aiden?"

Aiden put his hand to his throat. "It hurt when he took the words out. It hurt a lot. I don't want to sing anymore."

Kyle twisted his head sideways and spat dirt. He turned his amber eyes, pulled wide open and goggly, on Teagan.

"What's wrong with you, cousin? All you had to do was give him what he wanted."

"And let him kill my father, my brother, and Finn."

"You will learn to enjoy killing." He licked his lips. "It's good, Teagan. *Useful.*"

Had Kyle run with the pack, blood smeared on his chest and face?

"I don't think so," Teagan said.

"I know the world where you were born," Kyle said. "I walk there. That world craves the violence we were born to, you and me. It's everywhere in their imaginings and their dreams. They want to be us."

"Not the whole world," Teagan said. "Not me."

Kyle laughed. "Especially you. You were born to serve Fear Doirich. Don't you understand the power in a Highborn's words? That power reaches even past death. Your mother's mother's mother bound you to the Dark Man with her words, her will, and the sacrifice of her firstborn child. Fear Doirich is your god. If you will bow to him now—"

"I won't," Teagan said. "I'll never live the way you do."

"Then you won't live at all," Kyle said flatly. "Fear will send the shadows and the Sídhe to hunt you through the worlds. He holds the power of life and death over goblinkind."

Teagan ripped off another piece of tape and slapped it over Kyle's mouth. They'd better not meet anyone else she wanted to shut up. The roll was almost empty.

"Are we going to kill them now?" Aiden asked.

Finn looked uncomfortable. "I'm not sure I could do the deed with them taped up."

"They're really bad guys," Aiden said. "We should smash them with rocks like they were going to smash me."

Blood in Aiden's curls, and white bone shards. The image made Teagan sick all over again.

"No," she said. "We're just going to leave them."

"But Kyle said they'd come after us."

"We'll worry about that later, okay? Right now we need to get Dad home."

Aiden walked over and squatted in front of Fear Doirich. He studied the Dark Man.

"You're a stinking EI," Aiden said. "And you don't even sing good."

"EI?" Finn asked.

"Elvis Impersonator," Teagan said. "It's an Aiden thing."

Aiden stood up and pointed. "Are you going to tape him up, too, Tea?"

There was a Highborn goblin on his knees where the raven had fallen. He was as handsome as Kyle, in a beat-poet kind of way. He had short, dark dreads, and a soul patch on his chin. His clothes were rags, and his side was bloody from the thorn that had almost pierced his heart. The golden chain was disappearing into his body, melting into his flesh.

"You'd be Roisin's Thomas, then," Finn said.

"Hellhounds," Thomas rasped. He sounded worse than Aiden. "Fear . . . called the hellhounds. You've got to run. Save . . . Roisin."

"What's a hellhound?" Teagan asked. "Do you mean a dog-headed man?"

"Worse . . . devourers . . . soul eaters. They'll follow forever once they scent you. Even into your world . . . I . . ." Thomas pitched forward onto his face.

"Right," Finn said. He walked over to the goblin and turned him over. "He's alive."

"What are you doing?" Teagan asked.

"Bringing him along." He fumbled, trying to lift Thomas with one hand. "You think Roisin will leave without this pathetic bird? Mind your father, Tea. We've got to move fast."

"Let me see your hand first," Teagan said.

Finn leaned Thomas over his knee and held out his right hand. "It's working just fine. Skinned knuckles is all. See?"

"Your *other* hand," Teagan said.

Finn grimaced as he held it out. Teagan gently uncurled his fingers. His whole palm was burned, and blisters were filling with pus.

"We don't have time for this," Finn insisted. "I don't like the sound of these hellhounds. We need to be moving."

"You won't like not being able to use this hand again, either," Teagan said. "I've got to put antibiotic on it to keep it from hardening and scarring. You need to see a doctor."

She found the antibiotic on the ground where she'd dropped it when she was rooting through the kit for socks. Finn grimaced as she smeared the greasy compound on his palm. She padded the palm with gauze and held it in place with the last of the duct tape.

"Now will you help me get this fellow on my back?" he said when she was done. "It's hard to do one-handed."

They sat Thomas up. Finn squatted down in front of him, and Teagan draped the goblin's arms over his shoulders. He took Thomas's arm with his good hand, and Teagan heaved from behind as he stood up. Finn staggered a little before he caught his balance. Thomas was alive enough to mumble something about Roisin.

"You won't be able run with that thing on your back," Teagan said.

"Some of us won't be running." Finn looked toward her father. "I told you the man was warning us with the poem. We should have listened."

Mr. Wylltson was standing. He wasn't telling stories anymore.

"Tea," he said when she walked up, "what are you doing here?"

She was relieved he didn't start with the Blake again. But he'd forgotten it, hadn't he? It had been erased from his mind, like everything else that had come out of his mouth.

"He still thinks he's at work," Aiden whispered.

"Dad." Teagan took his hand. "It's time to go home."

"Five o'clock already?" Mr. Wylltson glanced at an imaginary clock on an imaginary library wall, and a smile spread across his face. "Your mother will be waiting! For some reason I missed her like crazy today."

"Mom's d—" Aiden started, but Teagan shushed him. All of those memories were gone, spilled out to entertain the Dark Man. All of the pain of knowing she was dead would come flooding back, all of the grief, new and fresh when he heard it again. It had almost killed him the first time.

He's forgotten, Teagan signed. *We'll tell him later. First we have to get him home.*

Mr. Wylltson put his hand to his head. "I know I'm forgetting something here . . ." His words drifted off, and the dazed look returned to his eyes.

"You'll be better," Teagan said. "Just as soon as we get you home."

"What about Lucy?" Aiden looked around. "Where's Lucy?" He ran back across the garden, jumped over Fear Doirich, and scrambled under the thornbush. He crawled out with the sprite cradled in his hand. "Is she dead, Tea?"

The sprite was definitely broken. Liquid leaked from a crack in her hard skin. If she was anything like an insect, that was bad. Insects needed their hydraulic systems working if they were going to move. But the lights in the eyes of the sprite Lucy had killed had gone out. Lucy's still had a flicker of purple and gold deep inside.

"Is she dead?" Aiden asked again.

"I don't think so." Teagan emptied the contents of the Band-Aid box and put the sprite inside with a little bit of gauze to keep her from rattling around. "But I don't have the things I need to fix her here. I don't even know if I can fix her."

"Don't worry, Lucy," Aiden told the sprite. "Teagan's just saying that. She will fix you when we get home."

Teagan shut the box and put it in Finn's bag, then slung the strap over her shoulder. "Let's go."

She looked back once before they went through the gate. Fear Doirich had his face turned toward them, the broad smile of duct tape plastered across it. He was too far away for her to see his eyes, but she could feel them.

She scooted past Finn and his piggyback cargo, and walked behind Aiden and her father along the path beside the broken wall. When they started down the hill, the path broadened and she took her father's other hand. He moved as if he were walking in his sleep, lifting his feet just enough to shuffle forward.

The dead forest stretched out before them. The path through it hadn't disappeared, but Teagan could already see the dark mists rising.

A IDEN," Teagan said, "which way to Yggdrasil's hands?"

"That way." Aiden pointed at the path into the dead woods. "Through the bad guys."

"You're going to have to sing," Finn said.

"I know," Aiden whispered. "The shadows are coming."

"We'll be right here with you," Teagan said.

"But you can't stop them." The corners of Aiden's mouth turned down. "They're coming." He took a deep breath. "If we get through the bad guys, and out of Mag Mell, you will find the things you need to fix Lucy, right?"

"I'll do my best," Teagan said.

"Sometimes your best isn't good enough."

"That's true," Teagan admitted.

Aiden studied the dead trees below. "If I do my best, and it isn't good enough, are you going to leave me?"

"Never, boyo," Finn said. "We'll be right with you, no matter what."

"Finn!" Mr. Wylltson's voice made them all jump. "What are you doing here? Aileen will be delighted. Who's your friend?"

"His name is Thomas, sir," Finn said.

Mr. Wylltson bent over to study Thomas's upside-down face. "Nice to meet you," he said, and then, in a stage whisper, "Is he all right?"

"Dad?" Teagan asked. "Do you know where we are?"

Mr. Wylltson looked around. "I never liked the South Side of Chicago," he said, "though your mother is fond of it."

"Let's go home." Aiden tugged on his hand, pulling him down the hill.

"Wait until we are right at the trees before you start," Teagan said. "That way you won't have to sing as long."

The black fog grew thicker as they walked toward it, swirling into man shapes and then melting, twirling, and forming again. Aiden clung to his father's hand, but Mr. Wylltson didn't seem to see the dead trees or the shadow men who stood like a solid wall before them, hiding the trail. They had almost reached the wall when Aiden started his song, but his voice was barely a whisper. Holes appeared in some of the shadows, as if cannonballs of air had been shot through them, but they didn't step back or drift away. They stood, waiting.

"You shouldn't be singing with a sore throat, son," Mr. Wylltson said. He felt Aiden's forehead. "I think you've got a fever, too. Let's take you home and see what Mom says."

Aiden looked at Teagan, tears welling in his eyes. She shook her head. She couldn't have her dad falling apart as he'd done when their mother had died. Not now.

"I have to sing, Da," Aiden whispered. "I have to."

"Why?" Mr. Wylltson folded his arms.

"Because . . ." He glanced at Teagan, then blurted it out anyway. "The monsters will get us if I don't."

"There are no monsters here," Mr. Wylltson said. "It's just an . . . unpleasant neighborhood. There is nothing here that will hurt you, son."

The tears splashed down Aiden's cheeks. Mr. Wylltson knelt in front of him and wiped them away.

"You see monsters?" His voice was gentle.

Aiden nodded. "Lots of monsters."

Mr. Wylltson looked around, clearly not seeing anything frightening at all. "All right. We know how to deal with monsters, don't we?" He swung Aiden up onto his shoulders.

> "'Tis of a famous highwayman
> A story I will tell . . ."

Mr. Wylltson's tenor swelled, filling the world around them.

> "His name was Aiden Wylltson,
> And in Ireland he did dwell . . ."

"Will you look at that!" Finn whispered.

The shadows were shrinking back, sinking into the ground. Teagan fell into step beside Finn, and they followed Mr. Wylltson and Aiden down the wide path that had been cleared by his song.

"But . . . Dad's no goblin," Teagan said.

"Your ma said your da was descended from the wizard Merlin, didn't she?"

"Myrddin Wyllt," Teagan corrected automatically. "He was nothing but a Welsh . . . bard . . ."

"And your da's nothing but a singing librarian." Finn shifted the weight of Thomas on his shoulder. "'A lover, not a fighter.' I heard the man say it himself. A lover of books and poetry, like Merlin, isn't he? That's Milesian blood we're seeing."

"Welsh," Teagan said.

"It doesn't matter, does it, then? It's from your da that Aiden gets his gift, not from your *máthair* at all!"

Mag Mell didn't wind and twist when Mr. Wylltson sang. The path she created was wide, beautiful, and surprisingly short. They hadn't completely passed through the shadows' woods when Teagan saw the tops of Yggdrasil's hands over the shorter trees.

Roisin was standing in the doorway as if she had never left it. She ran toward them, Grendal at her feet.

"*Thomas!*" Roisin shouted when they came out into the clearing. Finn lowered Thomas to the ground. Roisin fell beside him, sobbing and babbling in Gaelic. Thomas managed to lift a hand, and Roisin pressed it to her lips.

Suddenly a howl ripped through the air. It was the sound Fear Doirich had made, his animal scream, multiplied and somehow much more frightening. Grendal hissed and backed up against Roisin.

"What kind of siren is that?" Mr. Wylltson said.

It wasn't the howl of the hunt they had heard before. This was something worse. Something . . . hungrier. Hellhounds.

"Police, maybe?" Mr. Wylltson said. "I've never heard anything like it. No, it must be those new fire engines. Which way is it coming from?" The sound seemed to swirl around them, and it was growing stronger.

"Dad, sing," Aiden said. "Sing some more."

Mr. Wylltson started singing again, but nothing happened. Mag Mell didn't shift or move, and no passage opened for them.

"Tea," Finn said, reaching for Thomas.

Teagan pulled Roisin up. "Finn needs to carry Thomas again," she said, hoping the girl would understand. "We have to get out of here."

Finn grabbed Thomas's arm and jerked him into a sitting position. Thomas was either conscious enough or frightened enough to stagger to his feet, but Finn didn't wait for him to take a step. He picked him up and threw him over his shoulder.

"Let's go! Aiden, which way out?"

Aiden started running, pulling his father along. Roisin grabbed Grendal up and ran after them, her long skirt dragging in the dirt.

"The fastest way, Aiden," Teagan called.

"I know that," Aiden shouted back.

Teagan dropped a little behind Finn. The hellhounds were closer; she could *feel* them coming. She stumbled, then sprinted to catch up.

The ground they were running over started to grow spongy and soft, and then they were dodging the green pools and scrambling over the enormous roots and tree knees, and ahead of them Teagan thought she could see a shimmering in the air—the doorway to the park.

Teagan glanced back. She could see them now, two enormous black hounds bounding through the trees. They were the size of small bears, but sleek as Dobermans, their ears perked and their eyes glowing yellow embers. Their tails were long and thin, like the tails of greyhounds or whippets, and foam streamed from their muzzles as they ran. No one was going to make it to the park. The hounds—the soul eaters—were coming too fast.

I should turn and face them. If I slow them down, they won't take Aiden or Finn. They won't take Dad.

Teagan stopped. The fear was worse than anything she'd ever felt. Even facing the Dark Man had not been this bad. It made her legs weak and the air too thick to pull into her lungs.

I don't want to die.

Even as she thought it, she felt the toe in her pocket twitch. There was a way to slow the hounds down and live.

She dug the toe out of her pocket and ripped the wrapping off.

"Ginny!" Teagan shouted. "Ginny Greenteeth!" Ginny's head came out of the leaves that were hiding the deep water.

"Please." The goblin woman's pupils were dilated with fear. "Please don't. I won't hurt anybody anymore. I promise, I promise, I promise!" The water streamed from her stringy hair, running down her face like tears. "I'll be different, I swear."

For half a second, Teagan hesitated.

"Please," Ginny whispered.

The hounds were coming.

Someone had to die to slow them down.

Teagan felt something twist inside her as she threw the toe.

"By your flesh and by your bones, keep us safe, whatever comes!" It splashed into the water beside the goblin woman. Ginny shrieked as it writhed toward her like a water snake. She snatched it up and crawled out of the pond.

The goblin's shoulders were shaking as she turned to face the hellhounds.

Teagan sprinted after the others. She had almost caught up to Roisin when Ginny started to scream. Roisin stumbled, tripping over her long skirts. Teagan grabbed her arm to pull her up, looking back as she did so.

The larger hound had Ginny by the arm. He shook the water goblin like a rag doll. Ginny's arm ripped from its socket as he tossed her in the air, spewing a mist of blood. The hound threw back his head and gulped it down even as the second hound caught her in its enormous jaws. Ginny threw herself sideways, jerking away from the crushing jaws and wrapping her legs around the hound's neck, fighting for her life, and screaming in pain and fear.

Roisin clung to Teagan as they ran, while Ginny's screaming went on and on and on behind them.

. . . And then there was a prickling all over her body, and they were running across the park lawn in a Chicago late afternoon.

People coming down the library steps stopped to stare as Finn dumped Thomas on the sidewalk. Roisin knelt beside him, clutching Grendal and looking around wide-eyed at the buildings, people, and cars. A woman took out a cell phone, and Teagan was sure she was dialing 911.

Finn squeezed behind the gate and started rooting through the weeds, looking for his knife.

"There's no time," Teagan said. "We've got to get out of here."

"We could call Mrs. Santini for a ride," Mr. Wylltson said helpfully. "Or Abby."

Oh, god. Abby had only agreed to hide for a couple of days.

Teagan pulled out her cell phone and punched a number on speed dial. Even if they got away from the hellhounds, Kyle would be coming, too, just as soon as Fear Doirich was free. Kyle and all of his nasty friends. He knew that Abby was her friend. He knew how to find her.

"Dad," Teagan said as it rang, "I want you to take Aiden and go to St. Drogo's. The rest of us will meet you there."

"Where's your mother?" Mr. Wylltson put his hand to his head and winced. "Is she there already? Ah . . ." He winced and his face went ashen. "I'm . . ." He looked around wildly. "Where are we?"

"It's the library, Dad." Aiden sounded as if he was about to start crying again. "Don't you know?"

Abby's voicemail clicked on. "This is Abby Gagliano," she purred. "What can I do for ya?"

"Abby, it's Tea. Call me!" Teagan flipped her phone shut.

Mr. Wylltson had both of his hands to his head now. "Confused," he said. "I don't . . . understand. Where's your mother, Tea? What's going on here?"

"Hey!" Aiden pointed. "It's Mr. Schein."

Raynor Schein's '57 Chevy was parked by the curb, and the gangly man, dressed as a city worker, was making a huge pile of leaves with an old rake. He set the rake carefully in the truck and started toward them.

"I didn't expect extras," he said, stooping beside Thomas. "What do we have here?"

Thomas opened his eyes. "*Raynor. Conas ata tu?*"

"Speak English, Thomas," Raynor said. "This is Chicago, not Éireann. What are you doing here?"

271

TWENTY-THREE

I DON'T expect you to help me, Raynor." Thomas drew a ragged breath. "But help the others. Hellhounds . . . coming."

Raynor was suddenly in motion. "Everyone in the truck." He scooped Thomas up, none too gently. "*Move!*"

Teagan pushed her father toward the Chevy. He managed to get in, and Aiden scrambled up onto his lap as Raynor dumped Thomas into the bed of the truck. Teagan tried to pull Roisin toward the cab, but the girl started shouting and pointing toward Thomas. Raynor scooped her up, Grendal and all, and tossed her into the truck bed, too. She collapsed on Thomas's chest.

"In the cab," Raynor barked at Teagan as he ran to the driver's side.

"Finn!" Teagan shouted. He was squeezing out from behind the gate, knife in hand.

"He'll get here," Raynor said as the engine roared to life. He shoved the truck into second gear and slammed the gas pedal to the floor, clutch still down.

"Run, Finn!" Aiden shouted as the hellhounds came through the gate. Finn vaulted into the truck bed, and Raynor popped the clutch. The truck leaped forward, tires screaming on the asphalt.

The acceleration slammed Finn against the tailgate and banged Teagan's head against the rear window. She grabbed the sissy strap hanging above her and looked back again. Roisin was lying over Thomas, either holding him down or shielding him. Grendal cowered against the tailgate. Finn had his knife in his hand and was trying to hold himself in the truck bed as he turned to face the hounds.

The beasts were running down the center of the street, and people clearly didn't need second sight to see them. Cars were swerving around them and blowing their horns. Pedestrians were screaming.

"They're gaining," Teagan said.

"Not for long. Sing to me, Brynhild baby." Raynor tipped his head, listening to the engine's whine. "There it is." He shifted again.

"Stoplight coming up," Mr. Wylltson said. Raynor wasn't slowing down. "Stoplight, stoplight, STOPLIGHT!" Mr. Wylltson shouted.

"Go to sleep, John," Raynor said. Mr. Wylltson's head slumped forward onto Aiden.

They blew through the light, swerving to miss a gray Toyota Prius. Teagan glanced in the side mirror. The hellhounds were still coming.

"What are those things?" she asked.

"Hybrids," Raynor said. "Strange, aren't they? Half combustion, half battery powered. I think I might like to drive one. We all have to do our part for the planet. But I'm not quite decided . . ." He glanced at her. "Oh, you meant the hellhounds. I thought you were talking about the Toyota."

"Yes, the hellhounds," Teagan said before he could start in on cars again.

"You've heard of *evolution*, right?"

"Of course."

"Well, with the modern educational system, you never know." He shrugged. "Hellhounds are the product of—"

"Devolution!" Teagan said.

"That's right. They let hunger consume everything they once were. What you see is all that's left."

"What were they before they devolved?"

"The Dark Man's brothers," Raynor said simply.

"His *brothers*?"

"We're in big trouble," Aiden shouted. "They're catching up."

"We're not in trouble," Raynor said. "I told you—they can't out-run Brynhild. You just take care of your daddy, Aiden. Don't let his head bounce too much. It will give him a sore neck."

"When's he going to wake up?" Aiden asked.

"Not for a couple of days, but he'll be a little better when he does."

Teagan checked the mirror again. The hounds were falling behind.

Raynor made a sharp left without slowing down at all, and Teagan lost sight of them. He turned left again almost immediately, and left again, shooting across the street the hounds had been on. There was no sign of them.

"That was too easy." Raynor was frowning.

"Thomas said they would follow us forever, once they got our scent," Teagan said.

"That's true." Raynor checked the rearview mirror again. "They're messing up plan A."

"What's plan A?" Aiden had turned around so that he could hold his dad's head with both hands.

"Run them in circles until I can figure out a plan B. I'm tending toward getting on the nearest freeway and running their legs off. If I didn't have the lot of you to watch over, I might be able to take care of them."

"You could 'take care of' hellhounds?" Teagan groped in the crack of the seat searching in vain for a seat belt.

"One at a time. I'll have to separate them, of course."

"Who *are* you?"

"Raynor Schein." He glanced at her. "Did you hit your head that hard? We've met before."

"I mean . . . *what* are you?"

"A *caomhnóir aingeal*," Raynor said.

"A*ingeal* . . . an angel? What does *caomhnóir* mean?"

"'Guardian,'" Raynor said. "I'm Finn Mac Cumhaill's guardian angel." He checked the rearview mirror for hellhounds—they still weren't in sight—then gave her a disapproving look. "He never caused me any trouble until he met you."

"I don't believe it," Teagan said.

"A*ingeal* don't lie," Raynor assured her. "Well, *caomhnóir* don't, anyway."

"Finn lived on the street," Teagan said. "He got into fights!"

"You remember that, huh? That's the first time I ever had to intervene in person. Ever. And since then, he's been trying to fight the whole goblin world with his own two fists. As if that would work."

"It worked on Fear Doirich," Aiden said.

"What?"

"Finn beat that bad guy up," Aiden explained. "I stopped Kyle by singing."

"My little boy . . . beat up that *creature*?" Raynor grinned. "Where am I taking you kids this time, by the way? Gary again? Gary would be good, because the freeway entrance is right ahead."

"Mamieo is waiting at our house," Teagan said.

"Crap!" Raynor hit the brakes, throwing Teagan and Aiden against the dashboard and slumping Mr. Wylltson forward. The driver of the SUV that had to swerve around them made a rude gesture as he went past.

"Where are the seat belts?" Teagan pushed her dad upright again.

"They weren't standard on a '57," Raynor said. "Sorry about that. But we need to get back there fast. You three were with Ida. She's going to reek of you, and Mag Mell, too, if she's been using her dust. No wonder they haven't caught up with us yet. They're confused."

"They're after Mamieo?" Aiden's voice squeaked.

"*Might* be." Raynor was breaking the speed limit and blowing through lights again. "They might be after Ida, or they might be running in circles trying to find us."

"I don't want them to get my Mamieo!" Aiden sounded really worried.

"We'll get there as fast as we can. Why don't you tell me about Finn beating Fear Doirich while I drive, Aiden?"

"He tried to hit me on the head," Aiden said. "But Finn caught his stick. It was hurting Finn's hand, so I started to sing, but Fear was sucking up my words. Then Finn hit him, and he couldn't talk right. He couldn't sing."

"I'll bet it was an uppercut," Raynor said. "Finn's got a great uppercut. God, I wish I could have seen it." He glanced up. "I mean that."

"Why didn't you, then?" Teagan was looking down every side street they passed and trying to keep an eye on the side-view mirror. Not knowing where the hellhounds were was worse than knowing they were right behind you. "If you're his guardian angel, shouldn't you have been there, taking care of him?"

"I would have if I could. The last time I was in Mag Mell, it was with Pádraig."

"Saint Patrick?" Teagan said. "You were one of the two angels Mamieo talked about?"

Raynor nodded. "Pádraig was trying to raise a revolt against Fear Doirich. That fellow you dragged along with you—Thomas—was a captain in the Dark Man's guard. He pretended that he wanted to hear what Pádraig said, then captured and tortured him."

"And you were just standing there?"

"No," Raynor said softly. "We were not. The Stormriders are a powerful people."

Riders on the storm, into this house we're born. Raynor had sung it with Aiden the last time they'd ridden in his truck.

"You knew we were goblins," Teagan said. "When you picked us up on the tracks."

"Oh, I knew you were *sídhe* the first time I set eyes on you," Raynor said. "But goblins? That's a choice."

"What do you mean?"

"The Creator gave us all gifts. Me, my gift is being in the right place at the right time. The Stormriders have the gifts of—"

"War," Aiden said.

"That's right. But what you choose to fight is up to you. Thomas was fighting for Fear Doirich when he killed my brother Geert. I might not have gotten Pádraig out if Fear Doirich hadn't summoned Thomas before he got to me."

"Thomas *killed an angel?*" Aiden asked.

"Yes," Raynor said. "Then the Dark Man used the Highborn Sídhe's magic to lock Mag Mell up tight, so no other *aingeal* can get in. Only those who were there already can come out."

"There are angels in Mag Mell?" Teagan asked.

"Fear Doirich is an *aingeal* himself," Raynor replied. "And his brothers are, too. How could you have met him and not known that? He's fallen, of course. He was a *caomhnóir aingeal* to earthly kings in the time before time. Now goblinkind worships him as a god. I must say, though"—he glanced sideways at Teagan again—"you are more . . . *goblin* than you were the last time I saw you."

"I just know it now," Teagan said. "I didn't before."

"No." Raynor touched the brake as the traffic slowed still further. "That's not it. What did you do in Mag Mell?"

"Survived," Teagan said.

"Do goblins really have to do what Fear Doirich tells them to?" Aiden asked. "Because Kyle said we did."

"I know of three who didn't follow the Dark Man," Raynor said. "Your mother, your grandmother, and Drogo."

"Drogo was a bilocate, like Kyle!" Teagan slapped her knee. "Dad was right. He *was* sleeping in church!"

"He was still a saint—" Raynor was saying when Roisin screamed. The hellhounds had come around a corner right behind them, and they were close. Too close.

Raynor hit the accelerator, and Teagan saw Roisin tumble to the back of the truck. Finn caught her before she hit the tailgate.

Raynor swerved around a small blue Honda. The hellhounds came right over the top of it. Teagan could see the panic on the driver's face as their claws ripped open the metal.

Raynor was weaving through traffic like an Indy driver, gaining distance with each block. Roisin was lying on top of Thomas again, as if she could protect him, and Finn had turned to face the hounds.

"Traffic jam," Raynor shouted. "Hold on!" He spun the wheel, and Brynhild's tires complained as they went around a corner and into an alley. It was so narrow Brynhild's side-view mirrors practically scraped the brick walls on each side. The first pothole bounced Teagan's head against the top of the cab. She braced herself before they hit the second.

"Hold on," Raynor said again. "It's not too far to the next street, and we should be free and clear."

"Finn bounced out!" Aiden said.

Teagan put her hand on the ceiling to try to hold herself in place, and twisted to look at the bed of the truck. Thomas, Roisin, and Grendal were lying flat in the truck bed, but Finn was gone.

"Shit," Raynor said, looking in the rearview mirror. "Now we're in trouble."

He hit the gas pedal, and the truck jumped forward. They came out onto a side street, and Raynor slammed a rumrunner's turn. "Roll down your window," he said.

"What?"

"Roll down your window. I want Finn to hear us coming. Play *our song*," Raynor said. Wagner's "Ride of the Valkyries" blared from Brynhild's speakers.

"Louder," Raynor commanded. The Chevy blazed back down the alley, the music bouncing off the brick walls and rattling the windows.

Finn was running down the alley toward them. Teagan could see the hellhounds behind him, their necks stretched out like greyhounds chasing a rabbit.

"Slow down," Teagan said.

"Nope." Raynor leaned forward.

"You're going to hit Finn!"

The hellhounds had realized that the truck wasn't stopping. They turned to run, but Finn didn't. Aiden screamed and covered his eyes.

Finn jumped, catching a fire escape ladder that dangled from the back of a building. He swung his legs up and, as Brynhild roared under him, dropped onto the hood and bounced against the windshield like a giant bug.

"What are you doing?" Teagan shouted.

"Flesh and blood," Raynor shouted back over the blaring Wagner. "Hellhounds are flesh and blood in this creation, just like me. I can run them down." There was a sickening crunch, and Brynhild lurched as her tires bounced over what had been the slower hound. The side-view mirror on the driver's side threw sparks as it scraped against the building.

Teagan was sure Finn was going to be thrown against the wall, but he kicked at the hood, went over the top of the cab, and landed in the truck bed. Teagan twisted to see what he was doing. He grabbed up the old rake, and Raynor winced as he slammed it against the side of the truck, breaking the head off.

"It's coming back," Aiden screamed. Teagan turned back just in time to see the other hellhound jump.

Its feet hit the hood as it launched itself over the cab. Finn was on one knee, holding the rake handle under his arm, the sharp point up and the end braced against the pickup bed.

The splintered wood pierced the hound's chest, and Finn heaved hard, vaulting it over the tailgate. It turned like a cat in the air, landing on its feet, but the impact shoved the rake handle completely through its body. Still, it dragged itself after them until it collapsed.

"Play artist James Taylor," Raynor shouted, "softly." Brynhild switched from "Ride of the Valkyries" to "Handy Man."

"Those were fallen angels?" Teagan turned for one last look before they left the alley.

"What else would they be?" Raynor said. "Only Aingeal, High-born, and Fir Bolg are fully present in any and all dimensions. It's what we're made for—walking between the worlds. Your dad was dragged physically to Mag Mell, but his mind never left Chicago."

"So if you are fully present in this dimension, then anybody can see you?" Teagan asked.

"It would be hard to get a driver's license if they couldn't. And I've had one since 1903. I was driving before that of course, but—"

"What about Kyle, when he bilocates?" Teagan asked before he could start on the invention of the automobile.

"It's like astral projection, only with more mass."

"And the shadows? They can sort of touch things here."

"Those abominations are part *aingeal* and part something so foul I won't name it. Fear's own children." Raynor pulled into a parking space. "They've got just enough substance to make them useful to their father, but not enough to make them fully present in any dimension. Time for me to have a talk with Finn. You two wait here and listen to some music."

"I want to talk to Finn, too," Aiden said.

"Nope," Raynor said. "You stay here and take care of Teagan and your dad. I think they got a little banged up."

"You seriously need to install seat belts," Teagan said as Raynor got out. "It's the law, you know." He waved at her over his shoulder.

"I'm tired of holding Dad up," Aiden said.

Teagan was leaning her dad's head gently against the back window when her phone vibrated.

"Tea." Abby clearly wasn't happy. "Where have you been? I've been trying to call you for two days. If that street bum has done anything to you or Aiden—"

"He saved our lives a couple of times." She reached out the window and turned the mirror until she could see Finn. He was sitting with his back to the tailgate, listening to Raynor, his brows knit. Teagan tried to imagine the conversation.

Hello, Finn. I'm your guardian angel.

Finn didn't look surprised. Just tired. He turned and looked directly at Teagan in the mirror, and she felt a shock when their eyes met.

"—are you even listening to me?" Abby was saying.

"Sorry." Finn wasn't looking away. Teagan bumped the mirror so he couldn't see her. "I'm back now."

"I *said* I went back to my apartment to feed the fish," Abby said. "Some bastard had pinned my babies to the ceiling with toothpicks. They'd slashed all of my canvases, too. What kind of a sick person does something like that?"

"The kind I've been telling you about," Teagan said.

"You're saying it was a goblin?" Abby asked.

Teagan rubbed her temple. "I need you to pick up some stuff for me, okay? I need some Pedialyte, superglue, and duct tape. Can you get those and bring them to my house? It's really important."

"I'll get them," Abby said.

"He's ba-ack," Aiden said as Raynor opened the driver-side door.

"Will more . . . things . . . be coming out of Mag Mell?" Teagan asked.

"I'm an *aingeal*, not a psychic," Raynor said. "Speaking of which, I need to ask a favor. I would appreciate it if we kept the *aingeal* thing quiet. People just go nuts over that stuff, and it makes me very uncomfortable. We like to keep a low profile. Except for the fallen, of course. They all think they're rock stars."

"All right," Teagan said.

"And one other thing," Raynor said. "I wouldn't tell Mamieo what they"—he nodded toward the back of the truck —"are. Not yet."

"You want us to lie?" Aiden folded his arms.

"Never," Raynor said. "But there are two ways into a person's life: through their head or through their heart. Mamieo's heart is closer to her Creator than her head is. Let her take care of them and mend their hurts. If she's tended him with her own hands, her mother's heart will straighten out her Irish head when the time comes. I don't think Thomas is going to be talking much, and Finn is discussing the situation with Roisin."

"*Wait a minute,*" Aiden said. "We're goblins, too. Will Mamieo still like us?"

"We'll see," Raynor said. He didn't sound too optimistic about it.

Teagan picked a stray beetle leg and a small twig that Lucy had left behind out of Aiden's hair and tossed them out the window. *What would Mamieo think?*

"Stop it!" Aiden wiggled as she finger-combed out the last trace of the sprite's nest. "Lucy won't like it! When are you going to fix her?"

"As soon as Abby brings what I need." Teagan hoped the sprite was still alive in Finn's kit. *One problem at a time.* "First we need to explain things to Mamieo."

"How long will that take?" Aiden asked when he'd stopped wiggling.

"I'm not sure," Teagan said.

"I think I'll stick around after I drop you off," Raynor said. "Just for a little bit."

MAMIEO was sitting on the couch when Teagan came through the front door. The old woman was clearly expecting company. She was dusted with glamour and shimmered with *draíocht*.

To a normal person she would be very appealing. To someone with second sight, Mamieo glowed like a painting of a medieval saint, halo and all.

The saint jumped up as Finn staggered in behind Teagan, Thomas's arm around his shoulders. Finn was half dragging the Highborn, who managed to move one of his feet about one step out of three.

"You're alive, then!" Mamieo said.

"I am," Finn agreed. "And Teagan as well, as you see, and Aiden's coming along." Teagan stepped aside to let them through.

Aiden and Roisin came through the door next, and then Raynor with Mr. Wylltson slung over his shoulder.

"*John Paul Wylltson.*" Mamieo had grabbed Aiden in a hug, but she released him when she saw his father. "Is the man . . ."

"Just sleeping," Raynor assured her. "I'll tuck him into bed."

"And who would you be?"

"He's an old friend," Finn said, "and he's right about John. This is the one who needs your help now. We found him in the garden of Fear Doirich himself, no more than half alive. He still tried to help us, and the Dark Man struck him down for it."

Mamieo's eyes skipped over Thomas and went to Roisin, taking in her long hair and medieval dress. The girl shrank back against Teagan. Whatever Finn had told her about Mamieo, it had clearly frightened her.

"It's okay." Teagan patted her arm. "Mamieo is going to help Thomas."

"Show the man where to put your father, Aiden," Mamieo said, still looking at Roisin. Thomas chose that moment to pass out. Roisin jumped to help as his eyes rolled up in his head and he went limp.

"So that's how it is, then," Mamieo said as Roisin ducked under Thomas's other arm to help support him. "Let's take him in the kitchen. He can't be lolling about in the parlor. We're expecting company."

"Who—"

"Ms. Skinner," Mamieo said before Teagan could finish the question. "And it won't do to have her walk in on this, will it?"

"The Skinner's coming?" Aiden squeaked.

"I didn't know you were on your way, did I?" Mamieo said. "But don't you worry, pratie." Mamieo's voice was gentle. "She won't be here for an hour yet. When she comes, I'll set her right. Now, help get your father upstairs."

Teagan ran ahead of Finn to hold open the kitchen door. The room was spotless. Mamieo had scrubbed every speck of Kyle's blood from the wall.

Finn lifted Thomas onto the table, and Mamieo pulled his shirt open. When she saw the thorn wound, she sucked in her breath. It was green-blue and festering, weeping pus.

"Hold him tight, dearie," Mamieo told Roisin. "Hold him so he don't dare be slipping away from you."

She turned to Teagan. "Dial a number for me on that phone of yours, girl." When the phone connected to a Dr. Gorman's office, Teagan handed it to Mamieo.

"It's Ida Mac Cumhaill calling," she said. "Let me talk to Danny." Mamieo frowned. "Of course I mean Dr. Gorman, girl. How many Dannys are you keeping there? Just tell him it's Ida."

She pressed her hand against Thomas's forehead as she waited, feeling for a fever, and then against the side of his neck, checking for a pulse.

"Danny! I've a job for you, and it's urgent. I need you here *right now*. Teagan will tell you what you need to know."

Mamieo handed the phone back, and went to the sink for a clean cloth.

Dr. Gorman didn't sound as grumpy as Jackie the cabby had. He asked a few questions about the condition of the patient, then said he would be right over.

"Now, tell me what's going on," Mamieo said when Teagan flipped the phone shut. "It's sure these two never came from Chicago. Tell me everything."

Finn started with stepping into Mag Mell, and the paths that opened when Aiden sang, and about Lucy. Mamieo worked while he talked, washing Thomas's face and, with Roisin's help, getting his shirt off far enough to clean around the wound.

She said something Teagan was sure was an Irish curse word when Finn reached the part about Ginny Greenteeth. She stopped moving when he reached the part about finding Roisin in Yggdrasil's hands, and just listened.

Finn told her about the Dark Man's plans for Roisin and how Yggdrasil had kept her safe. He told how Thomas had fallen in love with the girl and sworn to love her as long as his heart beat.

"Didn't my Rory say the same to me?" Mamieo whispered, wiping Thomas's face again. "And wasn't he true to his word, just like this boy?"

Aiden and Raynor came into the kitchen.

"Did you tell Mamieo—"

Shut it! Teagan flashed in sign language.

Aiden's mouth snapped shut.

"Tell me what?" Mamieo turned to Finn. "What are you hiding from me, boyo?"

Finn wrapped his arms around her, lifting her in a bear hug.

"And what do you think you are about?" she said. "Put me down!"

"I'll do that," Finn assured her. "Just as soon as I finish my story. Time can run different in Mag Mell, as you've told me many a time."

"And what of it?"

"Aileen was Roisin's sister," Finn said. "Their father was Amergin the bard. Her *máthair* was Maeve, Queen Mab's sister."

Mamieo froze.

"My Aileen?"

"Yes," Finn said.

"The child of a goblin." Her eyes went to Roisin, where the girl stood protectively over Thomas. "And this boy on my table?"

"He's a gob—" Finn glanced at Teagan. "A Highborn Sídhe."

Mamieo went ashen. Even her *draíocht* halo dimmed. "One of those that took my Rory from me. One of the very creatures. Let me go, boy."

"The story isn't done yet," Finn said. "This one helped us in Mag Mell. He told us where to find water. If he hadn't warned us that the hellhounds were coming, the soul eaters would have had us."

"It's hellhounds, now, is it? And where are those creatures?"

"Raynor dealt with one, and I dealt with the other," Finn said. "It's over now, Mamieo. It's over. There's no more killing to be done."

"*Put me down*," Mamieo said, and this time Finn did. She walked over to the table and, after looking down at Thomas, turned and walked out the back door.

"What do you think?" Teagan asked.

Finn shook his head.

Mamieo was pacing in the backyard. Twice she stopped and shook her fist at the sky.

"That doesn't look good," Raynor said.

Thomas moaned and started to thrash. Teagan put her hand on his shoulder to hold him down. He was weak enough that it didn't take much. Roisin shushed him, touching her fingers to his lips and speaking softly in her own language.

When Teagan looked up again, Mamieo was standing very still. Finally she turned and came back inside.

"Are you going to throw us away?" Aiden asked.

"Your *máthair* was mine," Mamieo said fiercely, wiping tears from her face. "I'll not give you up, pratie, not to the devil himself."

"What about these two?" Finn asked, nodding toward Thomas and Roisin.

"He could be one of the very creatures that butchered my Rory. Even if it wasn't himself that did it, I know he's done other vile things."

Like killing an angel. Teagan glanced at Raynor, who was leaning against the wall, his arms folded.

"How could the Almighty ask it?" Mamieo whispered.

"What did he ask?" Aiden took her hand.

Mamieo looked down at him.

"'*Who are you, Ida?*' That's what he asked. 'I'm Ida Mac Cumhaill,' I told him. 'The widow of Rory Mac Cumhaill, the best man that ever lived. Done to death by goblins, as you remember.'

"But didn't he ask me again?" Mamieo said. "'*Who are you, Ida?*' 'I'm Ida Mac Cumhaill,' I told him. 'Daughter of the Fir Bolg, kicked out of their home by goblinkind, with every right to hate the bastards, as you well know,' I says. I thought I was done, but, '*Who are you, Ida?*' the Almighty asks a third time. 'I'm Ida Mac Cumhaill, fashioned by your own hand to mend and tend your creation, and don't you know it already?' I told him.

"'*Then tend my creature,*' he says. And isn't that what I'm going to do? Why hasn't someone put a pillow under the boy's head?"

"I'm going to check on Brynhild," Raynor said. Teagan went with him. Now that Mamieo knew the truth, there was no reason to leave Grendal outside, and she needed to check on Lucy.

A taxi pulled up as they stepped onto the porch, and a

round-faced young man jumped out. He was carrying an old-fashioned black doctor's bag in one hand and a collapsible IV pole in the other.

"I'm Dr. Gorman," the man said. "Ida called?" Teagan let him in, then followed Raynor to the truck.

"I think that went pretty well," Teagan said as she lifted Finn's kit out of the truck bed.

"Maybe," Raynor said.

"Maybe?"

"I told you her mother's heart was closer to the Creator than her Irish head. She's listening with her heart right now. But I wouldn't spring any more surprises on her. Her head just might take over."

"You're not going to take that guy to the hospital?" Abby whispered.

Thomas lay on a mattress in the corner of the kitchen, an IV needle in his arm and antibiotics dripping into his veins. Roisin was sitting beside him, holding his hand.

"We can't." Teagan sorted through the bag Abby had brought.

"Why not? Because you don't want Skinner to know about those two? That's why we're whispering, right?"

"You're the only one who's whispering." Teagan pulled out the superglue. They'd explained to Roisin that she had to keep Thomas quiet. Mamieo was in the living room talking to Ms. Skinner and Officer O'Malley, the cop Ms. Skinner had brought with her.

Dr. Gorman had been explaining his version of the situation to the social worker and policeman when Abby arrived: Mr. Wylltson had sustained some kind of brain injury while walking in the park.

He was now under Dr. Gorman's professional care and would be up and about soon.

Officer O'Malley seemed happy to drop the matter. Ms. Skinner was not as happy, but there was nothing she could do.

"So, why *aren't* you taking him to the hospital?" Abby asked. "He looks really sick."

"It's complicated."

"You're talking to an Italian about complicated?" Abby snorted. "There's ways to do these things. I keep telling you I got people I can call."

"Mamieo called people, or he wouldn't have an IV in his arm."

"The Travelers are like the Mob?" Abby asked. "They got people?"

"Sort of."

"So, you needed the superglue to save an invisible bug." Abby squinted at the paper towel on the counter.

"She's only invisible to you," Aiden said. "We can all see her."

"And why's that?"

"Because your brain isn't wired to see creatures from other dimensions," Teagan explained.

"Like it's not wired for calculus."

"Something like that," Teagan agreed.

Abby walked over and pushed the kitchen door open a crack.

"Eavesdropping is bad," Aiden said. Abby ignored him.

Teagan made a careful line down the crack in Lucy's exoskeleton, pressed it together, and then wiped the excess glue away.

Abby pulled the door shut. "They're leaving. But that cop was totally flirting."

"With Skinner?"

"With your grandma. She's one gorgeous old lady."

"It's magic," Teagan said. "*Draíocht.*"

"Magic," Abby repeated. "And the invisible she-cat that I keep tripping over is—"

"A *cat-sídhe.*" Teagan didn't look up.

"—and the guy outside crying over the scratches in his nice, shiny truck is . . . ?"

"A mechanic," Teagan said.

"And a freegan," Aiden added. "He wants to save the planet."

Lucy's eyes glowed faintly, and she turned her head toward the sound of Aiden's voice.

"She's alive!" Aiden shouted, then clapped his hand over his mouth.

"They're already out the door," Abby said. "You don't have to be quiet anymore."

The sprite moved her arms and legs weakly. Her exoskeleton seemed to be working again.

"She's going to need food, Aiden," Teagan said.

"There's always flies by the garbage." Aiden jumped down from the bench. "I'll get some."

Teagan gave the sprite a drop of Pedialyte on the tip of a swizzle stick. *Do sprites even have electrolytes?* She had no idea. Lucy sucked the moisture up.

"I saw that!" Abby gasped.

"You saw Lucy?"

"No. I saw the drop disappear."

The sprite refused the second drop Teagan offered her.

"So the invisible bug's gonna live?" Abby asked.

"I think so." Thomas and Roisin seemed to be doing all right as well. "Let's go keep an eye on Aiden." It was uncomfortable having him out of her sight, even if she knew Raynor would be watching over him.

"Wait up." Abby pulled her sketchpad out of her purse. "I'll come, too. I've got a bunch of character studies due in art class. I swear I haven't been able to draw a thing while you were gone. And I couldn't sleep, either. Too many nightmares."

Mamieo wasn't in the living room when they went through. She had probably gone upstairs to talk to Finn. Abby flipped open her sketchpad as they sat down on the steps.

"You're coming back to school Monday, right?"

"I don't know. It might be best if we get out of here. Get as far from Chicago as we can."

"Because there are goblins in the park?"

"Yeah," Teagan said.

"Bullshit." Abby sharpened her charcoal. "Dumpster boy's convinced you to drop out of school, that's what's going on. I'm not going to let that happen, Tea. I got a responsibility to the universe, ya know? Keeping you in school is part of it."

"You're not my mom, Abby."

"Yeah? Well, when's your dad going to wake up? I can't wait to hear what he thinks about this."

"Raynor said he should wake up in a couple of days."

"The mechanic guy?" Abby looked over at Raynor, who was working on Brynhild's side-view mirror. "What, is he a doctor in his spare time or something?" She started drawing.

"I've been thinking," Teagan said, ignoring her question. "If we do leave Chicago, you should come with us. Pack up and move to another town where they can't find you. Like . . . like your uncle Joe did when he went into witness protection."

"Joey the Squealer?" Abby said. "Not gonna happen. I got responsibilities."

"Like what?"

"Aunt Sophia and Lennie, for one thing. You and Aiden for the other thing. I know these goblin things are bad, Tea. They killed my babies, remember? My apartment felt"—she shuddered—"*evil* after they'd been there. Like walking into a remake of The Exorcist or something. I think their freaking filthy thoughts soaked into my walls, you know? But I don't run from bad stuff. And I don't leave my friends when they're in trouble. I get the superglue and the Pedia-lyte now, but duct tape? What's that about?"

"It's for Finn," Teagan said. "I used up the last of his tape in Mag Mell when we tied up Fear Doirich."

"I'm gonna clobber him if he touches you," Abby said. "Just so you know."

"Who? Fear Doirich?"

"Finn."

"I don't think you have anything to worry about."

"Oh, my god."

"What?" Teagan looked around, half expecting a dog-headed man, but Abby was staring at her.

"That *sound* in your voice."

"There was no *sound* in my voice," Teagan said.

"Yes, there was. Say it again."

"I don't think you have anything to worry about?"

"Oh. My. God. You're totally in love with Dumpster boy!"

"You can hear that in my voice?" She hated it when Abby jumped to crazy conclusions. Especially when she might be right.

"You know I got powers." Abby shrugged. "So is he in love with you?"

Aiden raced up to them holding a buzzing horsefly by its wings. He shoved it at Abby's face.

"I got a fly for Lucy!"

"Eww." Abby leaned back. "Don't let it touch me!"

"Hey," Aiden said. "You're drawing Mr. Schein!"

"Yeah." Abby held up the quick charcoal study. "An artist has to go with her gut. I got instinct, you know? My angel phase is over. I'm drawing mechanics now."

Aiden blinked. "Gotta feed Lucy," he said, and ran up the steps.

WATCH." Dr. Max tossed Cindy an apple.

"What am I watching for?" Teagan asked. "I mean, other than the fact that she isn't mad at me for standing next to you?"

"You'll see."

Teagan had been afraid she wouldn't get to come back, would never get to work in the clinic again, never even say goodbye to Cindy.

But when her dad had woken up still confused and missing memories, Dr. Gorman and Mamieo had agreed with Abby—they had to stay. Mr. Wylltson needed familiar surroundings to mend his mind. So Raynor had taken up residence in the library park like a homeless person. He wasn't letting anything nasty out.

"What am I watching for?" Teagan asked again.

"Shhh," Dr. Max said.

Cindy took a bite of the apple. Suddenly, the bamboo in front of her sleeping hole shook, and a short, dark, and hairy chimpanzee came out.

"Oscar?" Teagan guessed. "I thought you were going to keep them separate until they were ready to meet each other."

"It wasn't necessary." Dr. Max was beaming like a proud papa.

Oscar clapped his hands, then held them edge to edge, fingers together. He slid one across the other, as if he were chopping an imaginary apple, then clapped his hands again.

"*Share*," Teagan translated.

"It was love at first sight." Dr. Max chortled. "She forgot all about me the minute she set eyes on him."

"So you don't need me to play with Cindy anymore?"

"I still need you to observe them. You understand Cindy better than anyone else. And you need to get to know Oscar."

Hello, Oscar, Teagan signed.

My boy, Cindy signed back, and glared at Teagan.

"I'll leave you to it, then," Dr. Max said happily as he went out the door. Teagan walked to the far end of the enclosure, where the rail met the wall. She needed something to lean against.

Love at first sight. So it happens to Travelers *and* chimpanzees.

But not to goblin girls.

It hadn't been love that had made her throw up the first time she'd seen Finn; she was sure of that. So what was it? The self-preservation instinct, maybe. Goblin, meet goblin hunter. It took goblin girls at least a week to fall in love, even if the guy was totally awesome.

Teagan groaned. She *hated* it when Abby was right. And boy, was she right this time. Teagan was totally in love with Finn Mac Cumhaill. And it wasn't because he was hot, or even because of the sizzles. It was because he was some kind of wonderful she'd never met before.

The kind of wonderful who hadn't hesitated to go into Mag

Mell to help find her dad, even though he knew what was waiting there. The kind of wonderful who had dived into the pool to save Aiden, even though he couldn't swim himself.

The kind of wonderful who had moved to the other side of a dark culvert even though she was sure he'd wanted to hold her then as badly as she wanted to hold him now. But he hadn't. Because he didn't want to leave her with a broken heart when the goblins finally killed him.

She'd managed to avoid being alone with him so far. It wasn't hard with Mamieo living in the guest room; Roisin and Abby—who refused to go home because she was still having nightmares—in Teagan's room; Tea's father in his own room; Thomas on a cot in the alcove; and Finn sharing Aiden's room.

She didn't want to talk to Finn until she'd had a chance to think. And to cry. Because she didn't want to cry in front of him when she explained that Raynor was right. She was more goblin than she had been before they went back to Mag Mell.

"Focus," Teagan told herself. "You've got a job here." After an hour of being a fifth wheel while Cindy and Oscar groomed each other, Teagan was glad to head to the clinic.

"Tea!" Agnes looked up from the computer. "We were so worried about you! Dr. Max told me all about it. How's your dad?"

"Still confused. The doctor is not sure what happened to him, or when he'll get better. My grandmother's come to help take care of him and Aiden." She leaned on the desk. "Debunked any crypto-creatures lately?"

"I'm working on it. Check this out." Agnes was studying blurry photos of the two dead hellhounds. One still had the rake handle through its chest. "A Department of Streets and Sanitation worker claims to have taken these with his cell phone. He and his buddy were sent to pick up the roadkill."

"You have any idea what they are?" Teagan asked.

"Bears with mange?" Agnes leaned closer to the screen. "No, the snouts are all wrong. The crypto-nuts are going crazy over this one."

I'll bet they are. "Has anyone examined the bodies?"

"Nobody can track them down, as usual with this sort of sighting. Sanitation guys say they took them to the landfill. My theory is that they were sold to a dog food factory. Witnesses said they saw these things chasing a truck. There's even a video on YouTube." Agnes clicked from the photo to the video. It was Brynhild, all right. Fortunately the truck was too far away to identify any faces.

"They can't find the truck, either," Agnes said when the clip finished.

Abby had finally gotten to call her people. Raynor had cried when he turned over the keys to Leo, but he couldn't exactly park the truck in front of the Wylltsons' house after the show they'd put on up and down the streets of Chicago. It was Brynhild or Finn.

Angel and Donnie had assured the *aingeal* that they'd keep her safe. Rafe, in a dark blue suit that looked like he'd borrowed it from a teenage Michael Corleone, had punched Raynor's arm in a comforting way.

And then the Turtles had "disappeared" Brynhild, to somewhere they could get her a new paint job and some body work, and a new, untraceable license plate, just in case.

"It's a hoax, of course," Agnes said. "One I've been spending way too many hours on. You need the computer?"

"Thanks." Teagan typed up her notes on Cindy and Oscar before she headed home. It was strange how different the city seemed, knowing the people sitting beside her on the bus could be angels, Travelers, goblinkind . . . or something completely different.

The day before, when she'd walked to the store, there'd been an old couple shuffling along the sidewalk together half a block away. She'd turned her head for a tenth of a second, and when she looked back they were right behind her, staring with hungry black eyes, like a couple of octogenarian vampires.

Teagan had walked away quickly, and then flat-out run, but no matter how fast she went, they were always right behind her when she stopped and turned around.

And then she'd crossed a street and they were—*poof!*—gone. Teagan had asked Mamieo about the creatures, but the old lady had never heard of anything like them.

There are more things in the multiverse, Horatio, than are dreamt of in your philosophy.

Mamieo and Roisin were changing Thomas's bandages on the cot in the alcove when Teagan got home. Aiden and Lennie were in the living room arranging entire armies of Lego men that had been displaced when Thomas took over the den of boyhood.

"Aiden, what's in your hair?" Teagan asked. It looked like he'd sprinkled himself with red, green, and yellow confetti.

"The tooth fairy did it," Lennie explained. "Aiden says not to be afraid, even if you can't see her."

"The tooth fairy?"

Lucy flew into the room carrying a red M&M. She settled into her nest in Aiden's curls, cracked the candy shell expertly against her knee, then proceeded to peel it as if it were a hard-boiled egg, dropping the shell bits into Aiden's hair. *The tooth fairy. Of course.*

"Dad's still rebooting," Aiden said. "He's in the kitchen. Abby's asleep. She said she didn't sleep last night because of nightmares, so not to wake her up *or else.*"

Raynor had said that Mr. Wylltson's mind was sorting through the memories it had left, using them to help fill in missing bits and pieces. Abby was the one who had decided it was *rebooting.* Teagan found him sitting quietly in the corner where her mom's easel had once stood, reading his old copy of *Songs of Experience.*

"Aiden says I've read this before," he said. "I can't remember it, but parts of it feel so *real.* I'm going to ask your mom—"

"Mom's dead, Dad."

"That's right." He ran his hand over his eyes. "I can remember everything about her. Everything but that. I can remember some things, and then . . . it's like I've stepped into one of her canvases before she started to paint. All of the *colors* are missing, Tea. All of the shapes. I *know* the picture is supposed to be there, but . . . it's not."

Teagan put her arms around him and leaned her cheek on his head.

"You're getting better, Dad."

"Dr. Gorman thinks that reading my old books will help. But it isn't. I'm not finding the pictures that are supposed to be there;

I'm just making new ones. And they're not as good. God, I miss your mom."

"It is helping," Teagan said. "You're better than you were yesterday."

Lucy came through the open door, pulled open a cabinet, and disappeared inside. She came out a moment later with another M&M. Teagan gave her dad a hug before she went over to the cabinet. There was no way to explain to the sprite that too much chocolate probably wasn't good for her. They would just have to hide the candy where Lucy couldn't find it. She pulled out the counter drawer . . . and stopped.

The duct tape she'd asked Abby to bring for Finn. She'd never given it to him, just shoved it in the drawer when she cleaned up the kitchen. Teagan took the duct tape out, dropped the bag of M&M's in, and shut the drawer.

She couldn't hold it in much longer. She needed somewhere to cry. Teagan stopped in the living room on her way upstairs. There was no way she could just hide, no matter how much she wanted to. Aiden panicked if he thought someone had disappeared.

"I'm going to my Thinking Place," she said. "I don't want to be disturbed—"

"—unless it's a big fat emergency," Lennie said.

"That's right." Tears were already spilling down her cheeks as she went up the stairs. She locked her bedroom door so no one could follow her in. If Aiden needed her, he could just bang on it and wake up Abby, who was curled up on the bed, frowning in her sleep. Teagan tiptoed past her, careful not to let even one sniffle escape, went out the window, and slid it shut behind her.

She made it to the middle of the roof before she collapsed, hugging the duct tape. It seemed like a million years since the day Finn had told Aiden that duct tape could fix anything. Well, it couldn't fix this.

Teagan pulled her knees up, put her head down on them, and let the sobs come. They'd turned to hiccups when something touched her shoulder.

"Tea? Are you all right?"

"Finn!" She whirled to look at the window. It was still closed. "Where did you come from?"

"Came up the drainpipe," he said. "I heard someone crying up here and wondered who it was."

"You climbed up the drainpipe with your hand like that?" It was still wrapped in gauze and tape to help his palm heal.

"I can use two fingers." He wiggled them at her to prove it.

"Here." She wiped her nose on her sleeve, hiccupped, and held out the duct tape.

Finn took it and turned it over a couple of times. "You climbed out on the roof to cry over duct tape?"

"No," Teagan said. "I climbed out on the roof to be alone."

Finn sat down beside her. "You can do that. In a bit. But if you're not crying over the duct tape, what are you crying over?"

"I don't want to *hic* tell you."

"If you won't talk about it, girl, I guess I'll have to. What Roisin said that night . . ."

Teagan put her chin on her knees again. "It's true."

"I told you, I knew it was the minute the words left her mouth. It changes a lot of things, doesn't it?"

Teagan nodded.

"I think so, too. There's a Travelers' prayer I learned when I was little: 'I do not ask for a path with no trouble or regret—'"

"'I ask instead for a friend who'll walk with me down any path.'" Teagan finished his sentence for him.

"You know it, then!" Finn said. "That makes it all easier. So, do you get my meaning, girl?"

"No." He couldn't mean what she thought he meant. She couldn't let him.

"No?" Finn ran his good hand through his hair. "I thought it was plain enough. I'm the Mac Cumhaill, that's the thing, not a word man like your da."

"And I'm a Highborn," Teagan said flatly. "Go back to Mamieo and her Travelers' prayers and leave me alone with my goblin blood."

"Are you thickheaded?" Finn asked. "I know your blood, and the heart that pumps it. I'm saying I'll walk with you down any path, as long as I am able. I'd have told you as much that morning in Mag Mell, but you'd have thought it was my promise to Aiden talking, wouldn't you?"

"Maybe."

"I don't need magic to make me keep my promises."

"I know," Teagan whispered.

"I love you."

"You can't," Teagan said.

"Why not?" Finn said.

"You want to know what I was crying about?"

"I said I did."

"It's because I'm not good like you, Finn. I *am* a goblin. I fed Ginny to the hellhounds. Horrible, nasty Ginny Greenteeth kept her promise, and I *used* her to save my own life. She begged me not to. But I did exactly what Fear Doirich would have wanted me to, didn't I? Killing her was *useful*, just like cousin Kyle said it would be. Will you walk with me down that path, goblin hunter?"

Finn took a deep breath and let it out slowly. "Is that why you've been avoiding me?"

"Yes."

Teagan studied her shoes, waiting for him to walk away.

"Look at me, girl."

She looked up.

"I said I love you. That's not changing, no matter what you've done. But I need to know. Is that the path you intend to walk?"

"No," Teagan admitted. "I hate it. I hate what I've done. But I've started down that path, haven't I? It's in my blood."

"You've got choices, like any other creature," Finn said. "You can stumble down that road, pretending you can't help it. You can curl up and die of regret and sorrow for what you've done. Or you can get up and fight, even though the battle might be lost."

"Did Mamieo teach you that?"

"The Boy Scouts," Finn said. "Nothing could take it out of those two old men, not the streets, hunger, rags or curses. They *chose* their lives. They taught me to choose mine. If you start to walk down that path again, I'll do my best to bring you back, girl."

"That's what I'm afraid of," Teagan said. "My family is *goblin*, Finn. I don't want to drag you into it. I can devolve into something like Kyle. Thomas—a guy who killed an angel—is probably my cousin. I won't let you love me."

Finn scratched his head, as if he were considering.

"I may need your permission to kiss you, girl. But I don't need anyone's permission to love you. I choose it of my own free will, and there's nothing you can do about it."

Teagan shook her head. "You still don't get it. I know you thought I was your *a gra ma* whatever—"

"*A ghrá mo chroí*," Finn said. "The love of my heart."

"—but I'm not. What I did in Mag Mell *broke* me inside."

"And isn't it a Fir Bolg's job to mend what's broken, then?"

He reached out and traced a line above her bare arm, his finger an inch from her skin. The electric arc from his fingertip raised goose bumps as it followed his finger down her arm. It made her whole body shiver. "I've been wondering if you felt it, too."

"Yes." It was impossible to argue when she could hardly breathe.

"That's good." Finn nodded. "I'm just not sure what I'm going to do about it."

"*What?* Why not?"

"Because of the talk your da gave me that first day."

"But you asked if you could kiss me after that talk!"

"That's true," Finn said. "I didn't think I needed your da's advice then. I know I need it now. The man's had experience in this sort of thing." A door slammed below them, and Finn stood up.

"In what sort of thing?" Teagan could feel the heat flush her face. "Wait. You didn't ask *me* if I loved *you!*"

"Didn't have to." Finn stepped toward the edge of the roof and looked over. "I'm the Mac Cumhaill, remember? I told you I was going to change that plan of yours."

Teagan flushed. "I haven't changed all of it. I'm still headed for Cornell, and I'm not giving that up for anyone. I'll just have to figure out how I can focus on my studies *and* work things out with you."

"This might not be the best time to negotiate the finer points of our relationship," Finn said. He offered her a hand, and pulled her to her feet. "There's matters that need looking after."

"What sort of matters?" Teagan turned to look.

Lennie was standing on the sidewalk, holding Aiden up above his head.

"I see her!" Aiden said, and started waving his arms. "*Tea-gan!*" he shouted. "*Come quick! Thomas is growing feathers!*"

The Goblin Wars books are based on a reimagining of Celtic prehistory and mythology. I have borrowed the stories of Saint Patrick and Saint Drogo, and the life of Myrddin Wyllt, the Welsh bard who became Merlin of legend, as well as the modes and manners of Ireland's gypsies, the Irish Travelers, in order to fasten this story securely in our world.

I am indebted to the young Fionn Mac Cumhaill, the great Celtic hunter/warrior of myth, a paragon of Irish character. While researching this book I devoured the stories of the Finnian Cycle, soundly ignoring the accounts of Fionn's later life, when his character became questionable. Legend has it that Fionn, like King Arthur, will rise again when he is needed—so I didn't think he would mind that I woke him for the telling of this tale.

The Sídhe (pronounced "shee" as in *banshee*) of this book crept out of the shadows all on their own. I knew them before I met them in Irish mythology, and recognized them instantly when I did: a powerful people who fled to another realm when they were defeated by the magic of music and art. These are not fairies or fair folk, but creatures from older, darker tales, noted for malice and the stealing of human children for pleasure or sport.

Please remember that this book is merely a single storyteller's reimagining of what is, what was, and what just might be.

ABOUT THE AUTHOR

Kersten Hamilton is the author of several picture books and many middle grade novels. She has worked as a ranch hand, a woodcutter, a lumberjack, a census taker, a wrangler for wilderness guides, and an archaeological surveyor. Now, when she's not writing, she hunts dinosaurs in the deserts and badlands of New Mexico. This is her first novel for young adults. For more about Kersten, please visit **www.kerstenhamilton.com**.

IN THE SECOND VOLUME OF THE GOBLIN WARS TRILOGY,
THE BATTLE AGAINST GOBLINKIND CONTINUES . . .
BUT WHICH SIDE WILL TEAGAN BE ON?

Teagan, Finn, and Aiden have made it out of Mag Mell alive, but the Dark Man's forces are hot on their heels. Back in Chicago, Tea's goblin cousins show up at her school, sure she will come back to Mag Mell, as goblin blood is never passive once awoken. Soon she will belong to Fear Doirich and join them. In the meantime, they are happy to entertain themselves by trying to seduce, kidnap, or kill Tea's family and friends.

Tea knows she doesn't have much time left, and she refuses to leave Finn or her family to be tortured and killed. A wild Stormrider, born to rule and reign, is growing stronger inside her. But as long as she can hold on, she's still Teagan Wylltson, who plans to be a veterinarian and who heals the sick and hurting. The disease that's destroying her—that's destroying them all—has a name: Fear Doirich. And Teagan Wylltson is not going to let him win.

Turn the page for a sneak peak at

IN THE FORESTS OF THE NIGHT.

TEAGAN Wylltson blinked and tried to focus on her five-year-old brother. His best friend, Lennie—a pudgy, pimpled eighteen-year-old—was holding Aiden up so that he could see Teagan's perch on the roof of the porch. Lucy, the sprite who had taken up residence in her brother's hair, was zipping excitedly around his head.

"Come quick!" Aiden yelled again. "Thomas is growing feathers!"

"The man's shape-shifting," Finn said. He had taken her hand to pull her to her feet, and he hadn't let go. Every molecule in her was suddenly vibrating at a higher rate, and webs of electricity spread over her entire body. It felt good. *Really* good. But it did make it hard to focus.

"Where's Mamieo, then?" Finn asked.

"She was sitting beside him when I went through the living room," Teagan said, dropping his hand and stepping away.

Focusing would be a good thing right now. Finn's grandmother hadn't been happy when they'd dragged a wounded shape shifter out of Mag Mell, but she'd promised not to harm the creature—so long as he didn't do anything unnatural.

"Do you think she'll consider this—"

"Unnatural? I'm sure of it."

"She wouldn't—"

"Do away with the creature?" Finn rubbed his chin with the two good fingers of his wounded hand. "I doubt it. But I'd best go check on them just the same. Thomas might be needing some help."

"Finn," Teagan said, as he turned away. She glanced over to make sure Lennie had put Aiden down. He had. "I do love you."

Finn turned back, grinning. "I know it."

"But I'm not sure what I'm going to do about it, either. I meant it when I said that I'm still headed for Cornell. I'm not giving that up."

"You didn't think I'd go along with you? That's why you were crying."

Teagan shook her head. "I didn't believe you could love me. I was going to get over it, and get on with my plans."

"That's just like you. Sticking to the plan."

"Not this time. You turned my world upside down, Finn Mac Cumhaill. If Cindy hadn't fallen for Oscar at first sight, I wouldn't have been thinking about—"

"Why are you guys still talking?" Aiden yelled.

"Just one more minute, boyo," Finn called over the edge, then turned back to Teagan.

"Cindy and Oscar? Your monkeys?"

"Chimpanzees are apes," Teagan said automatically. "And they don't belong to me, I just work with them. They shouldn't belong to the zoo, either. They should belong to themselves. That's what I'm working for. That's why it's important that I go to Cornell. So maybe you and I *should* wait until things settle down a bit—"

"Tea." Finn looked grim. "Things are not going to settle. Your relations have come calling."

"You mean the goblins."

"And the Travelers. There's never going to be peace between them. And your family's in the middle of it."

"Are you guys *kissing*?" Aiden shouted.

"Not yet." Finn cocked an eyebrow and lowered his voice so only Teagan could hear. "But I can't wait to get to it."

"'Cause Mamieo said to hurry!"

Finn touched Teagan's face, then turned and jumped, catching the lamppost next to the house with his good hand. She stepped to the roof's edge to watch him swing around it as he dropped. She'd been coming out onto the porch roof since she was little, but her stomach still felt tight if she stepped too close to the edge. She would never just throw herself off it like that. Finn landed lightly in the patch of frost-yellowed grass between the sidewalk and the street, then looked up at her and lifted his arms.

Kissing. Teagan pressed her hands into her stomach to stop the trembling, which was threatening to spread to her knees.

"Come on, girl." Finn lifted his arms. "Jump down. You're just the right size for catching."

"Uh-uh." Teagan took a step back. "Not while you have a hurt hand."

"Well, then, could you bring my duct tape down with you?"

"Sure."

Aiden started for the door.

"Finn—" Teagan began, but he had already caught her brother by the collar.

"Not so fast, there," Finn said as Aiden tried to wiggle away.

"I want to know what's happening," Aiden said.

"Thomas is growing feathers." Lennie sounded worried. "Like a bird. That's what."

Lennie couldn't see Lucy and the other the creatures of Mag Mell who were only half present in this creation. But there were some unearthly creatures that were fully present in any of the worlds of the multiverse—angels, Highborn, and Fir Bolg—that even people without second sight could see. And watching a shape shifter transform would give Lennie nightmares.

"I'll take care of it," Finn assured him. "But I'll be needing two brave men to stand guard out here. Do you know where I might find them?"

"We're brave." Aiden stopped wiggling, and tipped his head as if he were listening. "Yep," he said. "There're bad guys coming. We'll fight them!"

Finn glanced up at Teagan, and she shrugged. Aiden had been saving the world from imaginary bad guys daily since they escaped from Mag Mell, sometimes by singing them away, and sometimes defeating them with stick swords and rocks.

"We will?" Lennie looked worried.

"I fought bad guys before," Aiden assured him. "I'll show you how." Lucy had decided the show was over and had settled into his hair again. She always played along with Aiden's imaginary battles.

"All right," Lennie agreed.

Finn looked at Teagan again, and she nodded.

"You two stay right here, then," he said, "until Teagan can walk you across the street to Lennie's house. Got it?"

Finn disappeared onto the porch beneath her, leaving both Aiden and Lennie looking up at her expectantly.

"Jump, Tea-gan," Lennie said. "I can catch you. I don't have a hurt hand."

"Thank you, Lennie," Teagan said. "But I'm going back in through the window. You wait there like Finn said." She wiped her tears on the back of her sleeve. Her eyes were swollen, and her nose felt like a blob. She picked up the roll of tape.

"*Aiden. Come to us.*"

Teagan froze. She knew that voice, and it made her hair stand on end. She stepped as close to the edge of the roof as she dared.

"Lennie!" Aiden said. "The *cat-sídhe* are here!"

"What's a *cat-sídhe*?" Lennie looked around. "Are they the bad guys?"

"Yep," Aiden said. "They're the kind you can't see."

"I hate that kind." Lennie picked up a stick and swung at the air.

Teagan was glad Lennie couldn't see the creatures on the far side of the street. He would have had nightmares for months. At first glance, they looked like large housecats. Dirty, diseased house-cats that stood upright. But if you looked closer, you'd notice that their mouths and hands were almost human. Bare skin showed in mangy patches through their filthy fur. The bigger one's ears hung in tatters. Maggot Cat. The last time she'd seen him he'd flicked maggots picked from his rotting flesh at her. The wound on his stomach didn't seem to be open, but even from this distance his bare abdomen still looked swollen. The *cat-sídhe* beside him was younger, and Teagan had seen it before, too. The half-grown *cat-sidhe* looked like it had been sleeping in an oil pan. Both of them had hunted Teagan, Aiden, and Finn through the streets of Chicago.

"Aiden, is Finn already inside?" Teagan asked.

"Ah, ah!" The smaller *cat-sidhe* pointed up at her. "Teagan!"

"Teagan!" Maggot Cat commanded. "Step down."

Her left foot moved a half an inch closer to the roof's edge.

"No!" Teagan said, as much to her own leg as to the goblin.

"Yessssss!" Maggot Cat said.

They can do that, Finn had told her, the first time the goblin creatures had tried to control her body. The *cat-sidhe* could move some people's muscles just for a second—long enough for a car to swerve into a pedestrian if you were driving, or for you to step in front of a train. Long enough to ruin your life. But you could learn to resist them, if you focused.

"Bones," the smaller *cat-sidhe* yowled. "Marr-ow! Marr-ow!"

"I heard something scary," Lennie said. "Like a whisper in my head."

"That's their voices," Aiden explained. "Don't listen." *Cat-sidhe* voices had never had any effect at all on Aiden, but Lennie was a different matter.

"Lennie." Maggot Cat tipped his head, looking at Lennie. "We know your name."

"Shut up!" Aiden said.

Teagan flinched. *Sidhe* creatures had more power to bend you to their will if they knew your name.

Lennie looked around wildly. "Where are they, little guy?"

"Leave him alone," Teagan said.

"Step down now!" Maggot Cat focused on her again. Her right foot moved a fraction of an inch, despite her focus.

"Let my sister alone!" Aiden yelled, and Lucy came out of his hair like an angry hummingbird.

"Sssssprite!" Maggot Cat hissed.

Sprites were *cat-sídhe*'s favorite food—at least in Mag Mell. Lucy zipped toward them. Though Teagan was too far away to see it, she was sure the sprite had pulled her tiny bone knife out of the sheath on her thigh.

"Ah! Dibs!" The smaller one leaped into the air, trying to catch her. "Dibs!"

"Let my Lucy alone, too!" Aiden started after her.

"No!" Lennie caught his collar. "We're not supposed to cross the street without permission, little guy!"

"Hold on to him, Lennie," Teagan called. Lucy was fluttering too close to the *cat-sídhe*'s claws.

She hefted the roll of duct tape. All she needed was a distraction until she could get off the roof. *Cat-sídhe* were not particularly brave. If she threw it hard enough to hit the wall above them, it might do the trick. The sprite could avoid the tape; she was designed for aerial combat.

A minivan blocked her line of sight for a moment, but as soon as it passed, Teagan threw the roll hard, aiming at the brick wall above the *cat-sídhe*. Lucy saw the tape coming and banked to the left, through the path of the tape. Maggot Cat twisted in the air, trying to follow her.

"No!" Teagan gasped as the tape hit him, knocking him head over tail.

"Yes!" Aiden cheered. "You got him!"

Teagan reached the drainpipe before Maggot Cat could catch his breath, grabbed onto the cold metal, and kicked the toes of her tennis shoes into the trumpet vine that wound around it.

"Ah, ah, let go, Teagan," the smaller *cat-sídhe* called.

"Get 'em, Lucy!" Aiden shouted.

Whatever the sprite did stopped the second *cat-sídhe* in mid-yowl. Teagan scrambled halfway down the pipe, then jumped to the sidewalk.

"I'm down, Lucy!" she called. The sprite zipped back to Aiden.

Blood dripped from the smaller creature's arm and shoulder where Lucy's blade had connected. It licked at it, trying to stop the bleeding. Maggot Cat leaned against the brick wall, panting. The duct tape had hit him hard enough to burst the swelling on his stomach. He pressed his hands against it, but pus oozed over his stubby fingers.

"You better run," Aiden said as Lucy settled into his hair, her eyes still flashing. "My sister's going to get you." Maggot Cat flattened his ears and hissed.

"Who is Tea-gan going to get?" Lennie's eyes were wild.

Teagan glanced at her front door. There was no screaming, so she assumed Finn had the situation under control. But she still couldn't send Lennie inside without knowing what was happening in there. She was going to have to take him to his own house— across the street, where the *cat-sídhe* were.

"You need to go play at Lennie's house, Aiden," Teagan said, taking the stick from Lennie.

"But I want to—"

Teagan gave him *the look.*

"Okay."

"Wait. Shake the candy out of your hair. Like you're putting in shampoo." Lucy had peeled M&M's in her nest on Aiden's head. Lennie might believe it was the work of Aiden's own personal tooth fairy, but Mrs. Santini certainly wouldn't.

Tea kept an eye on the *cat-sídhe* while Aiden leaned over and ruffled his hair with both hands. Red, green, and yellow bits of candy shell fell like confetti onto the sidewalk. When it either was gone or had settled to his scalp, Aiden took Lennie's hand, and Teagan walked them across the street, staying between them and the goblin cats, who were edging closer. She waited until the boys were safely inside and the Santinis' door was shut.

"I'm sorry," Teagan said to the *cat-sídhe.* "I was aiming for the wall."

"You missed," the small *cat-sídhe* pointed out.

Maggot Cat flattened his ears and hissed.

Their voices had less power over her when she wasn't in a situation where one move could be fatal. It was as if fear gave them that tiny bit of control they needed to cause a disaster. If she hadn't already been afraid of the drop, they wouldn't have been able to move her toward the edge of the roof.

"You're sick." Teagan took a step toward them. "I'll help you if you'll let me. I've had a lot of experience with sick or injured"— she almost said animals—"creatures. If you come with me to the clinic . . ."

"Fear Doirich says to bring Aiden," Maggot Cat said. "Bring Aiden to him."

Blood in Aiden's curls, and white bone shards. It was the image Fear had spoken into her mind in Mag Mell. She could see it if she closed her eyes.

"That's not going to happen," Teagan said.

"Keeee-yill." The smaller *cat-sídhe*'s lower jaw started to jitter. Teagan had seen a housecat do the same thing when it made a ch-ch-ch sound imitating the call of a baby bird to trick the mother into coming. "Keeee-yill, keeee-yill!"

Maggot Cat slashed at him, claws out, and the smaller cat leaped back.

"Bring Aiden to him, and Fear will let you live. He still wants you. *Bring Aiden to him.*"

"I told you, that's not going to happen," Teagan repeated. "And I know he can't come out and get us. There's an angel guarding the way."

"Keee—" The smaller cat began, but clapped his paws over his mouth when Maggot Cat narrowed his eyes.

Teagan started toward the *cat-sídhe*, but the creatures backed away from her, then flattened themselves, seemingly dislocating every joint as they squeezed through a gap barely taller than their skulls under the neighbor's fence.

Teagan glanced at the Santini house. Mrs. Santini had gone to New York to visit a cousin in the Bronx a few years back, and had come away with a healthy respect for rats. There wouldn't be a gap big enough for a mouse to squeeze through in her home, much less a *cat-sídhe*. Aiden and Lennie were watching from the front window.

Stay there, Teagan told him using American Sign Language. She'd had no idea how useful teaching Aiden ASL would turn out to be.

Aiden frowned.

I mean it. She picked up the roll of duct tape, and the foul-smelling smear the *cat-sídhe*'s wound had left on it made her stomach knot.

Her little brother had wanted to kill Fear Doirich and Kyle when they'd had them helpless in Mag Mell.

"They're really bad guys," Aiden had said. "We should smash them with rocks like they were going to smash me."

She'd been the one who'd said no. She'd wanted to get her family out of Mag Mell and home again. And killing Fear Doirich and Kyle had felt . . . wrong. She'd listened to that feeling, because Fear Doirich was bound and gagged.

Yet, not an hour later, she'd fed Ginny Greenteeth to the hellhounds to save her own life. It had been . . . useful.

You can curl up and die of regret and sorrow for what you've done. Or—

She would never do it again. She'd *never* let the Highborn come out the way it had in Mag Mell. Highborn were cold and calculating, born to violence, gifted in war. No matter what she'd inherited from her mother's twisted family, she would choose to be like her dad. John Wylltson was a lover, not a fighter. Teagan took a deep breath, then went back across the street and up the steps to her own front door.